About the Author

Nathaniel G. Sands was born and raised in Maple Ridge, British Columbia, Canada. An athlete and musician of youth, and intellectual and poet of late, Sands works as a lumberjack and self-studies in his free time, taking a keen interest in philosophy, religion, politics, and the social sciences, which is reflected in his writing.

He has an eight-year-old daughter, Leah, and a two-year-old dog, Bradley, with whom he spends much of his time exploring the forests, rivers, and mountains that surround.

Dedication

To the children of God

And that of my own,

Anthony Wilke and Leah Alexandra.

(Do it for her)

To taliah

Thanks for doing the amazing
Illustration. Cant wait to see
what you come up with
for Book two.

Your friend
Nathan Sauls

Nathaniel G. Sands

The Event Horizon

A Novel

Book One *The Abandoned*

AUSTIN MACAULEY PUBLISHERS™

LONDON • CAMBRIDGE • NEW YORK • SHARJAH

A CIP catalogue record for this title is available from the British Library.

ISBN 9781788233415 (Paperback)
ISBN 9781788233422 (Hardback)
ISBN 9781788233439 (E-Book)
www.austinmacauley.com

First Published (2017)
Austin Macauley Publishers Ltd™
25 Canada Square
Canary Wharf
London
E14 5LQ

Acknowledgments

I would like to acknowledge my good friends Bradley CB and Jonathan Z, whose thoughtful dialogues inspired many thoughts within.

I write to you,

Slave among slaves, peasant among peasants, man among
mankind.
My name, unrecognizable.
Sands of time;
Broken by his back;
Baptized by his sweat.
Despite faults and failures;
It is beautiful, and worthy...
The Sandman, I rightfully owe this life to.
The hourglass, a totem to be sure;
Constantly counting,
Sands falling,
Until...
Eventually,
It ends.
And I;
I take my place with those who've gone before me.

The Order

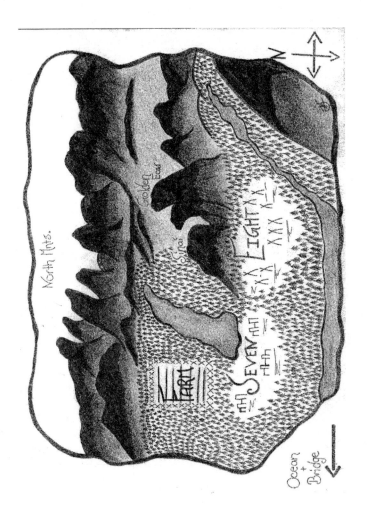

Part I

"And the Lord God said,
'Behold, the man has become like one of us,
to know good and evil.
And now, lest he reach out his hand and take also
from the tree of life,
and eat,
And live forever.'" -

- Genesis 3:22

Since the beginning, man has suffered. The fruit of true knowledge, of good and evil, a curse; and we humans still suffer from it. Anxiety, stress, depression... all from the root of knowledge — a plague on the mind, and a burden for mankind.

But, with the knowledge of good and evil in mind, can we truly understand one or the other? Is it possible to even know the difference? Or are we doomed to a life of conjecture, a world embedded in both, and destined to end in uncertainty.

Chapter One

Prologue

"A SPARK and life was created. The Spark ignites! Flames appearing, flexing, dancing in the wind; so chaotic yet beautifully unpredictable, relentlessly versatile, and eagerness beyond compare. The flames grow with excitement. The ever-devouring heat will not rest, it cannot sit still, it will consume until it can no longer.

Such a fire can never be quenched. It is doomed to end.

Without the fuel to maintain such a consumption, the flames lower... The fuel exhausted, the fire dampens, until all that is left is a soft glow, on its way to inevitable end.

Ash and ember are all that's left, and then...smoke appears.

In this new form, it rises to the heavens above. Swaying this way and that. But in silence it advances towards its completion. Towards the darkness above, and a world unknown."

This was a poem passed down from my ancestors in the latter days of the age of intelligence, when they saw what was coming, and were in grief and lamentation. It was my predecessors' beautiful acceptance of their impending doom, and our unending hope...

The world of human rule nearing its end.

But here in the world I now dwell, where no word can describe, nor mind imagine, I am.

I relive the memories, sometimes in shame at the hurt I've caused, and sometimes in contentment of the love a moment contained.

Keeping the good stored in the soul is the key to progression.

Yet sometimes I wonder: what of the Catalyst?

The mind bursting with memories and impromptu thoughts, never ending, eternally existing. How? And why?

Immortality is searched by some, but experienced by all. To receive Mother Nature's most precious gift: Rebirth; we must accept that we are obligated to die for this sacred tradition.

But many wonder: Could immortality be made possible in the flesh? The unsure and frightened, when thinking of what may be the end, either panic or suppress such a thought, and we live among such as these.

The thought of nothing scares me, but the thought of eternity... all the more.

The taste of blood on the tongue; my heart — the sound of a beating drum. And sight – a mixture of darkness and light.

Now, as I relive the pain of a long dull life, and the thought of the unknown that lay beyond – my next stop I am unsure of. Like jumping into a dark hole without seeing where it leads; shrouded in darkness, my spirit exits flesh.

But it is here, in my memories, that I truly feel...

If you fear death, it has already found you.

To understand death, one must first understand life. Life is fragile. One disease un-detained can wipe out an entire species. When a caste is experiencing technological advancements to aid in its physical evolution, it experiences a *de*-evolution, in its physicality and arguably its mentality. For, now the weak may reproduce, competing in an easier lifestyle, continuing the trend, onward and downward.

And as we work towards a fountain of youth, the possibilities of maintaining human life beyond those given by natural rights, those who seek to never die, will truly never live.

"Free conception – A warranted exception. Bold and boomed and bust. Mixed emotion, a warranted notion! And then udder demise."

We watch in awe and splendor, the ways of Earth's circle of life. We see it in autumn, as the leaves of bright colors fall to the ground. A gleam of snow over all things marks a time of rest and rebirth. The flowers close, the birds fly away; all seems to cease. Yet in the emptiness, peace is found.

We feel it, in shared stories of a loved one now gone. We remember their spirit, as we relive the story in thanksgiving; the inscription they etched into our hearts, their forever brand on a life. Connected in a curious kind of way. Here, as they perform their final duty, awaiting pure rest, contributing back to the cycle, Mother Nature receives the vessel it lent. One that was prosperous, full of good action and thought, now dust, preparing to rise from the earth once again, in an unknowable yet inevitable form. What an exciting way to leave it all!

To be sure, I am dead. And so are you. For here, at the end of life, all experience becomes simultaneous, yet asynchronous.

Yet, with all that I've seen and done, I am still unable to describe a feeling, an emotion of such a magnitude that something or someone can give you. Just as there are no words to describe the smell of a campfire, or the aroma of a forest, I lack the vocabulary to describe the feelings that dwell in my heart. Here in the hidden world I now call home, love stands still and everything is as it was.

As I reminisce, her smell, her touch, and the feelings I remember she brought; I am reminded that my love for her can never dampen... Her lost soul will never again be met with mine. This is the hardest thing to accept as I reach my inevitable death. She is gone forever, taken from me! But who is to blame?

I am unsure as to whom this will reach. In vain I may be sharing, but this message is for her and hers.

As a tree falls in the woods, the same fate awaits these words. Let its weight bring with it a boom of crackling and thumping! Let the bass of its sound enter through the feet as the earth shakes! Let it travel up to the heart, causing a skipped beat... Let the rustling of the branches and the leaves enter the ears and shape the listeners understanding. Take a deep breath; smell the freshly torn fibers of the gentle giant as it falls. Even if no one witnesses its death, the tree falls all the same, and leaves one life to supply another, fulfilling its ultimate duty to Mother Earth and Father Time.

My heart breaks for the fate of a once honorable species. Near its imminent end it scrambles to survive. A destiny that could not be avoided, yet experienced with a new sense of wonder.

I always imagined what the apocalypse would look like. The days of storytelling long gone. A man would once pass on his thoughts and predictions to his offspring. The children would stare in amazement, and wonder of what was and what could be.

History is not best told by the historian, but by the laity. The layman and intellectual, the slave and the owner have always been the product of Man's mortality. His developed ignorance, going back to tribal instincts.

Yet of these two, one emerges, a beautiful compromise between the meager and the eager – the *Artist*. He who recognizes the present struggle and uses inspiration to relay his ideas. Literature, poetry, philosophy, music, this is where mankind is found.

And I, another vessel, bringing death and destruction.

They say on death's door, one's life flashes before their eyes. The only thing I ponder now, does it ever stop?

Sometimes I wonder what the world would look like through the eyes of another man. Even as I reflect, and sift through my own history, this thought continuously re-appears.

Your own predicaments have placed you in such a position. You pride yourself in being right! Ha! It clouds your judgment. Can I even speak to thee? Will you not listen? Do you think you have all the answers? Look at yourself! The new you... who knows all things so well; the one so eager for change, so easily swayed and manipulated – Repulsive! And forming a life surrounded by opinion, the former self condemned; what does that tell you? How will your future-self regard you?

So listen! Do not interrupt! You fabricate the fight; you manipulate the result! No more! I am tired of watching, I'm sick of the score, and can stand this disrespect no longer.... And judgment is given by your own sword. You will be hung by your words!

Heed my warning, I tell you...

Do not be foolish! Learn how to discern!

At a certain point in history, there was a shift. The ability for one to imagine was lost in a world flooded with distractions. We raised a diseased society, selfishness it's illness, comfort the catalyst, and our own stupidity the fuel. In the mid-21st century, at the height of the de-stability, our doom neither began, nor ended there.

I, through the teachings of my father, had an advantage over most. I endured the wonders of a true earth! A world of uncertainty and chaos. One that had been abandoned for many years, left to rust and rot, for a world formed of our own imaginations — the newest lusts added to life.

The purpose of love and hope, is reflected in a man whose whole being cares for his people. As I reflect on the moments of anguish, the stories we shared, the life l lost to oblivion, euphoria sets in.

But here, and now, tears are a thing of the past.

Technically the past doesn't exist, and neither does the future. Does anything exist? Anything outside of the present? What is eternity? Continuous moments that exist, or memories built together?

As I digress, I drift; smoke rising above and wandering, from this thought to the next. I must remind you, to open your heart and your mind to a world not of yours, but of ours.

Here in the end, I am reminded of my beginning. Naked and blind, unsure of what is awaiting me as I cross over the boundary; complete uncertainty. But a sense of relief overcomes me! My task is near its completion. If my story is received, then I've done all I can in one man's life. A single man and his accomplishments mean nothing if no one is there to persist in his legacy.

I implore you! My one and only offspring, the only one who can possibly understand me, this is for you...

Perhaps I am nothing to you. Perhaps you would rather not be a part of it, a part of me; afraid of what it may be; afraid of change, afraid of truth, afraid of understanding. You may choose the life of ignorance, and none could burden you with blame. We lack any means to understand, but we are one and the same. A special bond no one can take, though some have tried.

Now in my last attempt to reach you, as I make my way towards death, and it's somehow alluring finitude, my mind wanders back, remembering the days my true story began...

Chapter Two

Parable

There is an ancient story I have not forgotten:

In a small village, a long time ago, twins were born to a loving King and Queen. In a seemingly advanced, but less moral society neighboring this kingdom, lived a rich man. He heard of the royal birth and used his means to have one of the boys stolen, as he respected but coveted the family and their accomplishments, and never had a child for himself.

Both boys grew up, and both were naturally smart. The stolen boy grew to be very powerful. He led the city, using slaves as his muscle and his cunning for combat, he expanded and grew his civilization.

The boy who remained grew into a great prince and ruler. He became a teacher in philosophy, math, and history. He was a powerful leader in the community and focused on advancing his people morally.

The stolen boy expanded and conquered many nations. When his forces entered the town of his birth, they raped and pillaged. Many men were killed attempting to defend their neighbor and loved ones. The city was decimated, and the survivors mourned their downfall.

The moral twin, now King, was brought back to the conqueror's palace. With his city in ashes, and his people oppressed and killed, he was brought in-front of his twin brother; and the stolen boy, the great and mighty conqueror, came face to face with himself.

On seeing the distraught reflection in front of him, he gets lost in thought. In prolonged silence, thinking about

20

his upbringing, he pieces it all together. His confusion turned to sorrow; falling to his knees in front of his own flesh and blood, he wept uncontrollably.

His reflection, utter morose.

***

The view from here: a decrepit, rotted forest, a once thriving ecosystem, laid waste to the industriousness of my people. The sound of crows nearby, mocking me in laughter. In spite of the jest, I am glad at least some species enjoy themselves.

The flight of the crow... Oh, what it must know! Civilization crumbles, and grows. But quoth the crow: "You reap what you sow!"

As abundant as the birds and squirrels are, the weight of extinction looms in the air. On this hill, you can see for miles. A demented forest – the trees distance themselves from one another; they stand lonely, unaware of the graves they take root in. Their ancestry, buried under them, as if they had never existed.

I come alone to this same mountain in this forsaken paradigm, storing within all the thoughts and feelings of a thousand generations before me.

Tonight, just like any other, I read through old literature, kept secret here on Mount Sinai, near the western coast of America. And as my mind once again returns to the pages from yet another digression, I come across a line from Jack London's *Call of the Wild* that reads:

"There is an ecstasy that marks the summit of life, and beyond which life cannot rise. And it came to Buck, leading the pack, sounding the old wolf-cry, straining after the food that was alive and that fled swiftly before him through the moonlight. He was sounding the deeps of his nature, and of

the parts of his nature that were deeper than he, going back into the womb of Time. He was mastered by the sheer surging of life, the tidal wave of being."

I've longed for such a feeling for so long, yet I'm met with sheer ennui as life passes by in this dark and dreary world I currently reside.

The start of the rising sun marks another sleepless night. The orange glow to the east no longer allows me to see the blue and white crest of the peaks I knew to exist just moments before. I close my eyes and feel the cool morning breeze pass over. An odd chill consumes me; such a chill I have not felt for some time. It suddenly and instantaneously takes over the body. Traveling into my spine, goosebumps fan out like a flame. It moves to occupy my arms. I look down to see my normally pale skin, tanned and freckled. The bleached hairs stand on end.

Eyes closed, I take a deep breath.

In...

Out...

Winter has come.

I usually come here at night, seeking refuge from a life of slavery. The only freedom found in solitude.

Using the moon as my guide, I enjoy reading the ancient ways of our kin. And most nights I am found here on Mount Sinai, looking at the stars and learning from celestials.

It is only safe for me to read in the dark, if anyone found me out here with the forgotten literature I possess, well, even I don't know what they would do.

Many believe in their own truths. I pursue the one and only truth. With so many truths to be discussed and deciphered, one must come to know solely through self-understanding.

But every night I again look up to the stars. I stare at that which once was thought to be a blanket covering the awe and wonders of heaven. The black veil, allowing only pinholes of light to shine through, unable to contain the beauty.

And among these heavenly lights, there sits *The Event Horizon*. To the untrained eye, one would be lost among the speckled sky, but I know the ancient map of our ancestors. And I loathe the massive block of human greed that sits out there, floating in the outer atmosphere, staring down in contempt at what it still depends on.

Sometimes I'll see small ships fly by in passing, which I feel must contain those of importance or of power, as they survey the land, that which they stole from the rest of us but claim to be Lord of, yet only know it by name. Their minds perverted, a symbol of what pride and power can achieve. Beings who know only the self by comparison, and somehow feel self-worth over the oppression of others.
A sick mind hovers over the face of the earth.

A Blue-Jay cackles violently above me, hiding in the trees, waking me from the state of dream. Fuck... shut up!

I cover and wrap the pages, taking care as I replace the novel in its proper place with the others. Rolling the stone back in its place, I quickly make my way down the hill.

The morning air is stagnant and moist, but I make it back to town before the general populous awakens. The smell of collective urine greets me; no rain to cleanse the town of its own befoulment. Glimpses of rotted homes make an appearance as the forest begins to fade, and the town I helped build becomes visible.
It looks nothing like it once did.

Home (if you can call it that) is a small shack that sits in the middle of an insignificant yard, wrapped by a four-foot chain link fence, surrounded by self-obsessive, delusional neighbor; row upon row of misfortunate souls, making up the general populous of the destitute village of Seven.

"Achilles!"

I keep my head down in hopes my neighbor Gus believes I don't hear him.

He runs up and yells again,
"ACHILLES!"

Even my dead father heard that one.

"Hey Gus, good morning." Hollow words seem to have become my norm. "Anything I can do for you?" I say as I approach my home, the dusty ground, unusual for this time of year, stirs up as I walk. I'm used to mud on my standard issue black boots; autumn, a relatively wet season for Seven.

"Well..."
He's a little slow.

"Well, Achilles..." He looks to the ground. I see nothing.
"Well, I was wondering, could you take me with you on a hike one of these mornings? You could show me what's so special out there; why you're always out for so long."
Now I look deep into his eyes, showing my seriousness.

Although he was just a little too much for me and my patience, Gus was a good man in my opinion. Big and hairy, strong and stupid (Our government loved guys like him). But he had very soft eyes, almost like he had just finished crying every time you saw him. His hair was curly and long. Always dirty but you could still see the shimmer of gold now and then. He took a liking to me, and I, reluctantly, took a liking to him. The closest thing I could call a friend.

"Gus, keep it down, will you!" I say in a serious whisper, looking around me, giving away my vulnerable position. The few up and in stir take no notice. A few boys run by in excitement. My eyes back on Gus and nostrils flared in a most serious tone. He looks at me like a child, unintentionally pissing-off his father. Noticing this I attempted to ease up on him. He acts like a child, and so, I must treat him like one.

"I told you, I don't think it's a good idea," I say with a smirk. "One day, perhaps. If you continue to stay quiet about me and what I choose to do with my time."

"Well..." he sighed in acceptance. "If you say so, Achilles."

We both stand in silence.

He's still learning social cues.

"So... I'll see you at work?" I say, eyeing my home.

"Yep! I'm ready to go! I could just wait for you here, and we could walk together?" His gaze of hopeful acceptance is pathetic, yet flattering.

"Okay, just give me a minute to get ready. Would you be so kind as to find me a hot cup of coffee?"

One of the only imported goods around here; the only perk I enjoy, and dare say, need.

Without a moment's hesitation, he was out of sight.

***

I'm not sure exactly where we are now, but it's somewhere south of the former province of British Columbia. My family moved North during the great migration. I was born somewhere on the western coast of North America. My father worked forestry, and his father before his. When we first arrived here, Dad said it reminded him of the stories his father told him. Reminiscing, he would almost smile thinking of his childhood.

Almost.

The dense and uncharacteristically untouched forest met us near our destination. He felt this was a good sign, an omen, showing promise, and pouring hope into our kind. He worked in optimism, and here, he would say: "We will flourish."

My father was incorrect. Wood became a thing of the past. Metals had become the jewel of the 21st century and my father, along with many others, worked where no one wanted to invest.

But much before me, and even before him, our dismal link to the past, our roots running deep through time, our family survived a world torn and broken. The time of *The Holy Wars*. Religious persecution was found all over the world. Persecution of spirit and, eventually, of body. Detached from the communal salvation, our ancestors drifted through the vestiges of wholeness.

That's what they called it anyways, "*Wholeness.*"

What many forgot is that politics stems from religion and philosophy the brother of both. We can't begin to live together without first exploring the ideas of good versus evil. But good and evil, too vague an idea, abandoned to a world of physicality. Spiritual thought and action was replaced by physical desires and intrigue. The here-and-now, instead of the what could be. Aristotle over Plato. Socrates, essentially taboo.

But history is so vague, a biased look is all one has, and in my case, a vague account of things are materialized as I attempt to understand my past, with no one but myself and the artist's pen for guidance.

We chose our shackles.
Or do our shackles choose us?

Chapter Three

C'est la Vie

Journal entry of Nathan, father of Isaac, father of Iris, mother of Achilles:

"Pity... Sadness... A painful grip on reality I live.
I look around, and all I see is suffering.
The mind of all... The sin revealed.
A nasty word, but nasty it must be...
For in shadow it lurks,
It plays the role of pleasure, ease and contentment.
Fear, that is.
It consumes the mind of the good and bad alike.
And manifests, and grows and becomes mankind alike.
And as I watch,
And ponder
At the world around me.
At the people who sunder,
And wander
And wonder,
And ache,
And lament in their minds.
Who cannot live in a world of peace,
Who cannot find a place of ease...
Who live each day regretting,
And Judging
And vomiting...
I sit and watch
The world at spin,
Regretting it all
And myself
Within."

***

"So, why can't I come with you at night?"

"Gus, I told you, it's necessary for me to be alone. If I were to bring anyone it would be you, believe me but it's not that simple."

I take the lead, coming to the edge of Seven. Gus walks just behind me as the path entering the wood begins to narrow.

Seven has grown and expanded. After graduating school, and showing my submissiveness to the UNA, I was granted freedom. *Freedom* here, a laughable concept. I feel ashamed thinking of the things I did to be granted such a shallow status.

"Well I feel like you're the only one who talks to me. You're not like the rest, but Achilles, neither am I!"

"Gus, until you unplug, you'll always be like them. Come on, we'll have to pick up the pace if we want to be early; I can't be late again."

The silence that ensues, most find awkward, or simply boring, but I find soothing. We take the long way to work through the woods. No one ever goes this way. Off the beaten path, away from the herd of workers and wayfarers. The leaves and branches sway as we push them to the side, walking single file on this dirt trail, headed north towards our lot of land, working for *The Man,* and his choice people.

Although I rest uneasily, mindful of my enslaved position, these are the moments that I live for. The pace of my breathing slows as we walk, deeper and deeper I inhale. The smell of the forest brings back wonderful memories. The birds chirping, sun shining; I close my eyes to take it all in. Here, in this beautiful silence, I feel at home. Here I have connection, roots and a family that goes further back then I can even imagine. As we move through the woods, leaves crumbling at my feet, sunlight bursting through the trees in seems; the air is perfect on clear mornings like these. I wonder in awe and amazement at the mind who could have imagined such beauty and the process of it all coming together. Here, living in a mystery, a state of never knowing what was, and what could be.

Sheer bliss.

I smile at this thought, and I don't smile too often. These moments help me forget my past. Our past, wrapped together in humanistic pain and suffering, one in which, it seems, all mankind is doomed to endure.

***

To understand my story, it seems I must start closer to the end. A dissonant summation:

I was born in the mid-2060s. But as far as I know, history always starts from some beginnings end, rotating, and thus never truly beginning. Besides this, the fact is there is limited information due to many reasons! But this arguably dates back to the first great famine, and the "Holy wars"; a time of disastrous population drops, which started near the first quarter of the century. I can't really say what caused the mixture of famish and cowardice, but overpopulation was my father's guess, who passed onto me many stories. My family line wrote about themselves and their current events all through the years, and as far as I know, I am the only one to contain any ancient manuscripts, after all the literature and historical documents were lost to the freezing winters of the 2050s, where paper was used for heat and the western forests decimated during the prosperity of the decade before. Any fuels, including books, were forcefully taken by the cold and dying people to burn. My father would recount how many times his father pinned over the stacks of painstakingly crafted fuel. The word and thoughts of a collective voice, writers and poets, artists crying out to him not to give in! And knowing that he must survive the cold, or die with them. Books were thought not to be of importance, as computers and global information could be shared through a sort of metaphysical screen. A hidden world of sparks and flashes, crafted through a miniature existence, albeit, destined to end.

But even after the burning of books and paper in a lazy order to provide fuel for fire, my grandparents and great grandparents, freezing and hungry, kept most of their books; hidden so as not to be burned; driven to preserve the history of our species. They predicted that all technological data would be destroyed, leaving no knowledge from history to continue. This prognostication became reality, in what was later known as *"the log out period"*, where the government took possession of all computerized machines in fear of what they called *an A.I. Spawn.* But even before this, the United States of North America, partnered with the Capitalist Party of Eurasia, were completely taking over the human inhabitants of Earth, and its history. A desperate people decimated by over eight billion dead of freezing and starvation. Propriety was a macabre of gruesome thought. Conformity to the concupiscence of the intelligentsia resulted with an ignorant laity. Our people have long forgotten the struggles of our ancestors, and rapidly so am I.

As complicated as it all seems, truly it is as simple as can be.

As for me, my mother died during childbirth. My father always had a hard time getting through the stories of her. His glossy eyes would mention her name before he did. His voice slowed and a subtle stutter manipulated his words. He could not look me in the eye, recounting her beauty, looking at the dust for his next word.

I can't help but pause to remember him in these moments. A man so shattered, I never knew him absent of a broken heart. His mind was sturdy as a stone, (Or he made it look that way) but I could tell he loved her, and would have given anything just to feel her touch one more time.

I remember this, because I too have someone constantly on my mind. Although, this one I have no closure, no certainty like he, that she is in fact dead and gone. I continue his sorrowful memories, but with hope that I may feel her presence before I leave this world. Hope that she might still be alive, and that I may still redeem my guilty conscience.

Our long journey to the district of Seven was a happy time for me. I remember the awe and curiosity of the quest! The excitement of a new world, every step leading to an inevitably beautiful home.

We walked as a group, an assigned journey to a people living on dead soil. At least a hundred of us walked, maybe more, along with our carts and buggies, livestock and animal companions. I had never walked so far in my life, but my dad said we were lucky, that most had to travel much further. He told me many were falling to exhaustion and that we should thank the spirit God for providing us with perseverance of mind and body.

He didn't have to teach me specifics, I learnt of God through his mannerisms. I remember seeing his constant smile as we bonded on the trek. The new scenery and fresh air awakened an ecstasy in life I now long for. Exploration, the unknowable world, yet attainable, just in need of pursuit.

We crossed a large river at an ancient bridge. Walking over the remnants of what once was our expansive culture, I marveled at the architecture. The wind blew strong and a light drizzle of rain greeted us at the gates of a long concrete crossing, undefiled by the vines and roots like that of the penetrated roads that we had traveled thus far.

As the bridge began to fan out near its end, we crossed the UNA (United Nations of America) checkpoint. Guards in balaclavas and camouflage stood still as we passed by; the dark frames embracing their weapons. I imagine my mother (if only she were alive) would embrace me like them, only tighter.

We were designated a plot of land along with others. Helping my father build our little community, the town of Seven was established officially. My father said that seven was a lucky number, in fact a divine number, and that God would one day redeem us and establish true provisions and justice.

The work was overseen by the government, constantly reminding us of its ownership – that we were building homes for us to stay, but on property not of our own. My father would say possessions we own end up owning us.

He didn't mind working hard. He said living such a way gains strength of character, and that was more valuable than anything a man could deem yours to keep. This was a gift from the unseen world, from the realm of truth, honor, and justice. This was far superior to a gift that could be seen, touched, or lorded over, and eventually rot.

In my beginnings of manhood, my father succumbed to some form of intestinal disease and died. We traveled with many, and built the community as many, but the community arguably died along with him. I remember burying him, just outside of the town, along with the graves of the others who went before him. A UNA representative shadowed the work.

I remember looking at Jacob, a man with presumed integrity, and he looked right back at me. The look of uncertainty and trepidation at the fall of Jonathan, the great leader and loving father of mine, and the burial of our hope in freedom and new life. We covered his body with dirt, load by load, and his eyes remained wide-open (as the dead so often refuse to close them), staring at me from within the grave. An image burned into memory, a sign, no doubt, but meaning hidden.

See, as I was on the threshold of puberty, I was unaware of the secret meetings my dad held. The townsmen were tired of the taxes brought on by the government, with little to no say for themselves. Also, the talk of a mind control device which threatened our way of existence; a very real threat described only by them as, *The Dream Machine,* which had already invaded the minds of the weak. A faded memory of a meeting or two remains. I remember, in the dead of night, the sounds of men in heated but whispered discussions over candle-light; the bastian, eviscerated by partisan.

Although these meetings remain fuzzy in memory, what I remember very clearly is the first night alone, the night of my father's death. The only night I would go to bed alone in the house my father and I had built.

That was when they came for me.

I was awoken with a start as the door flew open! Unable to move, I struggled to find a breath. Before I would find it, they had me. With my mouth held shut I was carried by a man, and all I knew was burning to the ground. I was whisked off to a world I never asked for, nor wanted.

Although my world was crushed and burned, my life taken from me, and my family all dead, the on-going existence of the books and journals my family cherished so much remained in the hills, hidden from all. Even Jacob and the other community leaders knew nothing of them.

I look back now and don't understand how he did it... How my father traveled, and lived so calmly. In our makeshift cart he carried scores of books — at least thirty or forty! UNA security was much more lenient then, I suppose, and never caught on. Upon arriving I could feel his anxiety grow.

That first day, as many rested from the long journey, we hiked. My father found what was perhaps an old wolf or fox den, a two-mile hike up Mount Sinai, as he called it. There, we traveled quietly and speedily, the first night, multiple times, just he and I, carrying the relics of our ancestors. Up and down. Back and forth. He rolled a boulder in front of the library, storing some of humanity's greatest minds at work. Here spawned my earliest memories. Learning by starlight, the importance of these books, and the role I had in preserving truth within the human species. We would come here together and he would tell me stories, share experiences, and motivate me to be all I could.

Sometimes, I sit and think of him. Tears recently absent.

My father's departure was a great misfortune, more so than just a boy losing a father. His death sparked the government's complete takeover of Seven.

Freedom is an ideal for the dead.

I became property of the UNA, along with many others. All the children whose parents were dead or murdered in the attempted revolution set out by my father and finally buried with Jacob.

We became what they wanted us to become all along. Some of us pawns, others, bishops or knights; but HE was happy, so long as we played the game.

He, known as 'The Great Alexander'.

School was repulsive. For two hours a day we learned what they wanted us to know. Revised history, basic mathematics, but mostly rhetoric proprietary. The rest of our days consisted of tilling the land, working various jobs on 'The Farm'.

Play wasn't normal. The sport 'baseball' was played, and the government workers loved it. They would even form teams to face the students. Those who did well were treated much better than the rest. And those who excelled, seemed to disappear, along with the brainiac's. They were taken away — promise of a better life and exciting futures, they succumbed to the flattery. Although it seemed to be the only real way of leaving the cruel life of a peasant, I showed no promise.

I knew what they were.

They were the enemy, and a life of satire is the life chosen by me.

Looking back, I only wish my moral convictions stayed consistent.

I showed no interest in anything. For years I went along for the ride, writing what they told me to write, working where they told me to work. Until the day she arrived...

As my hatred for all festered, and the thoughts of my father, and the kin I truly belonged to ached in memory, I felt a sense of responsibility, a feeling I was entrusted with some sort of truth or destiny. To this day I feel this great burden is mine to bear, and bear it I shall. I live in a world based on a lie, holding in my possession the keys to our history, the oppressed history, the truth! Yet all I can think of is the smell of her perfume, the look of her eyes catching mine, and the surge of nerves at her touch.

Two possible paths to take, and I chose the one most traveled.

Grace was her name, and I fell in love instantly. But the feeling of such joy is bitter-sweet, for I know the pain such love can cause, as in the end, all things inevitably separate. And now the result, formed by that feeling, the result of that smell and that touch; the product of two young lovers, so full of emotional energy, uniting in that moment of unpredictable chaos and creation. That feeling of awe and wonder over what two people can miraculously make out of nothing but pure love.

And I gave up. I gave in...

To the pressure of moral living among an endless barrage of tout concupiscence.

Like attempting to cross the sea during a storm, alone I battled the waves. And upon one look of her authentic beauty, I allowed the sea to swallow me up. Weak and weary, I battled no more. And because I gave in to the desires of the flesh, I was cursed! Grace, my one true love, left me... Instead of the lowly life of the peasant, one in which I gave her, she betrayed me! Forever burning a hole in my heart, she is now one of those, floating above me every night. The Event Horizon consumes one more, but the collateral damage put upon me. And now I walk alone. Forever remembering that I was not good enough for her. And the product of our love, my daughter, given away in a moment of discord. My little girl, *Solei* — oh, how I miss her!

With a dispirited heart, I continue. A life of moral conscience and obligation is partnered with a numb depression and inward turmoil.

This is my lot in life.

And every day I hear my father's words.

"They can take everything I have; my home, my books, my freedom, and my life. But they can never take my honor."

I only wish I could die with honor the way he did. The truth: I gave it away with my daughter, many years ago. And now I eagerly wait for redemption, for a chance to possess what my father called gifts of the unseen world, and perhaps, one day, to see her face again.

***

"Achilles... why don't you plug in, and how do you survive without it? And you refuse to let anyone else know. I feel so privileged that I know, but am so curious as to how..."

I cut him off.

"Gus, slow down and listen." He breathes deep to catch his breath. This is not out of the ordinary. "I don't like talking about it. Especially when they might hear us. And you figured it out, remember, I didn't tell you."
"But Achilles, you didn't have to tell me. I just saw you digging at the side of your house. You could have lied to me; I didn't know what you were doing!"

Recently I became paranoid that the UNA would find out I didn't plug in at night. Although, it seemed insane for any of us not to; for what else is there to do? One would simply go mad in a world without the comforting lure of a life far from the one of current reside. The freshet of life, all its glory dissipated within a false existence...

Dependent on a machine, but worse! Not a care that it is so, and the people go on! It is hard acting like the normal crowd. I am disgusted with the way humanity has become. How can one live continually within a civilization he finds repulsive? Daily disdain incarnated within the everything; surrounding, ruminating on the weak, receding into abyss. The leaders lord over the Farm arrogantly, as if they are enlightened, or envied perhaps. They peevishly watch as the living dead work the ground for them.

Well, not for them... for Him.

I live in constant fear my true nature will be discovered. If my eyes would reveal what is in my head, and my heart, and I be found.

And chastised.

Or worse.

Maybe I wanted Gus to know. But I couldn't just explain everything. No one believes what you say unless they figure it out for themselves. You can only lead a horse to water, and Gus is just learning how to drink.

"Well I couldn't take the chance you might tell someone, and I don't know, I guess I trusted you. I asked you not to tell a soul if I told you, and you shook my hand on that. Where I come from that's a deal; might as well shake hands with God."

"Who's that?"

"Let's just get to work, Gus."

Chapter Four

Abandoned

Loose-leaf Journal entry, no name or title attached:

"Within the ever-expanding people's, each given a square to squat, each handed their life and lot, the smell of fresh pot, and stale sweat overcomes the dead thought...

'It is only after we've lost everything, that we're free to do anything.'

I've discovered the air of freedom,
And find it hard to breath.
Each herein, counting down the days.
Each cell dying its last, only to reform, to be reborn;
To be resurrected.
Within the ever-developing being, unsure of its fate and what it all means.
As I go to sleep, although the body idle, the mind resonates.
This night so familiar, yet so unique, will soon be a shadow;
...Gone with the wind.

And what of me, and of my fate?
Ashes to ashes, and dust to dust.
I guess we'll know when I awake."

***

Work was more like a prison. A great big open space sectioned off in acres, with livestock and plantation. A *gross*, chain-link fence wraps around the entire perimeter, with only one entrance. I call it *'The Farm'* along with the others, and the management still wonder where this term started.

Here at the Farm we take care of animals such as sheep, bovine, swine, and, evidently, the UNA and its associates. We do their dirty work, and in return, they allot us a living quarter and nightly plug-ins.

Sometimes I think I am the only one who notices, or cares, that the people floating above us, watching us work and eating our crops, refuse, or simply do not plug in as we do.

We also manage the ground. The farm produces a variety of vegetation such as carrots, corn, potatoes, strawberries, blueberries, tobacco, and tomatoes. Apples and plums are among the fruits that grow as well.

As for me: I'm the bee keeper.

It was a difficult start, but this has offered me some significant advantages over others.

One: I get left alone to do my work for the most part,

And two: I can survive off honey, along with other scraps I continuously pursue.

It has been a long time since the mass starvations, but I predict another approaching rapidly. Even with the population seemingly down, we are still running low of provisions. Fewer children are being born among the workers, but more and more management (whom, as far as I know, don't plug in) have been sent down from above. And I fear that which occurs in history is destined to repeat itself.

It sickens me the way our ancestors abandoned us this way. Now, a forgotten race lives on what used to be a lush and growing world, raped and decimated. I stand on the corpses of the dead. Their lives a gross consumption of anything and everything, at whatever cost necessary. We produced more offspring, but put less into society. Multiple generations lived in cycles of greed and the exploitation of Earth.

My ancestors journaled much of this.

When our resources ran out, and our comforts receded into something of a dark age, we were too stupid and lazy to control this massive need. In turn, the government was given full control — autonomous power.

This is history, as I've come to know it.

Our history reveals the importance of great leaders, and the vast amount they can accomplish with such despotic authority.

I have a soured taste towards us. Those in control are just that. They control everything we do. And the population now so ignorant and lazy, would not survive a minute without the government to lead them.

Every night they lie down, the sun's energy harnessed and distributed into their bodies; a virtual world we chose to live inside.

Televisions became dull to the general consumer, and our technological advances allowed for a more realistic approach towards entertainment. *Plugging in,* you could now live in dreams (Those manufactured by the programs writers). As the population increased, our technology advanced; and given the physicality needed in the act of plugging in, it opened a world of a new, liveable resource. The sun's energy, harnessed, could now be passed into the mind of the consumer.

We became addicted.

That is my basic understanding of how it works... I try not to think too much about it.

No longer needing to work to provide sustenance, the people plugged in for most of the day. Food was rare, so only the rich ate. The rest were given artificial fodder. But, a bigger problem arose among the aristocrats. How do you get the much needed labor source to work?

Lacking moral fiber, my father's generation became drones; completely satisfied, they relied on the government and its management of the earth, their minds dulled and bodies weak, setting themselves up for death.

Apparently, this caused much of my father's revolutionary tendencies. He believed this to be a despicable action. An addictive means of control, laid out by those in power to constrain those with none.

As a child, years later in those UNA school rooms, I do not recall any of this being mentioned.

The UNA held its ground as leader and ruler, and built a ship called '*The Event Horizon*.' A massive project set out by the General to construct a large interstellar vessel. But because of the distance between us and the eastern provinces, we knew little of what was going on. Especially due to the abandonment of the *World Wide Web*, we were left virtually in darkness; my father, attempting to grasp information in the shadows.

The Dream Machine became regulated. My father's people (as many others I'm sure) unimpressed and dying daily, panicked as starvation was setting in; unmotivated to aid Alexander and his massive project, but cracked under the pressure.

Hard work — a thing of the past.

Plugging-in became the new generation's salvation. While my father and I traveled North, on the other side of the continent, men were working persistently in the mining, fabrication, and assembly of *The Event Horizon*.

As far as I know, my father and our rag-tag group were the last people to succumb to hardship, instead of kinship.

A complete submission to the UNA, evidently happened that fateful night, when my father died, and I was taken.

Our small population was given a choice by the UNA. And as I was allowed to return to my home town of Seven, Jacob and the others seemed to have lost the battle. With my father dead, and me missing enigmatically, apparently a life of submission was better than no life at all.

I can remember the voice of the man who would force me to plug in. I would scream, "take it off!", and his reply, in a monotone voice: "It's not going to hurt." Always, that same response as he penetrated my arm with needle in hand.

"It's not going to hurt."

Eventually I wasn't forced to do anything. I was surrounded by those my father hoped I would never become. But in a world where your morals are vastly different than everyone else's, it is hard to find company. I succumbed to the loneliness.

In my younger years I pursued the life of happiness. With a wife and daughter, I worked where the UNA told me to, plugged in at the end of the day, and repeated daily.

What a fool I had become.

Sometimes I am asked: "Would you rather live a life of love, and loss, or a life without love at all?"

I say: "It doesn't matter. For a life of love has been given. And an eternity of loss inevitably awaits. Yet a life of love and loss is what is, and we shall never, while here, know of any other way."

With my life came destruction. Everything I had and loved was taken from me, within my own ignorance and moral acquiesce. I still fall into dark memories of the past — a life full of love and loss. But I dare not dabble in specifics. Dark things dwell in the closed doors, the row upon row of incarcerated memories.

And finally, one day, all I did was listen to the wisdom of my forefathers. In a moral war that lasted for years, I quit plugging in, which had become undeniably unheard of.

Not in fear, but as an act of patience, I faked my way. An animal amongst drones, awaiting my moment to shine.

If you fear death, it has already found you.

***

As we walk, I note the warm morning sun claiming its spot in the sky, an undoubtable presence, penetrating all those under its dominion. A cool breeze shook the leaves. I take a deep breath to soak it in.

In such a moment, as the sun shimmers through the vibrant forest, life stirs. And I, along with it.

"What is truth?" Gus says quizzically.
I feel struck by his proverbial thought.

"That is a question that can't be answered, Gus. Truth is an Idea. By definition, it is abstract and so must become personally understood. Truth must dwell from within an individual, a purposefully self-generated idea of what is, and what is not."

And yet, all I know of truth, is that it becomes depression. An understanding above what is meant to be known. An Idea that is for a higher being, not the scum that is humanity. We fear the truth, and thus, we are not worthy of it. So it evades, and manifests, in the cursed and the damned.

Gus looks lost.

"Woah, what's going on?" Gus says as he raises his arm and points ahead to a crowd of co-workers uncharacteristically packed together outside the great fence. The large gate, keeping them without and the farm within. The mob regarded a wave; a single entity, flowing as many. My heart begins to race at this distinct change in predictable arrival I've experienced, day-in and day-out over the years. I approach not to a dull and empty mass of workers, but am met with a great anxiety, a high tensioned situation.

People were panicking! A great fear was resonating! Cries and whimpering could be heard, a dull panic overcoming the herd. And suddenly an unexpected excitement came over me...

I try to get closer, instinctively curious. But as I approach, a loud shot is heard, like a massive bullet flying over the head, a transport ship rips through the air! The sheer might of its power rocks me to the core, the bass blasting at my door! I feel the heat and the smell of rocket-fueled ash, as bits of singed pine float then drop to the Earth's floor.

I have waited so long for this day to come; my predictions seemingly brought to fruition.

The trees blow and crows fly as I cover my ears and crouch to hide. The sound still loud seeps through my hands, the feeling vibrates my whole being, causing my heart to jump and skip a beat.

Everyone fears what they don't understand.

Here you could smell it; and I longed for such a smell. For years these people have never felt such a potent emotion. The smell of fear awakens the inner animal and the surge of adrenaline, a necessary jolt for every man.

Is this what I have been waiting for?

Is this providence, the moment long awaited, yet never truly thought to occur?

I am the first to stand and can now see words etched into a flat stone, lying motionless on the ground outside of the wall ahead. My curiosity ripens, making my way through the cops, revealing perfectly cut words on a noticeably foreign object. Hands still to my ears, I approach it cautiously as it sits just beyond the crowd of early workers. I stare in amazement at what I would never expect.

A note.

I find it funny that someone would leave a note. Does anyone even know how to read any more?

The shouts and cries of fear are a nuisance to my ears! I can't read over the racket. My hands leave my head and in a waving motion, I signal all to find composure...

"Chill, everyone!"
I boomed in to cut off their chatter.
"Quiet down and I'll read what it says."

They all looked at the foreign object, obviously aware of its presence (they had probably already seen it, and examined it before our arrival) but momentarily distracted by the low flying dread. Instant silence as they all attempt to think, something they clearly haven't done in years. They knelt, staring at the closed gate, and the foreign markings resting just in front of it.

The eyes of hundreds now stare at me as more and more workers approach, noticeably perplexed. Surrounded by people of all races, age, and sex; a group so in need of direction – such a pitiful reflection. I knew the day would come, where those of us considered scum would be left to rot with the earth as those in power fled! Those disgusting elite – worse than us! But have they truly left us? The thought of being alone, I can only imagine, could send those around me into a state of panic! I fear they may kill each other or me!

As their shrieks of fear have ceased, a much deeper fear awakens. As each stare gravitates toward my confidant demeanor, pity overtakes me, and for a moment, I too feel fear.

I haven't been looked at this way in a long time.

For a moment, I just stare back. Me at them, and them at me. And a feeling of sadness overwhelms me. These people, my kind, MY people, have no idea what they've become. Their empty eyes look at me, yet I am the one who feels alone — glancing between each one of them... my family, my distant relatives – my people and home.

Me.

I feel pity alone. No anger, no judgment. They are just a lost and lonely species. So consumed in the idea of self, they've become lonesome, and loveless, just like you.

"Achilles, what does it say!?"
Only Gus can grab my attention.
Snapping back to reality, I first read in my head:

"

It ends abruptly.

Who could have written this, one of them?
Who could know about me? I've been so careful, so outwardly dull and lethargic; how could my cover have been blown?
And I wonder, "Who is Joshua?"

45

But no time for that...
The sheep are waiting.

What do you tell a people that are destined to die? How do you look into the eyes of a living thing and explain that their mother has abandoned them, on a ship full of the very ideals that make up the human psyche... I've thought of this moment before, but never could I have imagined the gravity emotion would have within me; the thought of all the good I've seen and read about, illustrated on their person. The authenticity of their souls could be seen through their eyes; righteousness hidden, deep down, but there to be sure.

The light within them; just an ember waiting to be fanned.

But I fear the worst! Paranoia – an abject feeling.

I think also of the closest towns, if there are any, and their inevitable abandonment. Will they survive? Will they come this way? And will they come in hostility or exploration?

A compact flash of the future and its perilous providence wraps within my mind.

These people couldn't survive a night. Their bodies are no longer a thriving cellular mass, warding off disease and fighting for survival. Weakness of body and mind creates a weak soul. Thoughts of what they are, of what I used to be, race through my brain. The pain and torture one endures to overcome a life of dependency.

But *I* did it, *I* overcame, or so I think...

I am not special. I was as weak as they are now, but I changed.

"And then, *a spark*!"

And I decide to believe in something... something I have long forgotten: hope.

Hope they can change, and quickly! If I inform them delicately, I may be able to lead them to survival.

I look through the gate towards the cold, stone structures of their stead. No management to be found; nothing but wandering livestock over a deteriorating enclosure; the last of the crops — fodder for the beasts.

And as my mind returns, I stare at them, and look around at their scared faces, just waiting for me to fix everything. The face of a young girl harnesses my gaze; the pale and defiled face, eyes red and hair knotted; the cold and distant stare reminding me why I must not give in to the darkness.

Do it for her.

This long pause has built an anticipation. Their hope is fading. No time to think, no time to react. They rest in my embrace.

Come on Achilles, don't fail now! This is the moment you've been waiting for; that ecstasy that marks the summit of life!

Well, here goes nothing...

Chapter Five
The Great Alexander

"Is it possible, I wonder, to study a bird so closely, to observe and catalogue its peculiarities in such minute detail, that it becomes invisible? Is it possible that while fastidiously calibrating the span of its wings or the length of its tarsus, we somehow lose sight of its poetry? That in our pedestrian descriptions of a marbled or vermiculated plumage we forfeit a glimpse of living canvases, cascades of carefully toned browns and golds that would shame Kandinsky, misty explosions of color to rival Monet? I believe that we do. I believe that in approaching our subject with the sensibilities of statisticians and dissectionists, we distance ourselves increasingly from the marvelous and spell-binding planet of imagination whose gravity drew us to our studies in the first place.

This is not to say that we should cease to establish facts and to verify our information, but merely to suggest that unless those facts can be imbued with the flash of poetic insight then they remain dull gems; semi-precious stones scarcely worth collecting."

- The Watchmen

***

General Alexander, United Nations of America.
Personal thoughts log: Day 220 year 2096.

"Open the door. Cross the threshold. The quietness of my abode welcomes me home. The days are filled with schemers, and the nights are filled with unending contemplation. As I shift from one to the other, it's as if a sense of self is reborn. As I walk slowly through my entrance and into the open room, my thoughts re-appear.

The most profound proverb will never possess spoken word.

A breath of smoke, a hack of the lungs, a life prolonged and love foregone. But no hatred manifests here... only sorrow.

Have you ever felt like you were doing the right thing, but for a selfish reason... and then wondered if you have ever done anything without a selfish desire?

Am I doing the right thing now?

These people with me, they are doomed. The earth passed its hope of survival a long time ago.

Desperate men in desperate times. I can relate.

It's surprisingly not hard to convince a people to leave billions of its kinship to die and rot. Mankind has *been doing it for millennia, and I am no different than those before me. The thing is, I totally believe in what I intend to do, and take full responsibility for each and every life destined to perish because of it.*

But these of my subordination are of the evil and ungrateful nature. Bent on personal increase, stopping at nothing to gain power and control over the earth; verily, they have received it. But this mission of mine is not for them.

Five billion people will die.

I lie awake each and every night to this thought, throbbing in my brain, the weight of the world dwelling in my heart — all the living beings who just went astray, who became emotionless. But five-billion dead is worth the survival of a potentially unending number of descendants, is it not? Besides, it's hard to call what they are human.

It is easy to condemn that which one does not understand.

A selfish species, whose only goal is self-pleasure; our ancestors ignored the signs, afraid of their own shadows — their honor rung out like a sponge the cur left dry and thirsty.

Now I bear their shame.

I live a life full of decisions they are too weak to make.

Too dark to envision.

My plan is the only hope for mankind's survival. I lead the greatest expedition of Earth's salvation never attempted before.

We are simply running out of food, and I refuse to let the technology of this age take control of my people. Plugging-in is man's simplest and most probable way to ensure survival. But I refuse to let it take over the conscience of mankind, turning us into a completely new species, no longer man but machine!

I will die before I give in to such dishonor.

They train you this way, they teach the importance of survival, and success by any means necessary.

Live by the sword, die by the sword.

But live by the shield, and rust with the dead.

I struggle to care about them. Every time I look at another I'm reminded of the sickened mind our evil people have inherited. Those on this ship, claim an expedition of peace, but bloodshed is in their eyes. They want a world for themselves. A life free of decline and hardship, of death and despair.

A life, free of life.

These are not the same eyes I see when I look into the lamps of a warrior. These eyes live a life of privilege, watching the world through a screen, feeling empowered by their weakened peasants, feeling content by comparison.

And I, I feel indifferent. Indifferent to the struggles of those on the fringes. Of the marginalized and meek. Collaterally, I feel indifferent to the responsibilities of the powers that coincide.

Indifferent to the Junkie, seeking and craving his next fix.

Indifferent to his Lords, profiting over such impetuous propriety.

Can this produce a world that is real? A vicarious victory over a brainwashed flock... The abandonment of the responsibility we were entrusted to? Giving up on the planet? What we have done the impossible through! The planet that housed millions of generations of species! The miracle of life, left to rot away in hope of a world that can't be found. A world we hope that will welcome us, as If we deserve a second chance.

All is detestable in this life of suffering, yet I press on. Lost in the instinct of survival.

And every night I lie awake with this as a reminder. As I stare out into the empty space, as I look out into the endless worlds far off; pictures of stars long dead still reach me from their grave, greeting me at mine. I feel alone in this samovar, even though I stand with half a million others. The most brilliant and powerful of the *whole human race stand beside me, yet who among them is worthy? We are all the product of a cold and calloused species. With this in mind, as I lay my head down to rest, the question again appears:*

"Am I doing the right thing?"

Every evening I go to sleep, hoping not to wake.

And as I log this journal entry, I attempt to bear it all.

Absolute power is a burden none should ever bear, yet I fear the power it could wield for another. That his conscience will keep him from doing what needs to be done. That he will be weak, influenced by his own personal desires. Or others', for that matter!

For something good to exist, evil must also exist. For without evil, good could not be. In a world full of evil, the vile actions must rise to become good. Have I become such necessary evil? Can I distinguish one from the other?

My heart is hardened from the years of bloodshed.

All must be considered when choosing to sit in the judge's chair.

The cries of souls extinguished! Faces covered in blood. Eyes void of tears. Mouths open only to gasp, or scream, or vomit – A restless mind remembers.

A pain only felt on the battlefield.

Sympathy, I now find to be a harmful weakness, with no place to be had among leadership. Yet I envy the eyes of a man who's never seen the things I've seen. The lackluster love for life. And it is life itself I reminisce... thinking of what was before it all.

The things I see within the deep recesses of my mind rival the beasts of the unknown. The horrors of the Leviathan, the terrors of the Titans.

I hope there isn't a God to count the bodies I've counted, and to witness the many more to come.

My hope in us is lost, but my faith in life pushes on. Time is eternal — it continues endlessly, or so it would seem...

Life itself: Can I maintain it? Can I continue its work? If so, am I prepared for it? For the sacrifice that is the culmination of all great men of renown.

Surely, I am prepared for mine own.

As I lay motionless, I remember my mortality. It's burned into me. Each detail a tote, misplaced and fuzzy, it lingers and floats.

Truly, there's no going back; and nothing left to do tonight, but to fall asleep in this floating tomb.

The constant hum of the ship, the overhead view of an earth so black; I look away from the window as my head begins to ache from the sight. The sharp pain of localized pressure hits the sternum. I'm sickened by the scene.

I have killed before, but my eyes have not seen such death as is about to be brought on by myself.

I remember many things, but nothing so burns in the back of my brain as the scorched jungle-gym remains... It stands erect, the dark smog filling the air; the skeletons of buildings, and buses, and bones; and the charred remains of a dress in my hands. I, leading a legion of soldiers, become motionless upon my knees instantly forgetting the duties of me and my soldiers — the rescue mission so callously sent on. An optimistic invasion into a mass grave. The black death of our destruction; the weapons of tyrants, claiming the lives of uncountable souls, one in which recently occupying that little dress within my hands. Vivid reality, darkness, suffering and death; and I wept.

This is my fault, as much as it is yours.

Baptized into humanity, compassion was overrun. Justice becomes the only occupant. A house once governed by the force of mercy, now lost complete control of the temple; and my inner being armed itself for the crusade.

But for now, eye's dry and drained, I lay my head down to sleep;

And pray the Lord my soul to keep.

Chapter Six

Private

"Would he purge his soul from vileness
And attain to light and worth,
He must turn and cling forever
To his ancient Mother Earth.

But the difficulty is how am I to cling forever to
Mother Earth. I don't kiss her. I don't cleave to her
bosom. Am I to become a peasant or a shepherd? I go on
and don't know whether I'm going to shame or to light
and joy. That's the trouble, for everything in the world is
a riddle!

-    The Brothers Karamazov

Alberta, United Nations of America: Year 2047

"Name, rank, serial number," the large man said in a
monotone voice, clearly not happy to be where he was.
The man in uniform eyed the young Alexander as he
approached the large rectangular-cut in the wall. Behind
the large man, Alexander could see an open room of boots,
fatigues, and equipment. He was at this point unsure of its
use. He also noticed steel framed gates, weapons locked
behind steel cages.

A freshly shaved face, although a shave hardly needed,
exposed his age for what it was. Alexander stood in front
of *stores* with anxiety as he came to collect his kit. The
recruit was just sworn in. He was followed by four others,
equally as nervous but eager to join the highly respectable
comrades, as they charged into the basement to grab all
the gear an infantry-man would need to get started.

They all looked like they had seen a ghost as the large man loomed over the counter. His confidence and beer-gut revealed someone with absent enthusiasm; a man who had lost the zest of the recruit as they, entering the military with angst and pep, had.

All things become dull over time.

"Private Seyer, sir! F25-" said Alexander, half snapping to attention, suddenly cut off by the large man.

"What the fuck did you just call me!" the man said without a moment's hesitation. The anger burned genuinely in his eyes as he leaned closer to Alexander, spitting as he spoke. "I work for a living; do I look like a fucking pencil pusher to you?" He pointed to the rank on his chest but Alexander stared at his eyes not saying a word. He wanted to answer the rhetoric but knew better than to outsmart a man who, in this world, invariably owned him.

"And 'F' no longer exists in your world, it's Foxtrot, you moron! Get it right next time...

"Alright private, here, just write it out, and sign for your gear."

"How do you spell foxtrot?" Alexander says with a deadly stare at the master corporal.

"If I wasn't so busy, I'd climb over this counter and Fuck you myself! Now get out of my sight, next!"

Alexander looked beside him, the young man, not much older than he, wide eyed and visibly sweating as he approached the master corporal. "Private Toman, sir, I mean!"

Alexander smirked and didn't look back.

***

"Room!" the high pitch squeal of an adolescent finding his voice was heard from the far end of the barracks. The stone walls only partially blocked off into cubes. The large, white-washed hallway led to small rooms, no doors, no windows, the early morning light shining through glass along the top of the dusty roof out of reach.

The voice was heard easily over the shuffle of last minute cleaning. The recruits scrambled beside their beds as their weapons laid disassembled on the ends of the perfectly folded sheets, and stiff bedframes. A moment passed as the voice traveled to the far end of the small building and back; not a sound was heard but the confident thuds of boots from the entrance.

An onslaught began as the section commanders invaded their recruits' rooms. Alexander stood motionless as he heard incoherent rabble from the air above. So he focused on his posture. He felt as if every muscle in his body was flexed to keep him in his rigid position.

"Are you kidding me, Rome? Is this dirt on your firing pin? How the fuck are you supposed to fire your rifle with DIRT on the fucking firing pin!" The sergeant of One-Section could be heard by all. Alexander could see movement in his peripherals as some of his comrades were shaking their heads.

"Fucking dust," whispered Private Lee, as he visibly turned his head towards Alexander. Seyer lowered his chin and shook his head to indulge him, but was sick of hearing the trivial judgment.

It had been over a month in these barracks with this same platoon; and every single morning the soldiers would stand by their conformed beds, getting chewed-out by a bunch of veterans, obviously enjoying the instant satisfaction of flexing one's power, and putting a lesser being under 'thine own' dominion. Every morning was something different.

Alexander and the others had spent their entire evening-previous cleaning. They mopped the floors, lubed their weapons, shined their boots, did their laundry, dusted virtually everything within reach, and then some. Nevertheless, there was always something to be found askew.

As the yelling became omnipotent, Four-Section stood in silence as their Section Commander approached. His easeful stride did nothing but add to the tension. The judgment of all their fellow recruits' faults became a distant memory as the respected man stood in front of

Alexander. The nine men of Four-Section, statues, careful to breathe easy and stand firm.

"Good morning, Private Seyer. How was your sleep?"

"Excellent, Sergeant!" He responded, looking through the hardened man, as if a ghost were speaking to him.

The grueling months of training have accumulated a collective debt of energy. All prayed there were no stray threads exposed on their uniforms, or lint visible on their berets. All the young men, nearly done their training, stood beside their disassembled weapons, hoping to God their mattress wouldn't be flipped on their final day of inspection.

"You've led your section very well, Private."

Alexander stood unfazed.

"The other section-commanders have been talking about our success. You've made quite a name for yourself, son." The Sergeant got much closer and looked into his eyes. The cockeyed smile, and almost angry looking eyebrows of the sergeant showed a happy man, who expressed a sort of pride in his student.
"Listen, Alex..."

Private Seyer's eyes now changed from the numb look of exhaustion to a jolt of adrenaline at this sudden humanness he was being shown. He brought his eyes from beyond the decorated man of might and power in front of him, into the eyes of a fellow human, the man of heart, standing a foot and a half away from him.

"You're a born soldier. And I would welcome you into my platoon any day. If you ever need..."

He paused.

"Somewhere to be?"

The sergeant welled up and looked away.

After a moment he turned, and left Four-Section.

As he walked away, Alexander felt a mixture of confusion and intrigue as Sergeant Gustoveson left the room for the last time. Most of the other sections were treated like absolute dirt, but Four-Section was led by a good man in Private Seyer's mind. He felt Gustoveson cared about each of his soldiers; a wolf, leading his pack.

Private Toman's eyes wandered so as to follow the Sergeant out of the room. He leaned to his left, peering down the open hallway to see the other sergeants still yelling at their trainees.

"He's gone," Toman said. "Alright boys, let's get 'er done!" He whispered.

Their blood started to fizz as the eight soldiers began to assemble their weapons. Alexander watched his brothers at work, feeling a warm sense of belonging.

If he was honest with himself, he would have admitted these were the worst days of his life thus far. Four-Section joked their course should have been changed from 'Basic Infantry Qualifications' to 'Basic cleaning qualifications'. The young men had spent more time with a broom and mop than learning field tactics. Toman joked that his rifle saw more CLP down the barrel than bullets. But then again, he usually had something to say.

The young men normally got 'Jacked' during morning inspection, but Sergeant Gustoveson never took it too far. Not like some of the other section-commanders. Alexander could recall one particular story of being discovered by the Master Corporal who ran Three-Section.

In this encounter, Joshua and his fire-team partner, Toman, were eating the beef jerky they had packed with them, sitting in their trench they had recently finished digging. A sergeant walked among the rows of sleeping soldiers, as dusk had come and each took his turn resting. "What are you doing!" said the Master Corporal mentioned, "Why aren't you manning your gun?" "We were told to take a break by Sergeant Gustovesen." "The right flank must always be covered! Get up! Out of your hole." The boys hoped out. "Now fill it!" What? "Fill it now!"

Alexander never forgot the rise of that morning's sun... He was just about done re-digging his trench as the star began to rise. He spent the entire night at the other end of a shovel.

Needless to say, Four-Section was grateful to have Gustoveson, and each appreciated his fine eye for imperfection. Most mornings he assertively reminded his men of this fact. His pinky-finger would always find dirt in someone's weapon, or a loose hair on the neck, missed in the morning's hasty shave.

But today was different. Their last inspection, their final morning of the dreaded and tiresome days, soon to be over as only one exercise stood between them and an actual status of Soldier within the army of the recently formed United Nations of America.

And the boys appreciated the Sergeants easy inspection of the morning. They needed all their energy focused on the task at hand; the final urban operations exercise was today, and they were excited to get their last *Ex* underway. The boys left feeling energized, not for the test of wit and will about to be had, but for it to be finished, followed by a well-deserved rest.

"Snap out of it buddy," Vermette said to Alexander, waving his hand in front of his lost eyes. Private Vermette's easy smile brought Alexander back to life, as he reassured his comrade of the ease in the zephyr. "Stand-to, my friend!"

Chapter Seven

Déjà Vu

"The Boast of heraldry, the pomp of pow'r,
And all that beauty, and that wealth e'er gave,
Awaits alike the inevitable hour.
The paths of glory lead but to the grave."

-Elegy written in a Country Churchyard

***

The convoy of trucks stopped after what seemed like an hour of driving. The chatter and jokes lasted about ten minutes. Nothing but silence afterwards.

The soldiers spewed out the back of the trucks to a bunch of angry yelling. Those who dropped their weapons regretted it instantly as a Sergeant screamed bloody murder in the faces of the weak. Those who couldn't find footing hit the dirt, as the flood of eager young soldiers continued, their showers later revealed bruises from where the boots of their comrades made dark impressions.

Private Vermette led Four-Section out of the back of the large, green canopied-truck to a defensive position he spotted about fifty meters to their right. Alexander stayed at the butt of the truck helping his men get out of the back. As the last boots hit the dirt, he turned to see the remaining three sections dysfunctionally assemble.

"Hey!" He yelled with a wave, signaling for them to follow. Four-Section established a defensive position as the rest of the platoon filed in. As Alexander reached the shrubbery he motioned for them to take up a spot on the ground.

The copse lived; it moved and spoke, and the occasional "ow!" or soft whisper came from the hiding spot. Private Seyer made his way towards the center of the oblong circle. Vermette was there already with his compass in hand and map flat on the ground.

"Find us yet?" Alexander asked quietly as he walked inwards, "I saw a twin peak roughly half a kilometer high and a kilometer wide, directly south from here.

Vermette went to his knees as he scoured the map for such a landmark.

"Smith saw power lines running north to south, maybe three or four hundred meters in the east." said Lonegan, One-Sections best asset upon entering the circle. He was put in command of the platoon and he entered with Smith from Two-Section, followed by Private Cass (the platoon's only female) and Private Holmes from Three-Section.

"Good eye, Smith!" Vermette shot out, still looking at the map, "I have us."

"How far are we?" said Cass, her voice was hardened by the constant male interactions she had to face. All the men of the platoon respected her, and thought of her as a great soldier. Despite her hair pinned back, and her face absent of any make-up, her natural beauty radiated from her as a constant lure towards the rest of the platoon. But not here. Not now.

"What does *The Great* think?" Smith said, not giving Vermette a chance to respond.

Alexander didn't much care for the nickname. He chose not to look at the young soldier who spoke with a smile.

"I think I want to be the first platoon to the objective, so let's do this quick." Alexander said towards Vermette.

"Alright, I've got it. We're ten kilometers out. We need to head north, my compass reads 0420 mils. Let's move."

***

The platoon took cover in the forest which Vermette assured was just before the objective. As the scouts returned, a jolt of adrenaline hit the single file of soldiers led by Lonegan. Smith and Toman had gone ahead of the platoon to survey the mock city they were about to invade. Upon returning, Toman pulled out the quick sketch he drew-up of what he saw from on top of the ridge, where he and Smith had stopped and observed for three minutes. (No more, no less). Both men saw no sign of enemy movement and returned with the information they were sent for.

Gasping for breath, they approached Lonegan. Coming from the rear joined Seyer and Vermette. Cass thought "What the hell," and joined as well.

Alexander grabbed the map, its lines and landmarks reminded him of a drawing made by a toddler; nevertheless, it showed some key information. The two runners went to their canteens for water, their tactical vests frustrating the thirsty young men. Smith rubbed his neck as he drank, apparently sore from running with the unwanted helmet atop his head. They waited for any questions, gulping the liquid in between breaths.

Seyer handed the map to Lonegan and Cass, as its ambiguous framework was of little importance to him now. He climbed the knoll the platoon had stopped behind. He signaled his comrades to rise, the soldiers in prone, hardly visible in the tall grass and hilly terrain, sprout up from the ground, like a mechanical sea of green and white and black. "The objective in the back?" Lonegan said indecisively looking up towards Alexander. He stood behind the knoll, looking out in a temperate eagerness.

"As far as we could tell!" Toman spoke, taking a deep breath mid-sentence, "There's the entrance. And see this rectangle on the building? That's the flag we saw. It definitely stood out... Don't know what that means."

"So let's enter cautiously single file, looking for any hidden enemy fortifying the objective," Lonegan said, looking for approval.

"Well then..." Alexander's calm response, "prepare your men."

Holmes led Three-Section through the chain link fence. The solitary gate was wide open, creating an unease within the ranks.

Although they seemed to have made it quickly to their destination (no sight of any others), Alexander couldn't help feeling they weren't the first to arrive. Slowing down and checking their weapons, (all had training rifles, a new replica designed specifically for exercises like this); the soon to be soldiers set their rifles to stun. Many fumbling with the safety as the adrenaline found in anxious fear took over most.

Private Seyer and Four-Section entered last. The barbed wire fence and brick buildings were a gloomy presence. The size seemed unnecessary and his mind wandered as to what this place is, or perhaps could have been. The large compound, a rectangular host of various abandoned buildings situated in the outskirts. A gravel road, seemingly infinite, lead from the mouth, into the fenced enclosure. Weeds and grass could be seen protruding from the dust, the dry air making each breath troublesome.

As Alexander approached, he couldn't help but feel somewhere else. In a different time, or a different place, as if he had been there before. As he surveyed a large brick building, its broken windows, graffitied walls and sagging fence revealed to him an unknown history. The emptiness opened up his mind to the possibilities of what could be or may have been.

"Déjà vu," he thought as he began to wonder where he had seen this place before. The imperfection, a remnant of history no doubt.

Over the shrubbery he walked, the smell of desertion came up from the dust.

"Was it in a dream?" he thought, thinking of the circumstances behind his sudden exposure to a world envisioned before, "Or am I dreaming now? Or perhaps, but a vision from a former life?" Alexander's mind wandered as this world awoke an inexpressible feeling he had been here before.

Upon seeing Lonegan directing traffic, the men all taking position about a hundred meters ahead, a bad feeling entered him.

"Four-Section!" shouted Private Seyer, as if suddenly snapping back to life. The young men all looked at him, rifles clutched tight, as if they had been staring at him for hours, waiting for his prophetic words.

"Take cover in that alley!"

Quickly they stacked against the building to the left. Hidden from the sight of the gate, only fifteen meters from the entrance. Alexander walked towards Cass, Lonegan, and Holmes, as each sections representative sought understanding.

"What are you doing? We have to protect that building!" said Lonegan in a panic. His red face expressed his nervous demeanor, remembering his responsibility of the operation. "Your section is to guard the rear as we take our positions inside!"

As if remembering a dream he had once had before, Alexander stood silently, within a town forlorn. For a moment, he was alone. The only sound, the dry summer wind; the only sight, the blue and white sky. He stood alone within a memory unknown.

"No, our objective has changed. Everything has changed.".".

Alexander crouched, a small dusty patch at his feet became his canvass. Cass cringed at the scratch of fine gravel (a sound she detested) as Alexander's finger penetrated the earth. Lonegan and the others looked towards Alexander as he painted a picture with his finger. The square buildings, arrows, numbers, and stones created the scene of what was to come.

The four leaders broke off, quickly collecting their men, taking their new positions.

Chapter Eight

Vive la Revolution

"And even those who were brought forth from the desire of lust for damnation, having inside them the seed that is lust for damnation, will receive the recompense of good things, and provided they decide to do so deliberately, and are willing to abandon their vain love of temporary glory so as to do the command of the Lords of Glory, and instead of that small temporary honor, they will inherit the eternal kingdom."

- The Tripartite Tractate

***

Virginia, 2058. Just east of the Appalachian Mountains:

"Stand to! Stand to!"

Chief Warrant Officer Seyer, also known as *'The Great Alexander"*, cried out as the whistles of mortar shells incoming could be heard. He felt the ground move under him and was awoken impetuously. Cold and wet, the sun just minutes from peeking in the sky, Alexander rushed to the front lines, eyes wide and heart racing.

Vermette was on the right flanks. The now-sergeant was nodding off, crouched in his trench. He quickly stirred at the sound of the whistles, and felt the earth shake from behind, and beneath. As debris flew over his head, he sprung up to his machine gun, instinctively scanning the earth in front of him. Down the open hill and into the forest movement and flashes of light could be seen; the sound of muffled mortar explosions, *Thump,*

Thump... from behind. He squeezed slowly and firmly on the trigger, tearing the air open, an onslaught of propelled hatred and anger.

Alexander was the only man out of the trenches. Yelling furiously, the men awoke from the screaming command, and the cries of the shells. They stood tall, shivering in their wet gear, not quite asleep but not fully awake either.

The sound of the machine gun firing to their right and the whistles screaming overhead caused the heart rate of each man to jump from one to a hundred. Many scrambled for their rifles while some began to take aim, the sound of popping coming from the ridge emerged, accompanied with the heavy bass of the rumbling earth, and the cries of dying men. The air filled with smoke and hot lead. The smell, so potent.

The earth and its inhabitants, torn apart.

Alexander jumped into a nearby trench, as debris from a nearby explosion nearly engaged him. Inside the trench, a young private (probably on the tail end of puberty) knelt, shaking as he attempted to cock his weapon.

The hardened commander said nothing, the warm breath made smoke in the air, speaking for him. Grabbing the soldier's weapon in haste, he prepped it to fire.

Alexander looked at the boy as he shivered — from fear or from the chill, Alexander could not tell. The earth moved, dirt and smoke filling the air. He could only hear the sound of his heart beating and his calm breath as all else became white noise and invisible vibrations. He felt pity for the young man for just a moment, shivering from weakness — unknowably mental or physical, but weakness all the same.

Chief Seyer handed the boy his weapon and smiled, giving him a solid punch to the chest. Looking him deep into the eyes, the young man felt the ease and strength of Alexander's behavior awaken an animal within, ready to slaughter. Losing all fear, prepared to kill or to be killed, his elbows reached the surface of the earth; his eyes over and through the weapons sight, seeing the enemy, yet looking at himself.

Blood is thicker than water;
The young Private would come to know this.

Standing in the puddle that was his trench, blood and mud thrown about; the young man took aim and shot along with Alexander, Vermette, and the others, killing the enemy — men just like themselves.

***

Alexander was at war with everything he once stood for. Born into a wealthy American family, he excelled at everything he did. He continuously sought for affection from his father, a doctor, and a part time professor at the State's University. His mother stayed at home, cleaning, cooking, or chatting most of the day. Alexander noticed early in life that his mother seemed to be more interested in her friends than in he. Hosting an array of parties, most going late into the night. The bass would overtake the quiet room of the young boy as he attempted to sleep, eyes red and body numb, wishing someone would just come to him and say goodnight.

He loved history and remembered the stories of ancient warriors he read. Stories where mortal men faced sure death and despair, only to overcome, emerging immortal as legends. Lands in crisis, a single warrior fights wholeheartedly, and claims unquestionable victory. All such men were men of old, from an ancient law he learnt not in the class-room. And so, he left the path his family paved, and sought his own truth and glory.

Declaring war on one's enemy, virtuous.
Declaring war on one's family, divine.

Alexander fought for years. He was the leader of many battles and wins with the Senate controlled UNA. But as time went on, the enemy, he would see, became those he used to kill for. The closer to power he climbed, the closer to corruption he found himself.

Words marked by the soldiers who heard his cry before the battle's lore:

"...The result of a people so desperate for comfort, so eager to become one with the system. All complied to their rules and thoughts and ideas, with no time for criticism, no time to question, no time to decide for themselves!

They brainwashed us into submission, and now I say we forcefully take it back! Like the ways of our forefathers, who fought for honor, for glory, for truth and for justice. Not for Money, or possessions, or manipulative power!

It's been long enough! I say we do away with it, before it destroys us forever!"

Not long before the revolution, the young Chief Warrant Officer became a piece of the UNA's largest act of genocide ever recorded, which went beyond any nuclear warfare ever consorted. These records were quickly erased as the empire declared all technology to be banished. The nuclear destruction was deemed an internal act of terrorism. And at first, the United Nations of America maintained control.

Rumor was circulated of an *Artificial Intelligence Spawn*. Propaganda or not, no one could find blame... every major opposing-forces country equally and utterly obliterated, along with many allies. A decimation of all around the world, dead by the craft of a power-hungry people, blaming incompetence as the means, and ignorance surely the agent. Billions, and Billions wiped away, like bacteria sneezed into a tissue, and flushed down the toilet.

Alexander Seyer, a young Chief Warrant Officer, along with his obedient men, overthrew their disgraceful leadership.

True patriotism: To kill or be killed for one's beliefs.

As the world burned (the people along with the earth itself), the aristocrats in fear hid within their wealth. From behind carefully-calculated closed doors, they watched as families buried one another. And propaganda momentarily abandoned, along with the age of technology.

Alexander witnessed the disgrace. His regiment traveled from city to city, raising a *Coup d'Etat;* Alexander's message hit everyone with an ear to hear, and his stories were printed for all with eyes to read. The Senate no longer had power over its citizens, as their most important piece, Alexander and his men, no longer accepted orders.

The people had seen too much death under the Senate; and Alexander's *coup* succeeded after the culminated battle, dug into the eastern side of the continent.

Alexander was given credit for the victory. The new and disfigured world and its intellects stood behind the moralistic young warrior, who fought the world's most feared enemy, and won.

The young General was given complete sovereignty. But instead, abandoning absolute power to observed democracy, in a form of anarchist's state of governance, the continent and its foreign subordinates ruled at the lay-level. Collective communities, the distribution of power, and the destruction of the class-system were universally accepted. But the world only fell deeper into depression.

At the beginning of the next decade, Alexander the great, Lord Seyer, vanished from the seen world, becoming a shadow to the public eye. An impression of his leadership stamped on the world as it moved, but exercised from a distance. The spirit of Alexander seemingly hidden.

For another year the diminished populous ached over the earth. The worldwide smog of the nuclear-decimated world started to lift, and the tired and worn out survivor's yearned for hope. Aware of all that occurred, yet allowing free will in each individual. *Plugging-in* became the world's last option; the hungry and desperate majority chose to allow its use once again.

The bill passed with approval and quickly after, a new project circulated, prepared by Lord Alexander Seyer himself — the warrior in recluse.

The legends of him passed by word of mouth, and repeated speeches gave the man divine status. His letters sprung-up within people a new hope! Seeking approval, Lord Alexander Seyer revealed plans for a great ship to be built. The ambitious proposal to rival the tower of Babel, and was an excitable topic discussed all through the modern world. A vessel to be called, *'The Event Horizon.'*

He proposed that mankind would not survive much longer the way things were going. That sooner or later the battle for self-preservation and needs, would once again lead to such sorrow and pain as witnessed in recent history.

"The heavens are our only option," he would say pointing up. "We live like barbarians, fighting over scraps of land when we were meant to explore, above and beyond!"

This ushered in a new age. A time of seeming progress, where the mines were opened, projects invested, and bright minds hard at work. Young, cold, and weak, Alexander and his empire went to work, just as eager and prepared to die as the day he started.

On the battlefield, nothing mattered but the brother beside you, his blood baptizing you into the faith of old.

Kill or be killed.

And Alexander would be haunted forever, a new world exposed to him through the years of fighting, remembering his baptism all too well, back in the training compound of the UNA, so many years ago...

***

Cass and the men of Two-Section took up watch behind Four. The westernmost-building they occupied covered most of the objective they were to control, as well as overwatch of the alley Alexander and his men stood. Flush against the wall, rifles pointed towards the center of the compound, Alexander stood with his men in anticipation, knowing he was not to react instantly on sight, even if he wanted to.

It seemed as if time stood still for the men. They became nervous in their anticipation — the wait eternal. Rifles hung from tired arms, gentle whispers echoed through the men passing time in a forgetful manner. The *Chug!* sound of water splashing from within the canteens signaled a relaxed platoon, a company of undisciplined men without a care but the immediate present.

Alexander stared at the street ahead, watching and waiting.

It was in this uncertain amount of time that Alexander remembered his dream. The feeling he had stood on this spot before, with these men behind him, manifesting a mystery within that would live on, invariably until his last breath.

As he found himself, lost in the thought of what this might mean, the snap of a shot woke him from the dream. He could hear each ball of energy as it passed his eyes, along with the thump of his heart beginning to pound in his chest. It seemed now, his heart beating, and breath repeating, was louder than all else.

He remained motionless, kneeling at the front of the stack, not looking at the men behind him; hoping they were ready, hoping they would not yet spoil their cover. A jolt of adrenaline came over him as a lean man in dust colored camouflage took cover in their alley. Not seeing them, the soldier fired towards One-Section's gunners on the main drag. The enemy advancing forward, beyond the corridor. And the solitary man, standing erect, his left hand against the wall, stabilizing his sinister weapon, right hand pulling the trigger, aiming at Lonegan's men. He took a few shots, then ran forward.

Unseen as he had hoped, and the silence reassuring his plan was in motion, Private Seyer imagined the two gunners, Young and Wald, retreating from their position as planned. The two were to fall back to the rest of their section, who waited patiently out of sight upon the roof of the building just beside their objective. As Alexander and his men waited, fingers patiently resting on their triggers, five or six more men passed the alleyway.

Alexander waited for the signal.

All of a sudden, he heard his men from the back of the fortification shouting and shooting. He rose to his feet, not diving in to the numbness and tingle in his legs which were on the verge of collapsing from the dull and static position.

As the enemy advanced towards the objective, where a hail of blue volleys came from One-Section, the enemy overcome — no shots returning. To Alexander's front a man turned sharply toward him, rifle aimed to kill. Seyer fired his rifle and hit him directly in the chest. Like a paintball, a blue glow protruded from the enemy's now rigid body. He, falling to his back, revealed another target directly behind. Almost in sync, a hail of shots from above — surely Cass and her section eager to join in.

Alexander became undoubtedly aware of what was to come. Disconcerted, his memory of the dream flashed over him. He at the front of the stack prepared for his fate. Toman, directly behind him, raised his rifle over Alexander's shoulder. The tip seen in his peripherals, quickly double-tapping his trigger at the enemy who sprouted towards them, now aware of the hidden presence.

Alexander stepped away from the wall, shooting his rifle at the now visible army, stacked as they on the other side of the brick barrier, the building all seemed to hug so tight.

Private Seyer could see this was not another platoon in training — the enemies' fatigues of foreign design.

All of a sudden, a shot went by his head, hitting the brick behind him! Alexander instinctively returned fire and stepped back. No blue glow was seen to his left. Although his realization of the true peril encountered only lasted a minute, Alexander saw the damage the wall endured — soon to be his brother. A bullet had flown by his head; and as if preparing to say something, perhaps halting the operation, Alexander watched benumbed as a dark soldier bounded from the hidden street, and shot him directly in his thigh. The sound of the shot was forever remembered in his mind, as well as the initial pain of the bullet as it penetrated his skin. In the cold winters that followed, an ache in his left leg would remind him of the event. Again, and again he would relive those final memories of the operation, as he was knocked to his ass, the sight of his friends fighting at his side.

Before all went dark, blackness overtaking the senses, he remembered seeing his friend, his brother Toman, standing erect with his rifle firing — in an instant crumpling to the earth; his body an architectural mess against the opposite wall. The blue storm fell heavy upon the assailant and any others who were caught in Alexander's ambush. The dust floating about and sticking to the sweat and the blood on each man. A river of their body fluids flowed as Alexander held onto his leg, looking over toward his brother — already departed. And the overwatch, unaware they were taking down a platoon of foreign invaders. The blood shocked their senses. Later records would reveal a detriment to the UNA's military from this continental incursion. Alexanders platoon suffered but one casualty, and one wounded. Much better odds than the platoon in training, who got caught headed towards them, not fifteen minutes behind.

Soon after the battle was won, Cass cried uncontrollably overtop Alexander's still body, and looking over to the mess of skin and blood and bone and fatigues that was now Toman; the pools of blood on the dry ground left an outflow of prints as it clung to the boots of each soldier, who wandered and wondered as to what had happened.

And as if it were all a distant memory, Alexander woke up, once again, as if from a dream.

Déjà vu, all over again.

Chapter Nine

Event Horizon

Journal Entry of Michael, father of Jonathan:

"What is God?

If we approach the question in such a way, describing the idea as What, rather than Who, does it bring the idea to a broader level? If we limit the Idea of God to a Who, or more specifically, a 'He', we put a humanistic limit to what It is, or could be. We limit God to a basic understanding on a human level. If we alternatively see It as a What instead of a Who, we can see a unity of all faiths and religions... From Jesus to Baba Nanak, Allah to YHWH. Krishna to Osiris.

We act as though we live fully in spirit, yet we cannot live undeniably materialistic. We are so caught up in matter we cannot comprehend a life apart from it. We still look at the body and see matter in control, flesh and blood, proteins and nerves, functioning in a miraculous yet fully graspable way.

A microcosm of true existence.

When we assign the title of Good (for many, this is a unified description of God), and give it a gender, we bring this huge concept, one that cannot be defined in language, manifested by our finitude, and limit it to human description.

Everything we see and touch is reduced to a gender. Le and La, He and She. And apparently, God falls under such dominion.

Is this the story of God? Was this unexplainable force, so great and mighty, put into stories of old, simply given a gender assignment? Helping the listener to identify the unidentifiable?

The idea, more ancient than writing itself; is this the understanding we currently possess? Have we developed any sort of better knowledge of It? Or have we continuously drifted, as a single consciousness, barely grasping the cusp of what It could be. Still reducing this unknowable force to a materialistic understanding!"

***

"Attennnnnnnnntion!"

The mass crowd stood all at once. Minutes already read, the mundane and unimportant eagerly ignored. Those who love to talk had taken their time and the elected officials stood in silence, waiting for the conclusion. After a few heated debates and even one fellow who stomped out, the meeting continues. Not unlike most assemblies, the men and women acted as infants, dull in mind and body.

The rustling of papers, a few whispers cut short, and Alexander enters the room.

His *Thump! Thump! ... Thump! Thump* broke the silence. The wounded veteran's steps were in tune with everyone's heartbeat. The suppressed excitement filled the room, the energy monitors spiked.

He was in control.

Man has always played war. It's built into us.

And the ancient war of politics, an important attachment. And these more specifically just the latest version... But soon to be executed.

Lord Seyer couldn't stand these things. Their game of politics was now just theatre. Bystanders watch as the veil of democracy bows to the dictator as he enters.

You could hear a few *gulps* in between each echoed step he made. No eye dared look into that of Alexander's. The silence spoke volumes to the reverence pulsating in the room.

"At ease, everyone," he said rather lightly approaching the podium front and center. The mic was there but wasn't needed, they listened to their entrusted emperor in awe

and wonder. Yet he always looked back at them with the same manner. His heavy-laden eyes looked up to meet the gaze of nearly half the ship's population. The others watch from their suites on board. This was the moment they were waiting for.

Their solution cleared his throat...

"Hello all. We have called this emergency meeting to discuss the future of your survival, and your children's survival and their children's survival."

Pause for effect.

"The rumor of a shortage of food is true. We will not make it another harvest. Our consumption and rapid growth rate here on The Event Horizon cannot be met and we must act quickly.

"This is not the first time we have needed hasty action. Within the last few hundred years our kinds has been plagued with the disease of our ancestors; we have been fighting a losing battle against our mother, Earth. I hate to say it people, but our mother doesn't want us here any more. She's made her decision, and it's time we flew the coop."

A few soft whispers were heard, but not for long. No one dared upset their god speaking in the flesh.

"Our forefathers decided our fate years ago. Our leaders globally failed to act, they failed to create peace and perseverance. We drifted aimlessly towards extinction. But then we made a choice. We chose to act. We formed a new means of running the world. Under a

NEW United Nations, supported by all other major governments, we created true Wholeness. We reverted back to tribal days and appointed the leadership to one man.

"One man, to care for humankind, collectively, under one banner. What great honor and responsibility bestowed upon me; and such responsibility I endure as a burden not meant to weigh upon any others. You chose me to act, and act I shall. And now, I declare this a new age!"

His voice, starting to raise, passion taking over the melancholy man.

"We will leave this planet! In its dust we shall choke no more! Man is too great for such a home. We leave in search of one that we will not only survive on, but thrive on! We regret what our forefathers did to us; they cursed us and this planet. They thought they were so smart, yet they could not predict our obvious end. We can no longer stay with our mother, we've been suckling her tit far too long. She doesn't want us any more, so you know what I say...

"We don't need her!"

Cheers were now heard. Their trust in Alexander was so great they didn't care what needed to be done. They were happy to leave what most of them had never seen and what Alexander had seen too much of.

Alexander's passions started to simmer at the height of the cheering. Most felt this and quieted down a little, perplexed at this unforeseen shift in mood.

"There is one thing that remains to be mentioned, those who still walk upon the Earth. Those who chose a life of our ancestors; disillusioned by the promise of happiness, accepting their prison sentence. We cannot allow them to feed off our lives any more, for the future of our children depends on this need for action."

He said this as if to convince even himself.
We have never been a true match for the ego.

Moved for the people who worshipped him, and as a cheer erupted, Alexander's mind fell deep into thought:

Is it because of fear they don't kill me? Fear of death, of life? Of pain, sorrow, hatred, displeasure?
"Death itself is no one's fault, for all are destined to rust and rot.
"I hold mankind itself within my midst. Whether by war, famine, ignorance, age, frailty... all are doomed to perish. And I, merely involved within the process, instead of an ignorant passerby.
"The question of 'Why?' remains outside of my power. But the question of 'When?' realistically mine to answer.
"What shall be my ending?
"All things must surely end, and I along with them. This age is sure to end, just like all ages that came before it. Ushering a new era, when will The Time of Alexander reach its fin? Shall it continue? On into eternity? If so, can I last much longer? Can I survive the torment of this position for years to come? Seeing the life and death of those within your control, your influence and power, manipulating the entire being of a species...
"I stand unmoved, lost in a detached humanity. A society of animals."

"This world and these people are doomed! But each one of you will survive. This is the last time many of you will see me, as each one of you will be placed into a cryo-unit. As you sleep, Captain Lenore will lead this ship into the unknown. Our handpicked team of scientists will remain at work and will not sleep until they find us a new home."

Energy continued to build in the huge auditorium.

"We have had faith in all that they have done. These minds have not let us down yet. Working night and day, they seek to find us a new home, but we can no longer do it here, we must move on, and I know they will find a home for us. Perhaps not in my lifetime, or perhaps not even in theirs. But I assure you, when you wake-up, in the future, you will open your eyes to a new world.

"And we will endure!"

Part II

Where were you when I laid the foundations of the earth? Tell me, if you have understanding.

Who determined its measurements? Surely you know!

Or who stretched the line upon it? To what were its foundations fastened?

Or who laid its cornerstone, when the morning stars sang together, and all the sons of God shouted for joy?

Or who shut in the sea with doors, when it burst forth and issued from the womb;

When I made the clouds its garment, and thick darkness its swaddling band.

- Job 38: 4-9

Wherein lies salvation?
In the heart, in the mind?
In the body, in the spirit?
Perhaps our descendants, or our forebears...
Can there be true salvation
From the sorrows of this world.
From pain and grief, destruction and death?
Is true salvation from the woes of one's life,
Graspable?
Attainable?
Can I hold such a thing within my hands?
Can I see it as I wake?
This question has puzzled me for far too long.

Every human must face his own sorrows of this world.
For some, a moment;
For others, a lifetime.

Chapter Ten

Maan

Nature, or nurture? Are we built structurally, by the very fabric that makes me, *Me*? The deep seeded code I inhibit, and inhibit alone?

The only personal touch to such an impersonal world.

How can someone truly know themselves, if they know nothing of their etiology? Of what or who they stem from... How can one know themselves if they know not the genetic code, imprinted within their foundation; written at first life, passed on through countless lives before.

All things, split in two.

But the personal is nothing without the impersonal. The essence of the structure is necessary; yet we've become so focused on the structure, we forget the unpredictable world inside.

Joshua, my one and only son, the only such peace I can find in a hostile world as this. My adopted son, sharing not my blood, but the blood of a coward; nonetheless remains one of mine, another abandoned baby boy given over to the Government; the one I loathe to serve day in and day out.

Another life rejected;
By their hands... into their hands.

They say with age comes wisdom, but to me, all makes less sense every night I lay; only to attempt sleep with eyes open, drifting in and out of thoughts and memories, and the horrific future I envision.

One thing I will admit: I saw this day coming a long time ago.

I sleep here in my quarters every night. The soft glow of the moon shines through the barred windows as it travels across the floor and rests on my bare walls. A little wooden dresser holds all I own. Inside the drawers contain the few possessions that remind me of a forgotten world. One of visions, dreams, and goals. On top sits an FM radio, now considered an artefact. I've worked hard to maintain its working order, mastering the craft of electronics for most of my life.

My mastered craft, the source of my incarceration.

Many nights I lie awake, wondering when the end will come, hoping to witness its inevitable climax. The end that I've been waiting for, yet unsure of its personal significance.

Too long I've watched as we've sucked this planet dry. Too long I've internally struggled, living and serving under a selfish breed: The Human of the 21st Century.

Death reaches us all;
But extinction...

This is my fear.

The God of my fore-fathers, the Christian God who died with the ancient religions... I can't help but feel he also has left me for dead; abandoned along with the world we destroyed.

And I, a spoil of war.

My plan of escape has always hindered on one aspect: my willingness to make an attempt. To make a break for it, risking the punishment, knowing full well the consequence if I shall fail, the only reason I lie here once again.

Well, not the only reason.

I lie here, another night among countless others, staring at the moonlight. The silence, my companion, as not even a cricket chirps in the lonesome darkness.

I see the day as trivial, and my thoughts nothing but internal torment. Am I the only one who sees the horrors of this world? Who sees the oblivion that awaits me and all others? I'm curious as to if any are like me. If any question like me, seeking a better way, a better future, sick of living in a bleak present...

Am I alone?

Perhaps others share my sorrow. Though we speak not of it. I wonder if this is what the peasants of Seven see. The lowly slaves of those in power. Their eyes seem empty, as do mine.

But the eyes of one, unlike the others. The one I've learnt to be known only as, *Achilles*.

Does he see what I see?
Does he feel as I feel?

Of all species upon the earth, it would likely seem, Man has conquered all.

We became ruler and governor of all that lived and breathed, subduing and lording over all. A virus, a plague, on the earth and its inhabitants.

But, long ago, there existed a day where we roamed as a protector of the world. We stood together to survive with all species.

Until that is, the time of Adam and Eve;
The first enlightened ones.

Near the beginning of the 21st century, the market for capitalism was nothing but debt. The governments began to take control of the populous more firmly as they grew concerned of internal revolt; converting the mob into workers for their respective countries. The loyal consumers would resist the purges of the poor, and the politicians would turn them against each other when needed.

The Dream Machine took over the entertainment world. It became an unbelievable success. The company drove the stocks into record breaking numbers, consumers were hooked, and it developed new models constantly. This type of expansion self birthed complete manipulation. At the same time, the Governments of the western world lived in fear as terrorism from anti-capitalist and anti-religious groups became no longer terrorism, but fully fledged war.

And the most effective weapon of war: propaganda. The UNA ultimately controlled the company and its device, plugging in became a weapon of mass destruction.

My grandfather would tell of how they fought for control over the entire world as we knew it. Aggression and stupidity scared its foes until the ever-expanding United Nations of America made the largest undeclared act of terrorism in the history of human beings, unleashing an array of nuclear warheads; all major countries virtually wiped out, on July 5th, 2057.

The world, as was known to me, wiped away;
But my war continued.

Signing of The Artificial Intelligence Protection act, the senate of America quickly stated, through verbal and written proclamation, that all computer systems were condemned. Suddenly, the world of all the lay folk came to a halt. Sparking another famine, as the product, *The Dream Machine,* was no longer needed, nor accepted.

And so came the revolution.

***

As I return to the task at hand, the thoughts of the past seemingly relentless upon eve's fall, the sound of boots on the ground stirs me into a frenzy. For some reason I knew tonight was the night. And it was confirmed as I reached the front door of my chambers.

These darkened hallways alight! Each barred opening I pass, gleaming from a light not of our moon. I reach the stairwell, each step counting down the anticipation of freedom.

What does it all mean?

It's as if I've lived a life of holding my breath, waiting for a savior, anything to take me away. The sun once shined through these windows, but now only shadows remain. The stillness and darkness lures.

Whoever wasn't awake before, surely would be now.

The large heavy doors burst open as three soldiers come through in a line. I stand paralyzed as they advance, rifle lead, into the dark corridors of the factories living quarters.

Somehow, in my motionless fear, they pass me without notice.

I waste no time to exit. Startled by two men standing outside, I stand but for a moment in between them. Both like magnetic opposites, rifles pointed towards the outer darkness, looking perhaps for a runner.

As if anyone shall be of such courage and bravery.

Perhaps luck, or God's manipulation, somehow I hobble silently towards the front gate, like a ghost, present, but only to the chosen. I dare not turn, as the calls and cries from my fellow inmates are heard.

Fellow inmates. *Mates*, I wish I could call them.

But my one friend, Joshua comes to mind. My adopted son, the poor devil.

Left to rot with the rest, out there beyond the hedges.

He propels me forward.

Reaching the high, chain link fence that contains me, like a rat being observed, incarcerated, I stop and think aloud;

"What am I doing?"

How could a man, old like myself, wasted away by time, and haunted by history, climb this fence and miraculously reach the outer world. The world, I've observed to be even more incarcerated.

It would seem I've grown soft over time.

He, along with Achilles and the others, would be out there preparing for their day's work, in complete ignorance, but if my intuition is correct, left in solitude, as Alexander makes his final decisions. My guess: Deserting Earth to its inevitable demise.

Abandoned, but abandoned to freedom.

Perhaps they won't make it. Perhaps the ways of the past will eat them up. Maybe time will prove to have weakened them so much as it has me. But, maybe they will find the inner spirit, the strength God gave humanity, so long ago. The strength that still dwells somewhere within.

And perhaps my task is not over. Maybe I was destined to be taken along, boarded upon the Event Horizon, as a prisoner of the tyrant, *Le Bon,* Alexander; *The Great* Seyer.

Of this, I have no doubt. And as far I can see, the only chance at ending his tyrannical rule, hope in karmic justice, and perhaps, my involvement.

Hope, the only thing a man has when all else is taken from him.

But the question remains, how do you fix a broken world?

Would it be ethical to kill? To end the life of a man who has ended so many others... To lie to get to him? To cheat and deceive, to manipulate the manipulator; a life sacrificed to sin, for even the slightest chance at looking into his eyes, and seeing to their departure?

Although I realize what I must do, if the day comes where I look into the man's eyes, what *would* I do? If, with the odds so overwhelmingly against me, I managed to see into his dark, dead eyes, could I accomplish what I know I must?

As I finally understand my lot, my destiny, I unshoulder my bag, search for a flat rock, and grab my *Boulder Buddy,* (A product of old I worked frivolously for).

The sound of boots begins to rise over the sound of my pen, the smell of the charred rock causes my eyes to water. The smoke, no doubt a signal to any who perhaps searched for me but knew not where I was to be found. Frantically, as I hear a voice yell from behind me, unsure of what I wrote, or if it even complete, I muster all the strength from within, toss the rock over the fence, raise my arms in familiar instinct, and suddenly a pinch in my chest, and all becomes black.

Darkness surrounds everything.

Chapter Eleven

Over Hill, Under Foot

Journal entry of Michael, Grandfather of Achilles.

How long will the god of sorrow torment me?
Is pain not enough, but to pile up?
Like a single brick in the foundation,
Buried under all the hurt.
It goes unseen, untouched, for far too long.
Trouble has been following.
My words grow in uncertainty. Condemning me with every syllable.
Yet as I sit silently, here once again, what is to come?
Nothing of good, and nothing of bad.
I search words of wisdom, but to understand takes wisdom.
I act a wise man, but live a lie.
The master of inequity permeates the clock.
Eating at these precious minutes, like bacteria on a corpse. Rotting, even before death.
Those who have never heard the cries of children in the masses, weeping in pain, pleading for mercy as their rib cage protrudes from the side;
And the silence that ensues, as these children lay awake, greeted by maggots at death's door;
And such as these, living naively in ignorance, can never claim to have met this God I know, and have yet to experience the suffering that is to come,
Shared by all.

***

Earth, third season of the Nineteenth year of the new age.

In the early mornings, everything stands still yet stirs; the quiet motion brings a warming calm to the self, reminding the host that the beauty of the other is where true life lies.

I still remember the day, twenty years ago; that fateful day we were left behind. As I stood there, back at the entrance of the Farm, with all those eyes staring at me, I had no easy answers to give. And as they stared, waiting for me to offer some glimmer of hope, some words of comfort, some divine salvation, I had no idea what to say.

So, I started at the beginning:

"Look around everyone at what you see... Before all this there was nothing.
Matter didn't exist, and neither did we.
Then something happened, something unforeseeable.
A miracle!
The creation of the cosmos',
Rocks and dust, water and air, and undeniably, us.
Some force, a great power managed to make something from nothing. We can't explain what it is or who it is, but what we know is that when we, life, became aware of the sacred right, we learned that we adhere to certain laws...
This mandate is to function in a way as to keep all matters consistent. In order for chaos (as is the universe) to be systematized it has to adhere to certain laws (or principles), governance, and hierarchy.
And listen when I say, truly all is chaos...
And so, one day a rebellion occurred, and these laws were broken.
Early members of our species did something; they broke the rules. They became thinking and moving flesh! This is how we came to be. Matter, (and when I say matter, I mean all things graspable by the senses, evolved in the realm of creation) learned how to move and operate.

Like a rock learning how to swim.

We don't know how this happened but we are here! I can see you, and you can hear me. But other than this basic truth, all we have is recorded speculation. Science, just a tool to observe such chaos, manifested in space and time, and manipulated by good or evil ..."

After my introduction, my energy and enthusiasm was met with perplexed minds, but attentive nonetheless. I proceeded to tell them of our history, from Gilgamesh, to Abraham, Pharaohs to Kings; cultural differences, technological advances, religious movements; political uprisings – as far as I had come to know them.

As I told many of these stories to the people, they sat in awe of my words.

This brought me hope.

My one fear, that plugging in had killed their minds along with their imagination and human spirit.

A lot of them didn't understand the words I spoke, but they were so captivated and so in need of hope, they sat for hours as I spoke.

They still talk about that day. Here, in the community, it's being told to the children. My ideas of keeping our race surviving, passing on our history, of utmost importance to our development. And as part of our educational workshops, we learn about our clans beginning.

As I sit up on the hill, the same hill I've awoken to since I can remember, the sun begins to rise. The orange glow brings peace of mind. The spirit passes through the air, and I sit and wonder... What is it all for?

It's been twenty years since that fateful day, the day we were left to our own vices; and tomorrow marks the anniversary. To celebrate, the greatest post-apocalyptic night of partying will commence at sundown. We've been preparing for weeks, arguably for years.

As we learn about that day and the importance of the years that followed, I'm reminded of the years of ache, the struggles we've incurred, and endured, together.

You can't quite describe the state of constant mourning. One knows the need for three days to grieve, the heartache all must face sooner or later. But when daily? This, a damnable sight.

For us, a day without death became warranted jubilation. Times were tough, but we held on tight. Soon, it was three days free from death. Things looked better. Then seven days, and all seemed brighter.

Man lives, toils under the sun, and dies. A vicious cycle of pain and hard work. Why? What does it all mean? The question I ask myself daily.

We've fought starvation, political unrest, torture, slavery and oppression. And tenfold after the UNA left... Times were hard, we had to start from the ground up! Learning together how to hunt and fish; trapping, horticulture and such; learning to survive took years! Then introducing astronomy, history, medicine, art... We used the few resources I had kept secret, now free to be shared and absorbed for all, yet maintained under me and my order, the small group of men and women, who've chosen the life of solitude, as I, upon Mount Sinai.

Much of our workable land remains at the farm. Although it first seemed the symbol of oppression, we needed to utilize its resources. It soon became not the symbol of oppression, but a symbol of liberation.

But freedom always comes at a price.

After I learnt of what the sign meant, and as Joshua and I spent many nights in discussion, we agreed to temporarily install me as Chief. I assured him it was temporary, until a proper council or senate could be instated, or when *Maan* would return.

Maan, the name of my scribe, my messenger, an angel, according to Joshua.

I walked the darkened doorways, the home of Maan and the other management. The cold walls revealed a prison of slaves just like me. A people, just as dependent on the system as us, only a little bit closer to the one in charge, behind the scene, running the show.

I was quite fond of Joshua when I met him. His stern facial features made him look as if to be constantly on alert. He would observe the world as it spun, yet repeat every word you had ever spoken.

Sometimes, I wish he'd just smile.

But smiling is for the living, and he (as I), dead inside.

***

I approached Gus as he read allowed to his pupils. It wasn't often these days that I visited classes in session, but the thought of seeing an old friend, especially as he read my favorite book, *Fight Club*, brought me to the small clearing in the forest where he read to the grown children. The much-deliberated novel a very odd choice for my father to keep, but was so popular within us, '*The Abandoned,*' as we call ourselves now. Here among the classics, historics, and scriptures, breathes a small paperback, visibly eroding from time and use.

Aloud, Gus read:

"*What you have to understand, is your father was your model for God.'*

Behind us, my job and my office are smaller, smaller, smaller, gone.

I sniff the gasoline on my hands.

The mechanic says, 'If you're male, and you're Christian and living in America, your father is your model for God. And if you never know your father, if your father bails out or dies or is never at home, what do you believe about God?"

A pause.

"Well, what do you believe about God?" I chime in from behind. Gus, unaware of my presence, turned rapidly; the young teens snicker, and I, smiling on approach, walking-stick in hand, leaves crunching underfoot.

"Yes, well that's part of the homework for today," Gus spoke directly to me, noticeably off-balance, and then to the class: "We will finish the chapter tom-"

"No, no, I would love to hear the rest, please..." I insisted.

And with a wave of my hand, he continues.

His reading voice was fantastic. I sat down with the children, but quickly realized the distractions. I could see the young mind wander on far away things, like the games they would soon be playing, the care-free lovers they would soon be chasing, or simply the cool autumn breeze, waiting to be breathed in solitude.

But I sat listening to every word, enjoying the outcome of what my father would surely have wanted. And in that, at least, I may be proud of.

A pause.

But now I have become suspicious. The feeling of success, joy more prevalent in the population-increased; and better living in general for all...

But I worry.

For times of good are always in a shadow. The loom of darkness that seems to torment me, even in prosperity. The future sits and waits, watching to see destiny unfold. And I cannot shake the torment, the inner demons, the Incubus inside.

Why? I wonder and can answer not. For perhaps I am cursed, walking alone; the moon a reflection — As we both drift in circles, watching history unfold, yet far, far away.

The thought of starting fresh scared them all. I walked down from Sinai, twenty years ago tomorrow. Joshua at my side as I went right for my *Dream Machine*. The people slowly emerged outside of their homes to the smell of burning plastic, masking the smell of burnt cedar, as the fire in the town center roared, causing a great commotion. Kids danced and played around the flames; their crooked teeth showing the infectious. I looked around at an alien, a foreign ferment. There was an emotion present I had not observed for so long, and had thought ceased to exist.

The people were excited.

Without a word, they all joined in.

Without a word, they made a choice. And they chose humanity.

Homes were emptied in free will, the decades of comforted evolution combusted; the smell filled the air for miles. The flaming liquid led the way as neighbor gathered; greeting each other, exchanging names, and celebrating the day.

True liberation being had.

Although celebration that day, the months of suffering ensued. Learning what life truly was changed everyone. Death like that in store had not been seen for quite some time.

For certain, people died in the community under the UNA, but the management would quickly take them away, creating an almost confusing idea of the subject of death itself.

It's like we forgot the inevitable conclusion of every story.

But now, parents watched their children cease to cry as their lungs emptied. Men: Cursed to the troubles of the mind. Women: to the pain of the flesh. The old accepted their fate, hoping their next life would be better than this, while those in the middle wept, angry that they must suffer such a fate. Food was scarce, many went to their graves in hunger and pain. But we remained hopeful. Well, I did anyway.

Surely now, hungry no more joined together in the foundations of the earth, these brave souls now free from the bondage of flesh; free from all the suffering this world causes. And as a community we still honor them in prayer, hoping their spirits have found rest, as surely ours would soon to be theirs as well.

And after those dark years came abundance, known as the time of prosperity. We were able to reproduce. Swine, cattle, chickens, goats. Our battle to maintain these animals, even while facing starvation and death; this act of will and attrition was one of my greatest attributes (in my mind at least) as leader to date. But mixed thoughts on the subject have arisen, as my actions as leader are now put into question.

A man with absolute power, is still a man.

And while many went hungry in a cold and fruitless winter, I prayed their souls find rest, while others claim me the source of their termination.

For twenty years I've sat as judge. Gus is part of the new council, but the future of this clan rests not on him, but Joshua. He was young in the beginning, (I guess we all were) but was eager to help and had a strong heart. He now sits as the new favorite in the upcoming election. I am excited yet nervous to give away my seat of power.

Finally, my burden to bear is nearing completion. I feel at ease knowing I've done my best and that I had an important role in the future of our species.

But here in this moment, I still think of her. Her flesh is gone, no doubt, but her legacy remains. In my mind, I replay her story in times of ease.

Comfort and age betray me.

Here in a life of peace, I can't help but be reminded of my pain. And I fear the dangers a completely peaceful society may cause itself, and I.

Even in times of prosperity such as this, I become suspicious; suspicious of what's in store for us. We as a species have a knack for fucking things up.

This world, one that we create;
A villain, whom we must face.
An emperor, expanding his reign and power;
Posing as a loving and caring monarch.

Peace Keeper, friend. Giving you what you need and keeping you warm.

But in the warmth you drift, in the ease, you grow soft...

How long will you sleep?

Comfort brings boredom, inner darkness manifests.

"How long will the god of sorrow torment me?
Is pain not enough, but to pile up?
Like a single brick in the foundation,
Buried under all the hurt.
It goes unseen, untouched, for far too long.
Trouble has been following.

My words grow in the uncertainty. Condemning me with every syllable.

"Yet as I sit silently, I'm wrapped by an unknowable thought: What is to come?

Nothing of good, and nothing of bad.

I search words of wisdom, but to understand takes wisdom.

I act a wise man, but am living a lie.

The master of inequity permeates the clock, eating at these precious minutes, like bacteria on all those corpses.

"Rotting, even before dead."

Or maybe it's me. Maybe I stand in the midst of a beautiful society in which I've created, yet can't shake this devil that haunts me. Am I cursed? Destined to walk the end of my days in worry and doubt.

And the thought of my former life rushes through me once again.

Her moment of birth marked an ecstasy never felt before or since. Upon entry from the darkened doorway of nothing, she emerged. A flawed perfection! My little girl.

If you've never seen the birth of your own child you, can't quite understand, this feeling that marks the pinnacle of existence; the living definition of a miracle.

But the devil inside ruined all that, and cursed me to a life of solitude and despair. And now I must pay back my debts to God.

I have never been able to understand what exists after death. I have learned the answer has, and always will be hidden from us. But I pray the thought of her eyes rests in my soul for eternity. The long years since we've parted, and the long years to come, are just empty time, filled with void. Events are layered and layered. But underneath those layers, I see her, waiting for me.

Chapter Twelve

Boy

Later that day, I find myself again on Sinai, meditating, praying, and having a smoke from my pipe — anything to pass the time. The mid-day sun passing overhead, some warmth much appreciated. And then, a shadow... Gus approaches.

"Sir!"

I look back with contempt. "Gus, you're my oldest friend, I told you to stop calling me that."

"Sorry Achilles, you're right. Ahh you know how it is, a seasoned guy as myself. Hard to teach an old wolf new tricks..."

Gus, a wolf... debatable.

"Anyways, Joshua and his men are due to arrive any moment now. You should come join the welcome party."

I take a deep breath and survey the land once more.

The leaves are changing color, the blossoms receding. Another winter approaches.

"Hey, Gus... is it as you imagined?" I ask, looking out to the same land my father viewed and adored.

"What do you mean, sir?"

"Twenty years ago, you asked to come here with me; is it as you imagined?"

We both stare at the open landscape, hills of colored maple trees, and green from the evergreens. Snow caped mountains far to the south-east. The River of Plenty clearly seen, shimmering vibrantly. Pure beauty.

"We should get going, Sir"

I bend over with a sigh and a few cracks, pick up my walking-stick and make the slow descension of Sinai; down to the bustling community of The *Abandoned*, the only known civilization left in the area, and as far as we know, Earth itself.

The population has been growing, and expansion begun. The hunters, no doubt will be coming from the east. To get there I am lead by Gus through town.

I enter into a living organism. The old neighborhood, my stomping-grounds, the town of Seven.

I used to walk through the camp as a God. All were silent and stared at me with much honor, respect and acclaim. Now I'm not even noticed. No one looks twice at the old man who kept them all alive till now. But that's a good thing, I guess.

Moving forward...

I get to my log home and begin to change into my party clothes. A large covering of a bear's fur that we took down a few years back hangs above my empty fireplace. Well, I shouldn't say we, Joshua took him down, nonetheless, I proceed to wrap the great beast around myself. This coat marks me as their leader, given to me by the greatest warrior the people have ever known. The last thing I want to do is parade myself around in the skin of such a fierce beauty, but it must be done, for the good of the people, I guess.

As I return to the open skies and smoke and chatter, the ambiance feels enlarged. All with smiles, chatting and flirting, but with a sense of urgency, prepping for tonight's celebration. Near the center of town they prepare the fire pit, that same spot we burned the remnants of a devilish governance, where many tend still to gather; I see two men blowing on a red ember, two more to the side cutting firewood. No doubt, this is where they will celebrate tomorrow. But as for me, I stop not here.

I step-off towards the northern trail with a bit of a jump in my step, noticing Gus stopped to chat to a lovely brunette. Ali is her name, if I am not mistaken.

The ache in my body quickly reminds me of my age, and I enter the trail, which banks east, in solitude. This is where the path to Eight lies. My new home. Our new home.

As I walk through the trail, the newly formed path towards Eight, I feel free once again. Alone, and at the will of nature, a sense of peace felt once more.

As I make my way into the quiet town, I see many at work. Here is where the new center will be. Closer to the river to the south, and the furs of the east, the final project I intend to live out.

I head through the town towards its eastern border, many a mother and father pointing toward me, a whisper in the air as they fold themselves down towards their children, informing wide and colorful eyes as to who I am and what tonight is all about. A despicable sense of pride sends a shiver up my body, as I pretend not to hear the whispers, and not to show my arrogance.

***

"Well, what's the word, boys?" I ask a pair of young men upon reaching the eastern-border (Ziggy and Dagu, if I'm not mistaken). Leaning on my staff, I breathe heavily. The two sentries on watch don't seem to notice me, looking out as if lost.

But they do respond:

"Nothing boy, go wait with everyone else." Ziggy turned to see my big smile stare right back. His eyes gulped, I could smell his bowels move.

Did he just call me boy?

"Judge Achilles! I mean, sir! I-I d...."

"Did you just call me boy?" I said cutting him off as he stuttered.

This, a negating term used amongst the new generation — "Boy."

"I thought you were one of the townsfolk. I'm sorry, I didn't see you co..."

"That's fine," I say cutting him off again. "Now, has there been any sound or smell?"

The dirty young man shook at the question. Ziggy thought only of his foolish statement made towards the most important political figure of his day. Dagu's mind, no doubt, on the party and the available girls it would surely bring.

But the sound of laughter and cheers were heard, as if the answer came at call, faint but growing...

Somehow, in seconds, the whole city fermented. The sound of the Warriors on approach became the sound of the mob at my back. If you were to scream in my ears, not a sound but the smooth and continuous hum would be heard; like rain, where all voices stand for one. All individual drops, yet collectively rain; one in motion and trajectory.

The energy produces a euphoric awe.

The men came into sight through the trees, as if glowing as the setting sun met them head-on through the bush. Dogs straggling in with them, sleds harnessed with the week's kills.

The effective hunters have become such fantastic support to the city's economy and morale. Living among their fellow people, *The Warriors* hunting and sacrificing for nothing but full stomachs, too much ale, and the glory and honor all men seek their whole lives for. Revered by all, they lead the town from a surviving barbaric tribe, into a hopeful community.

When young boys aren't in their studies, they could be seen playing with makeshift spears, wrestling one another and working on animal-calls and sounds. All the young wanted to become Warriors just like them. But as these boys matured, many left the thought for things just as important: raising children, woodcraft, farmhands... But none were so talked of as that of the Warriors; the hunters, the woodsmen, the mysterious tradition, the wondrous secrets kept between the men and the trees.

Those who leave for such trials as these, come back after the seven days as either a member of the group or dead. Buried nonetheless, in the ground from which they came.

The glow of the men, surrounded the air as they were seen through the bush, I couldn't help but gawk along with all the others. Trying to count them as they pass, I look at each man in the eyes as he enters the ecstatic community, checking to see if all made it back safe and sound.

Each man bowed his head as he ran by; I bow respectfully in return.

Again, that despicable pride...

Then I notice the young Lukas stroll by; the recent trainee, yet observably a different man. The dirty face smiles at me as he passes, which now looked not to be of a boy, but of a man. He looked now more like his father (May he rest in peace) than the boy who left one week ago.

My eyes then draw to the rear, toward the leader, the last to approach. With his dog Buck in the lead, Joshua's strides turn to a walk as he hits the threshold of people awaiting his arrival.

The eruption behind me livens.

He stops at me, turns, and bows to one knee. I can see the dirt in his hair, matted and woven, his dark wavy locks and dreads flowing over his hard face and stern chin. The Warrior was just about as tall as me on his knee. And as I stare at the motionless act of respect, instinctively I drop to one knee as well, and close my eyes as I bow.

Darkness is my sight. All I feel is peace as the crowd goes silent. In this moment, we are one, and everything stands still; but suddenly, an old memory appears...

The little blue boy.

I vaguely remember him. His soul, still present, as I reminisce, to that first winter, the original age of the Abandoned.

Chapter Thirteen

Black and Blue

Journal of Ryan, Uncle of Jonathan:

"A Conversation with God:

So... I've come to the state of loneliness many time before, as you must surely know...

So they say God loves us! That there is a purpose for us!

But, what do I see?

And what do I think...

I look at what I dislike. I walk, a reject of mankind — just looking, searching, and hoping in what I dare not define.

So, because of my loneliness, I reminisce...

I remember a specific day. A moment in time. I was a child, surrounded! A sea of people known, and unknown. And I envisioned a personal friend, one of the imagination. I envisioned a true companion, one who would, in that moment, simply play with me. And that he desperately wanted to be my friend, and would be content just being with me.

I mentally see him; another boy, perhaps my age, or just a tad older.

Why did I crave him so?

I guess, because I have never experienced true brotherhood, no reciprocated bondage. I have, no doubt, experienced brotherhood, but only a low one in perspective. One of lesser form. A father, a friend, a co-worker. But none perfect, or even close to such a concept.

But maybe, I could just imagine.

It is very possible that there is a creator behind life. Stranger things could be, like the possibility of life itself –

infinitesimal! And as it goes, a lesser chance of existence itself, the thought that something incomprehensible, the source of it...

Yet I,

Mocked among intelligentsia.

Gnosis, a rare gift.

But that being said, I've always been a coward (as surely you must know), a product, perhaps of my environment. Just another organism in bondage to the law.

I also have created life, and witnessed its arrival. And if you created me, in which such an event I also (perhaps to a lesser extent) have participated in;

Causing me to wonder... what do you see?

Alas, you won't tell me.

Yet, in my weakness, in my flesh, I grasp! A glimpse of love for the imperfect. The imperfect view, longing for more, craving reciprocation...

Is it so weird for a man, then to proceed as if another were present, beside, accompanied? — dark, and silent, and complete..."

***

As we sat and stared at the great blaze, the cracking and popping, drowning out the sounds of stomachs pleading to be filled. The fast approaching darkness surrounded the circle of discontentment. My eyes periodically wandered from face to face, reveling in the pain of each gaze, and the power of fear, which death controlled still.

All of us had become detached. Burials of the old and young were daily, and the cold nights, and hungry days, created a beautiful acceptance I now only comprehend. The feeling where all control was lost. That anyone could be the next to go, and that in this moment, we would just be with each other.

The cold dominating my being, taking over my thoughts; the chill, a welcomed feeling amidst the agony. The body fighting so violently, a much-needed awakening.

Oh, how I so violently shiver!

The snowflakes began to drop, floating slowly one by one to the ground below. A young boy to my left, Michael, as he was named, griped my arm with his cold little fingers, jolting me back to the material world.

The child looked to be two or three, or perhaps even six for all I know. He hadn't said a word for days, and I had already begun to forget the sound of his voice. The thought of so many voices I cherished, faithfully (and unfaithfully) departed.

I looked down at him, watching as he shivered. I wrapped my arms around the cold boy as he looked up at me with a sad sort of look. His dead eyes appealed to me from within my bosom, searching for an answer. An answer to his struggle, if there could ever be such a thing. I looked back at the cloudy, blue sting still left in the young boy's eyes, attempting to speak to his internal cry for help.

I had no answer to give. And so, I sucked back a tear, held him close, and breathed unnaturally with my head above his. The tears of heaven fell as white fluff, melting in his curly brown hair. The boy moved his gaze towards the expanding glow in front, the desperately hungry fire. Sparingly it danced for its deprived creators, as I could do nothing but hold him yet tighter.

His ribs, protruded from his side, making him an uncomfortable partner in heat exchange; and my mind wandered as to what he must think in such a time. How the young could witness death daily, and meeting it with such a powerful visage. If only he could make it! If only he could overcome! Truly, he would be a better man than I could ever dream to be.

Burdened, his gaze forever burned in my brain.

He looks up; not at me, but past me.

He seems so distant. The burden of true life, felt at such an early age. What does he feel alongside such pain? Does he curse the world, wishing it to end? Does he curse God, wishing to escape his cruel clutches?

I remember breathing slowly, closing my eyes, and doing something I hadn't done in a long time. I prayed. I appealed to the God I had assumed abandoned us, long before the UNA did. The God rarely discussed by my father, and his community of the followers. *"The Way"*, they called their following. And as I pleaded for the life of the little boy-blue, I drifted into a slumber, forgetting the world around me.

I awoke seemingly as quickly as I had fallen asleep. The fire had diminished slightly, and the night was darker. I remember feeling wet, as the fire kept the frost at bay, melting the snow in the immediate area. I looked around at my family, the diminished community members, who I deemed, *The Abandoned.* Many asleep, and many awake. Although un-alert, they stared at the warm glow in front. The quiet night, was made quieter by the thin white blanket that surrounded our circle, all breathing as one entity.

Here, those of us who remember the hard days of old, experienced true life, and true death; in humble recognition that the world was dangerous, full of each; death, and life, and everything in between. My muscles ached as I came back to the soul within my grasps. I no longer felt a shiver in my side, but a cold and damp body. His vigor, gone. The fight for life painfully ended. A small, blue boy rested in my grip.

Such an unpredictable end to such a beautiful first act.

I looked at the pale white face, the blue lips, and the soft wet hair. At a loss for thought, I pulled him again tighter. Not able to contain my despair, tears dropping, I felt such a feeling as can only be described as human. A feeling I now reluctantly envy.

***

The loss of such sorrow in my life again breeds ennui, and I find myself often remembering Michael. And his beautiful face comforts me, reminding me that life is but a breath, and that I, a mere man.

I am at the mercy of death, but must fight to preserve life.

An honorable man will always feel the presence of his errors as time unfolds. And a true man fights back against such darkness. The thing is, I may have been responsible for many lives; and because I cannot see the future, though I pine over the effects I may have poured onto humanity, as time continues to exist and shape all things new, these thoughts mean nothing! Decisions were made, and lives were affected, for better or for worse.

They looked to me, an ordinary man, for guidance and wisdom; yet only one soul still looms in my mind. Although I made countless negative results in the lives of those around me, they are all but a drop in the sea that is the life of my little girl.

Solei, how I miss thee.

Taken from me without a fight, I am ashamed of the man I once was.

So consumed within myself, I lost sight of the truth. The truth that within her was locked away all for me, and all of me. I had the key all along, looking for it in all the wrong places. The key I gave away, and can never replicate. The all that's missing from within.

Now the true fight exists as I drift, the moral man in me haunted by the soul entrusted, yet abandoned to selfishness. The lusts of the world called to me, and I answered.

But for Joshua life was lush, it was vibrant, constantly on the move, and never a dull moment. The Warriors walk like Gods before men.

Lay-men stare covetously, lusting after the lives they imagine; the world unknown, full of wonders and dangers; the only men of the Abandoned tribe, who stand face to face with death every day, and more importantly, with absolutely no fear of it.

And the women stare with hearts racing. The tough, muscular and handsome men pay no attention to the gawking girls; the lifestyle more *grandeur* than the most beautiful of women. Their rush came from life, and the idea it could end at any moment.

They walk through the greeters like conquering heroes of old. Saviors, from the realms of the unknown. Followed by a trail of carcasses and seven days' worth of accumulated stench. A mixture of sweat, blood, and death. But here, that's the smell of victory. A smile on all the people's faces, especially Natalia's. The pregnant wife of the team's leader was waiting in her tent. She could smell the scent of ceremony as it appeared.

The leader of The Warriors, and surely the new Judge of all Abandoned, was finally home.

The campaigns were coming to a close, and the newly appointed Judge would surely be her husband. Natalia, although pregnant and in no mood to be discussing politics, couldn't help but be pulled into all the surrounding community gossip. As all the men discussed her husband's position politically (as if that were what she wanted to discuss), and all the women, his brute strength and seductive mystery (as if she wanted to hear their lust for the father of her unborn child).

She knew he was steps away, before he even approached the tent. As he walked in mechanically and abrasive, stiff from the days of marching, she didn't recognize the skin of the man — only his eyes! Black from dirt and soot, his hair matted and wet; he dropped his gear caked in mud with a clank at the entrance. She suddenly sat up on her bed, as if there were something she knew she ought to do or say, but couldn't figure out what it was. Her heart raced as she looked at him. His muscles bulged, and his waist narrowed, (seven days in the woods always caused a slight change in his physique). She recognized his teeth as he smiled; the warm smile she missed, the smile she lamented upon departure, knowing she may never see it again.

She smiled back at him.

His eyes grew soft and he entered without a word. She stood and approached. A bucket of water sat at the entrance near the feet of the great man. She reached him, not taking her eyes away from his.

Natalia bent down with a rag in hand and plunged it into the water. They both conceal a *gulp*, as if nervous yet lascivious, as Natalia proceeded to cleanse him.

Chapter Fourteen

The Beast and the Scarlet

Journal entry of Ryan, son of Jacob, Great-Uncle of Achilles:

"My mind, a weight.
A great weight,
and it takes hold.
It crushes all it caresses.

Not freedom, but slavery I live.
Like all men who discover the true nature of it.
The true nature of It.

But I,
I wait.

I envy, the man who lives free of this bondage, this curse, this sin!
I long for it, while he resides in it.
I yearn for his freedom, but here, I remain;
Unable to live any other way,
Finding it in all, except in me."

***

No one can ever explain to you how your memories become a ghost. Haunting your thoughts, day and night, years after mistakes are made. A man of integrity will battle inner demons his entire life; especially a man of high worth. The more responsibilities embraced, the more mistakes made.

It is impossible to avoid.

We, as emotional beings, are incapable of leading a perfect life. We may know what we ought to do, but doing so is one thing; and not doing it, quite another.

To know what may become of any decision is for the gods to discuss. As for me, my decisions are a weight anchored to my spirit; holding me back and bringing great struggle as I push forward; reminding me of the mistakes I've made, each one causing a ripple in the sea of humanity.

The moon hovers, it hallows, and follows as I walk, anticipating my movement, watching me from afar.

The night, a weight upon my spirit, keeping me within its grasp. Another sleepless night I fester, apathetic and detached.

Some nights I wonder of Joshua's *Maan*. The one who wrote the message. A message of hope, which we have buried. The thought of *Maan's* return, just another wound in the flesh of our people's future. But surely, something remains of the one Joshua refers to. I felt him as I entered his cell; a barred cube, a sad estate. There lived a man I had not understood before. The management of the farm, I so ignorantly bigoted.

His room was dark and damp. A small dresser with a few remains, along with a cot is stuffed into a tiny room. Although the building itself provided quite a few aids towards our advancement, *Maan's* dresser of trinkets offered little more than a few coins and pencils. As well as a photograph, which caught my attention. It was a scenic picture, one that no doubt took his mind away from the horrors of his home. The clear water, blue and white mountains, and lush greenery brought calmness to the soul instantly.

Picture in hand, I sat on his bed to marvel at the vivid colors of the grass, and the orange hue of the sky. I felt something under the mattress. I had sat on a small brown book, hidden under the sheets, *Holy Bible* written on the front.

The power of law, is no power indeed. The law evolves, along with mankind... And power, accordingly. For, as the law moves and grows, it succumbs to the will of those in power. So easily influenced, so regularly broken. And the laws of the previous century, nothing but a confusing array of jargon and vagueness. Ready for any, and all who are willing to take advantage.

A timeless truth: law is truly within the individual. A power that does not take form, or possess spoken word, but manifests itself within the complexity of life itself.

Etched into the soul of everything.

Within such a moment, I pause to ponder, how not long ago I had condemned such a man to selfish pride — working for the UNA in a tyrannical way. Yet as I sit, and open the contraband, I realize our brotherhood, our similarities, our connection!

And sometimes I wonder of his story. Of how he got here, and where he is now. And at night I look up to the stars, wondering what became of the face that watched from above.

I talk unto myself of a world just out of reach, where everything is silent and timeless, and dead. But alive is the brightness, the moon's light I gaze upon. Yet, not of it, but of another. The star over the Earth's day, the energy of all, and in all alike. It brings with it an inaudible cry, along with all creation:

Endure!

"In the early mornings, such as this.
When all is dark, and cold, I seldom fear.
For surrounding me, strength in numbers;
A beast as ceased to invade.
A plague, destroyed by our spirits.
A life of lust and greed.

Yet as I walk alone, under the late sky;
I walk the ground, equally dark and distant.
Surrounded by obscurity;
Unease passes through the man.

Courage,
Just a word."

And life, a scary thing, yet must be. For we humans thrive on fear. It is our greatest curse, but a curse of life nonetheless; and to know... fear from the one who created it.

The fear of God looms. My life thin and vulnerable. And in such mind-space, I find unity with the fearful...

Heavenly.

Awaiting that fearful day of departure, marveling at its purpose, and many times, envy there-in.

***

As the moon and stars disperse, and their blanket becomes red and gold, Joshua met with his friend Atenacious at the local Social House, the neighborhood pub.

Two young women sat on the ground near the entrance cross legged. They looked up and giggled at Joshua as he entered. He smiled and walked past the two blondes towards his mate; Atenacious barely visible near the back. The Warrior, and friend of Joshua leaned on his side with two clay mugs of foamy drinks. The rich aroma, along with the sight of his friend relaxed Joshua's senses as he plopped down by his side.

"How's the brew today?" Joshua said with a sigh, gracefully reaching the ground. His lips touched the foamy beer, and the bitter drink (which was formerly crafted for the UNA) went down hard but crisp.

"You tell me, brother. How's the wife?"

Joshua took another big gulp.

"She missed me." He winked and smiled at Atenacious.

The two roared in laughter! Looking over, they noticed the young women giggle, obviously observing the dignitaries as they celebrate another homecoming. Atenacious produced a pipe, and before he put it in his mouth, a lovely young attendant approached with timber, flame aglow at the end of a stick. Atenacious took a deep puff and passed it to his friend.

"We must speak softer old friend; the birds sing constantly through the streets. By sundown this conversation may reach even Achilles." Atenacious said this with a seriousness that showed a downcast eye towards the ruler.

"That would mean nothing to me, old friend! The man maintains my utmost respect." Joshua imposed his strength as he said this. Not that he could help it. The big man's face and voice reflected his sheer might.

Atenacious recoiled, not trying to overstep. "Well, the elections are here, you must at least speak of him. Do you think he will just give you the throne? He's held it too long – the man has become mad! He sits up there on that hill with his followers and claims he knows what's best for us?"

"He claims nothing!" Joshua said aloud.

The place fell into silence. The young maiden running drinks midway between the kitchen and the men stood frozen. Joshua softened as he realized she was on approach.

The young woman attempted to say something as she placed the fresh drinks to their side. An inaudible mumble; and the two waited for her to leave. Joshua could not look at her, embarrassed at his outburst. All he heard was a faint "us" from her direction. He caught a glimpse of her dirty feet visible under the hem of her dress as she walked away.

Joshua gulped down the remains of his pint, and started his second, helping him recuperate. "He is a wonderful man and has been a great leader for many years. Do I think his time is up? Yes, but so does he! He has no intention of letting the elections swing his way. He has made no real presence among the commoners for years and doesn't show signs of intent to overtake their vote."

"Change is his motto, my friend. I just don't trust a man who sits on the throne. But you, my dear friend! Stoked for you headin' the clan! As well, I feel I would be of great assistance! A mighty adjutant and humble advisor! A friend who would help a friend no matter what the situation. We have killed, and been killed. Together, you and I! Blood is thicker than water, and the blood we've spilt into the soils of the Earth echo our bond."

Joshua finished his second mug as the two sat silently. The smooth texture of the clay reminded him of his mallet, and a momentary memory entered his mind. All he felt was the pressure-built energy exerted into striking a death blow. The warm and bitter drink as it entered his mouth reminded him of the blood he has so often tasted in the wood.

Atenacious spoke truthfully, the two had shed blood many times on the battlefield of the animal kingdom. The memories of the slain, the flashbacks of the hunt...

The mind is a dark place.

***

Thump! Thump! Thump! Thump!

The angst of the hunt. The normally calm sounds of the forest, the birds chirping, trees rustling, momentarily suspended. All drawn, to the deafening:

Thump! Thump! Thump! Thump!

Joshua and Bradley were on pursuit. The smells trail had led to the darkened forest. The leaves dreary, cold breeze dropping leaf after leaf. Atenacious, the young mate of Joshua followed. A makeshift spear accompanied each of the vigorous young men. Bradley continued to sniff along the path, but Joshua's instincts felt it before Bradley's nose could smell it.

The young boy of five had disappeared. The older boys lost track of him. So the search party went out, tracking his whereabouts.

Joshua gripped his spear a little tighter as they walked the brim of Mt. Sinai. A sense of revulsion caused him to call Bradley to his side. Silently the three predators crept along the wet leaves, until the muffled sound of an animal feasting accompanied the *Thump! Thump!* Mapping the sound, the three inched their way in its direction. Joshua in the lead, then saw what is now only a disturbing memory — a large cat, tearing apart the bloody mess, devouring the entrails of the dead boy.

A nightmare — eternal torment.

***

Joshua could not dream of what would happen to these men if they could not kill again. What could man do, with the ingrained lust for blood? How could he function in the life of a commoner, the boredom of the certainty that is the day, and its comfortable vices?

The life of a politician.

In silence, he gave his mate a nod, left the tent, and made his way towards the warrior's commune, preparing for the busy day ahead.

"Buck!" Joshua called firmly and sharp as he left the tent.

The road he walked, a strip of dirt, hiding asphalt half an inch below. The newly established city of Eight was not yet awake. The sun just starting to produce its heat reminded Joshua of autumn's fight against winter, an ancient battle going back to the dawn of time itself.

Buck arrived with a sharp halt. The two-year-old mutt was energized at the call, and eager to be of service to his master. The two walked side by side through the tents and piles of bricks. The remnants, relics of an old world made anew.

Along with the sight of children beginning their day's play, and the smell of smoky fires beginning the day's events, people began to stir in the street.

"Buck, come here!"

The city's stir had begun, and Buck's tail began to wave as he came closer, arriving at his master's heel, tongue out and wide eyed. Joshua grabbed the dog's mouth and pulled both heads toward each other, then pointing to his eye with his free hand. Buck looked at him, then away, then back again — tail waving apprehensively.

Joshua's right index remained on his cheek. His eyes burned towards Buck's. Buck again looked away, then back again.

To the layman, an odd game.

Joshua stared into his companion's eyes in amazement. *"If only I could see the world through his,"* he thought. *"The seemingly endless blur of pleasure and pain. A world surrounded by survival, and survival itself being the world. The vague sense of where to be and what to do, led by the cohesion of experience and internal knowledge. The primordial knowledge of good and evil. Good being survival, and evil, apparently the grave.*

The freedom of ignorance, acting purely for good. It's only through this feeling we will find salvation for despair. The thoughts of men, a plague upon the race.

A gross idea of supreme being.

I envy these eyes I see..."

Joshua, lost in his thoughts began to walk, Buck started along as well. The early-birds beginning to merge seemingly noticed the two. Many, surely praying Buck would come to greet them, saying "Good morning!" apart from words. This would make their day, something to tell their co-workers and families, solely for the sake of creating envy.

Buck shook his tail and walked up to a pretty, young woman, dressed mostly in cloth (some of the ancient remaining fabric left by the UNA), along with a wool over shirt and deer skinned sandals, she smiled and looked down at him, revealing a perfect set of teeth rarely seen. Joshua smiled and walked up to the two of them.

"Good morning, miss."

She blushed as she gently placed her hand on Buck's head. He used a little more force as he pushed up with his nose, landing her palm on his left ear. He looked up at her in blissful joy, the black-haired face, tongue hanging, his breath creating a smog.

"Can't complain," she made out softly.

Joshua upon hearing it was instantly astounded. Never had he heard such a soft and beautiful tone, the melodious words felt like poetry upon his ears. He examined her, in a tasteful way, he made sure.

"Are you new around here? I don't think if I've seen you before," he made out finally, intrigued at the young beauty.

"I just finished school in Seven. She said looking only at Buck, rubbing his neck. Then up at Joshua.

She didn't look at him the way others did, he noticed. She looked directly into his eyes. Unaware of his status, and so strong in herself, she continued to talk as if he were just another man of the town.

"I along with four classmates have a plot of land just to the east." She pointed (more towards the south) then looked to the sky quizzically.

But only for a moment. Eyes, back on Joshua's.

"We intend to build a home. And we came to serve and be a part of the community here at Eight. Today is my first day! Figures with the party tonight and the haul of animals I hear awaits. I'm on my way to the kitchen where my mother got me a job... Maybe I'll see you around?" She said sincerely.

Joshua starred with a grin of confusion. "Yes, you will!" he said, trying to figure out what she meant.

As she began to walk, Buck started her way as well.

"Lovely to have met you," she said at a half turn, revealing her lovely smile and rosy cheeks.

"Yes, you too!" Joshua dialogued inaudibly, watching her as she turned.

As he began to walk, only a few paces away he turned violently! "Oh, and what's your name?"

"Isla," was her response. "And you?"

"He doesn't talk, but his name is Buck," he said with a stare, trying to sell the corny sarcasm.

She instantly looked down with a smile, blushing again, she said: "Well, bye Buck." And blew a kiss to the young dog. Isla turned round, and began to walk to a new life. Her red and blonde hair shone as the sunlight gleamed from her healthy locks. Joshua watched until she turned a corner, then out of sight, he turned south.

Chapter Fifteen

Travail

Journal of Vanessa, Daughter of Ryan.

"And we sit, and we fester. Pent up anger, a common understanding of a species completely settled. Not wanting or unwilling to understand themselves and the world around them. The definition of the 21st century man: A time bomb, waiting to explode.

Capitalism, the demise of the human race, the beginning of selfishness, the idea of ownership. The possibility of possessing more than one's neighbor, flaunting what one has but all want. And the possibility of using that to own another, disgraceful! Trapping them into the lure of obtaining such treasures, only to become indebted to the one who Lords over it all."

***

The attitude of the oppressed reflects that of the oppressors.

To Joshua, a dog likewise reflected its master. The loyal companion becomes, in his mind, the one un-manipulative specimen a man can truly trust. A man may attempt to deceive those around him, pretending to be someone he is not, but if he is accompanied by a canine, his true nature will always be revealed. Joshua understood this as he looked at Buck, the way he understood it as he looked at Bradley years before. He understood that his dog was like a copy, a primordial revelation, himself in its intended form. A reflection, absent of knowledge, but equally a slave to his master.

He was fascinated by this thought, and he lived with an appreciation of his companion's submission. He was grateful, that was understood. And so, Joshua strived to be the best master he could be, a true leader, caring for that which he leads.

Joshua and Buck walked through the new growth of forest to the south of town. Through the trees, a gentle slope opened to a flat ridge — the home of the Warriors.

But something felt off. Buck stood like a statue at the edge of the forest, tail stiff, tongue hidden, eyes focused. Joshua grimaced as he approached slowly and silently, curious as to what may be happening before him.

Okuna and Mathias were silent.

The two faced the jittery snarl of a local straggler. A wolf left for dead stood defensively, fighting for survival as he faced the pair of hunters.

This small male had a silver hide with patches of black, regarding a shadow upon its shoulders. His eyes, shallow and fierce. It seemed to emanate an understanding of death's imminence within battle, and our desperate means of procrastinating its inevitability.

Okuna held a sling, moving slowly to his side, seeking cover behind a nearby tree.

Mathias held a large wooden mallet. He lifted it high in the air, waving it like a banner.

"Come on!" he yelled, catching the attention of the tall, but thin canine.

The dog drooled as he growled at the man — a low and menacing sound accompanied by a sinister stare. His teeth protruding like snowy mountain peaks, equally as tall in the mind of Mathias. His mien strictly business, as the two eyed one another. Two beasts, wondering who would make the first move.

Mathias bolted forward! The man sprinted full force to the carnivore, a full-on assault, grabbing the animal's absolute attention. The animal crouched, preparing itself defensively, when suddenly a surge of pain emanated from his side; a piercing blow, agony brought through unforeseen opposition.

The rock, no larger than half a fist, had flown so rapidly, at such precision, that it caused the beast to *yelp* aloud. His attention directed to the right.

Before he knew what hit him, Mathias held him down, while Okuna tied him up.

Part of the Warriors training is such exercises as these. The group regularly sparred within its commune, the legendary training area sought by all, especially the young boys of the Abandoned, hoping to one day enter ceremonially. This space of land belongs to the Warriors, and so is treated as such. The laws of Eight, although ambiguous and more so a product of the judge's rulings, had no effect out here. This land was run by ancient laws, those ingrained in all animals; humans and beasts alike.

Joshua approached as the mood lightened, the men freeing the good sport that was the dog, lying helplessly in the ring. Those who watched in fascination now discussed the events, most speaking of how they would have done something different; others worshipping the two at their victory.

The flock watched the battle with a fascination as one watches a fire. The silence, accompanied by the crackle and pop that is energy and conflict, followed by humanities second favorite pastime, gossip.

Joshua walked towards the wooden fence which housed a large training area, as well as provided a seat for the onlookers; for Joshua, something to lean against. Upon approach, he realized most of those in attendance were young boys. No sign of any young maidens as of yet.

"What's next?" Joshua asked a boy to his left as he approached the hysterical crowd. Buck at his feet, also looked up at the young teenager. Over the chatter, the boy managed to hear him; turning, he stared dumbfounded.

"I... I'm not sure, sir." He said in a respectful fear, not to fake an answer as a lie would incur great wrath (he presumed). The boy must have been thirteen or so, somewhere near the age of recruitment.

"I think the suit.... But I'm really not sure," he added to Joshua.

Joshua looked toward the ring as the two young men in the center began to walk to the side with Shadow. Shadow, as the wolf went by, was discovered in the east near Gold Creek. He was ferocious upon sight. Both Joshua and Atenacious were part of the team who ran into the dying dog. He stood, growling softly, as if aware he was helpless, but too weak to defend himself. The men looked on him with pity, approaching him with a piece of smoked meat, and a warm smile.

Unlike Shadow, many groups or stray dogs needed to be taken by force — most killed in battle. Buck, the product of one such occasion. Almost five years ago, his mother, only an adolescent, was taken as the warriors collided with a pack from The Red Mountain. The team stumbled upon the den as they sought to expand their map of the terrain. Many wolves and two humans were injured badly. Okuna survived his wounds, the other, Borodino, died of infection. But with each mistake, improvement is made.

The Warriors understood their might, but humbly they attempted, even upon battle, to show kindness to their foe.

Mercy is unforeseen, yet respected subconsciously by all.

But no matter, when the group returned after each of their expeditions, there was great celebration for the added family members, going away boys, and returning as men. As well as great sorrow for a life lost. Souls departed. Body's back to dust.

Returning to the arena, a bear now walked into the center.

Joshua noticed groups of his companions approaching from all directions. Dogs alike walked with their masters, the great men emerging from the wood, stole the attention momentarily from the crowd.

A single man in the middle approached and stood like a great beast. The horrific sight, a man partially infused with a bear, for indeed he was! Bear hide coated his arms, creating a protective layer, like a gladiator prepped for battle. His head was encased within a Grizzly's, the upper Jaw unhinged revealed a face black and red.

Emerging from the crowd came Fierce, aware of his master in the ring, and the suits implication. The gladiator's own beast and the man himself squared off, looking at each other with well-intended aggression, as if this may in fact be a fight to the death.

To be sure, on this ground, deaths have occurred. The art of training for battle consumed enough lives over the years, but was a protection for all others. Joshua tried not to think of the blood that had been shed, the two sparring on the sacred ground he had seen so many injured before, even instant death, as both types of animals became lost in the heat of training. A real warrior emerging from within.

Joshua was not in the mood to watch. As cheers rang through the crowd, many young boys watching in excitement, he turned away, looking towards those approaching.

"Much too early for games," Joshua said loudly towards Bruce not fifteen steps away. The man was older than Joshua, and had been with him in many situations before. The retired Warrior now lived with the dogs, keeping order among the bitches, studs, and pups.

"Well, not everyone is coming home from the hunt," Bruce said to his friend, "We wouldn't be coming just for games anyways. Look at Daisy, she's not too happy..."

Bruce was cut off by the cheering crowd as he pointed to the young female. Neither men looked towards the middle but looked to comfort the frightened girl. Buck wagged his tail, beginning to walk around her in a circle. Unexpected contentment emanated from her eyes as the big black dog's tongue protruded. All of a sudden, she bolted towards the open field to their side! Buck following in pursuit.

The two men smiled, watching the young love, or young lust, or young playfulness, whichever it was, as they began to wrestle.

"Atenacious is to give the report of the hunt and state of affairs," continued Bruce. "That's what I was told, anyways,"

"That's true." Joshua knew this was custom after a hunt, "But that doesn't mean you had to come. You've done your time. She should be relaxing with the pups, and you with them!"

"Don't tell me about relaxing, Brother. When are you going to take some time for yourself and enjoy the family life? You do enough with the Warriors, and the council, and isn't Natasha pregnant?"

Joshua smiled at Bruce's honest inquiry, despite the wrong name.

"Yes, it's true," Joshua responded. "And to answer your question, sooner than you might think! Let's go for a walk with the dogs, all this testosterone is worse than being on the hunt. I need some quiet conversation with an old friend," Joshua said with a big smile, revealing an array of white and black, one or two teeth missing here and there.

"Well, I shouldn't miss what Atenacious has to say this morning. I heard we lost none, but that there is some major topics of discussion"

It was true, there was lots to discuss. The party that night. The newly initiated members. A call for recruits; But mainly, the Abandoned's upcoming election. All this Joshua knew, but didn't want to hear.

"All you need to know is said by the trees, and exclaimed by the wind," Joshua said smiling at his attempted insight. "Let's go for a walk with those two young lovers over there, and when we return, if you're still curious, I'll tell you what news was shared. Don't forget who the alpha here is!"

As the men surrounding the arena cheered, and the two in the middle jostled, one man and one beast, becoming one entity, the way wind meets rain, becoming a storm. As the two continued, like a bull and his fighter, fueled by the crowd's vibrant noise, Joshua put his arm over Bruce's shoulder, and the two walked into the light.

***

At the corner, Isla could see her destination. The big, triangle-shaped tent, sticking out much higher than the others, not more than one hundred feet further. She gulped in its view. The young lady was as the ancients put, "Green".

She had decided to join the city of Eight as it began to flourish, hoping to find a new life away from her home, not four miles in the west.

Our Genetics create an elusive past, a history of the self never truly certain.

Although she felt angst at home, and the inherent need like all animals as they reach a certain age to fly the coop and tread the path of their own choosing, she missed the life of old. Every morning her mom would go to the blueberry fields and Isla to the classroom with the others — students of Seven, just like herself.

Her father died many years ago, before the days of the Warriors, and she knew only the stories about him, and the struggles of her parents' generation throughout the last few decades.

Her mother would often bring her to the fields on her back; this she does remember. The joyous times she spent with the other children, in an age that started seeing progress. The youngsters would run around in the sea of purple, blue, and green. The sun brought a smile, and the clouds brought inner peace. They would eat and collect, and enjoy the time with each other.

When Isla began school, she found that she loved to learn. She looked at the hard work her mother did and decided it was not the work she wanted for herself. She wanted to work with her mind. She was especially intrigued by history; she saw all that had happencd, and how it leads into all that does happen.

The good and evil that befell mankind.

She wondered at her existence; her ancestors' strength to survive such terrible times.

Unlike the other children reaching their early teens, she saw only an easy lifestyle, built on the backs of those who suffered. She felt no suffering until she saw the history books. The death and suffering of so many; of the wars, crusades, torture and famine. She genuinely grieved her inner past. She embedded herself among humanity's catastrophes. The struggle of the human, to suffer through not just her own life, but the life of her people; in full knowledge of both, and the necessity of compassion. And she marveled at it all, but could not escape its truth. She lived a quiet inner turmoil, unable to escape its presence in her life. She was determined to master it, and to teach others. But first, as a young woman, at the age of fifteen she had to start somewhere, and the kitchen she felt, would teach her much about herself, and the ways of her people.

Before one can teach, one must know.

Isla approached the hut, bustling and warm; the cool morning at her back, the heat of an already working unit to her front. Nervously looking inside, she attempted to collect herself and peeked in to see the women sorting animal entrails, meats, firs, and fats; a network in motion emanating purpose and progression. Before Isla could get a good look, she was startled as she reached the front door.

"Hey, you Isla?" the tall wrinkled woman said to her, pronouncing hey name like *Eye*, and a French "*la*" put together.

"Yes," Isla responded, almost visibly shaking.

"Alright," the woman said with a sigh. "You're late, we've been hard at work. I saw you coming but thought I would'a seen you much earlier. Did you get lost?"

Isla blushed. "I didn't know you started so early. It won't happen again."

"It better not," she said sternly. "I'll give ya anoder chance but don't disappoint me again."

The tall wrinkled woman walked to the right. Isla forgot all she had just seen and followed as the woman walked stiffly around the side towards a roaring fire. Isla could smell the smoke as she walked, but was caught off guard as the open view behind the kitchen revealed a true hearth.

She saw ahead of her the monumental amphitheater. She learnt of its power in school; the site of many debates, trials, and votes, a hallmark of the progressing civilization. As she walked a few strides behind the wrinkled woman, she marveled at the grass, and at the curved wall that led up to a mount. A wooded area, the sun directly above it, "This must be Mount Sinai," she determined. The historic mount, less famous than the arena below, but more revered in her eyes. Talk of the new village was discussed endlessly at her former home, but the beauty of it all, never mentioned.

"Ay, Lass!" Isla couldn't tell if she mispronounced her name again or if the term *Lass* meant something.

Isla snapped to. She now found herself standing over a pile of meat on the floor beside a stoking fire in a large pit. A few wooden stakes held up a large stitched tarp covering the area. The kitchen held a position right on the edge of the amphitheater, but Isla now only saw the hot sweaty women to her front, bloody and chatting, as if nothing were out of sorts. All working and laughing, a bustling community accomplishing the task at hand, and seemingly enjoying their work. Isla felt lost and nervous as she attempted to embark in something she knew nothing of.

"Oh, 'n hey, try not to blush." Isla looked into the wrinkled woman's eyes as she continued, "You're pretty. You'll break hearts with a blush like that."

Isla's rouge remained.

Chapter Sixteen
The Sea of Rorschach

"One thing would be awful, to bind oneself forever to a suffering man. It would be everlasting torture."

-       War and Peace

"...Listen up all. We have come to gather this special evening, as today marks the 20th anniversary of our freedom!"

Joshua's voice booms over the crowd along with instant cheers from the masses. He, being born to do this, always captured the attention of his people. His strong neck supported his large head, full of scratches and scars. Years of hunting and physical training built a specimen of a man most could not imagine. Standing six feet tall, his face mostly covered in hair, a dark visage passionately addressing the people:

"This is a great day for the *Abandoned!* We have been left for dead and abandoned by those who were entrusted to protect us. They lost sight of what was important. They forgot about the collective we, and focused on the repulsive self. But there was one man who saw this. There is one man, we follow, who understood what he saw, and the rotten hearts of his peers. That great man and prophet of God pursued a life dedicated to truth. He died a death worthy of acclamation. Hear now as I read the words of Ryan, great-uncle to our leader Achilles..."

Joshua had given up on Maan, and the idea he would return to us. Originally, he had hope, but hope only last so long. Time wears on all things alike.

Joshua pulls out an ancient manuscript.
The front reads: "Rorschach's Journal, 1985"

Flipping through he finds the spot he was looking for. Pausing, he surveys the crowd. At this pause a chorus of instruments begins behind him. A quiet awe was left over the people as the beautifully soft music of a violin began. The antique instruments were discovered by the Warriors a few years ago, in the ancient homes of the natives who must have dwelt within.

Certain children in the community were chosen and brought up from an early age to perform and maintain such important pieces of artistry. These musicians had been practicing for months for this occasion, and shook with nervous anticipation, facing the biggest audience they had ever seen.

The music did something to its listeners. The sounds, which transcended generations, created unity. This unity was felt in the heart, in the feet, and in the ears. All felt one with each other.

Joshua clears his throat, and begins to read:

"You see me when I don't see you,
You hear me when I close off all else;
You're there,
when I'm not here.
I sense you, but don't see you;
I long for you, but can't find you.
Where have you gone, Oh God!

Hear me when my heart breaks.
Heal me when emotions crumble.
Pick me up when I fall down.

When I am alone, do not abandon me.
When I turn to you, do not turn away.

I ask, but take no action.
My presence you crave, yet I ignore.
You speak to me, but I do not listen.
You reveal, yet I look to the ground.

My heart is hardened from the evils of this world.
My mind wanders through the index of flesh and desire.

I ask and you hear me.
You ask,
and I tarry.

When, my God, will I follow you?
When will I obey you?
If not now, tomorrow?
In a month? In a year?
This eternal circle of shame brings me to this moment
Over
And over
And over...

Only you can break the cycle.

I am too weak.
Corrupted by the ways of this world.
Eaten up by HaSatan and his influence.
Consumed by the media,
And wasted by the years of ignorance.

I am alone, even when I accompanied.
I am forsaken, though you take me back.
I am guilty.
I am empty.
I am in desperate need.

Let the spirit of life enter, follow me, guide me,
influence and lead me.
Cover, protect, endure forever!
Pick up the ruins of my shattered life.
Start with the cornerstone.
Fill these walls with joy;
May peace flow through its windows;
May these doors accept all who enter.

All have abandoned your name.
All have found comfort in denial.
All have turned from the eternal ways of truth.

But I will stay true to your name.
I will not let this world tear me to pieces,
As the wolves tear the unguarded sheep.

You hear me God, though I do not speak.
You listen, God, though I do not pray.
You heal me, though I am not ill.
You love me, though I love not myself."

"This martyr, this great patriarch of our people, true prophet and protector; made all this possible. By preserving the ancient writings and beliefs of the peoples of old, who cared and preserved truth and justice, we live on today through his great sacrifice. I read from his final entry...

"And here I go
Walking into the abyss.
The great sea of fear
Its waves have reached my toes long ago
But alas, the tide has risen.

What awaits me out there?
In the sea, all that is mysterious.
This home of so many who have traveled before me,
Calls to me.
And like all others entering, fear takes hold.

Yet from here is where I rose!
This is where we emerged.
Out from the fathomless recesses of the deep.
And to the place of origin is where I seek.
And so, I walk...

A chill rises up the spine, as the breasts meet their
new home.
Fear takes form as I witness,
Its magnitude and beauty.
Its chaos and imperfection.
It's creatures of darkness and death.

But now I tread.
I tread towards the setting sun,
Its glow brightened by the eternal waves

No end in sight.
No;
End in sight."

As Joshua continued to woo the crowd, I find it odd...

I wasn't asked to say anything.

"We are a nation, united by a very strong brotherhood of perseverance! Our people have overcome the tyranny of the so-called United Nations of America. This form of corrupt government took control of our parents, our grandparent, and most of us standing here today. This authority manipulated us into a greedy, possessive, disengaged, disheartened, depressed people... Living a life of dependence and torment, envious of the dead."

Joshua, becoming as I.

"But tonight..."

All eyes upon Joshua as he paused to breath; the crowd pulled in by his words. His voice and delivery rivaled his appearance as a man of importance. If you had just seen him for the first time, you would understand why he deserves the respect he has earned and is given.

"Tonight..."

He repeats now, letting go of the intensity in his eyes. His cheeks lift and his teeth exposed. Some in the crowd begin to feel a surge of energy.

Many in attendance remember the history of turmoil and terror throughout the years of horrified memories, as tears of heartache transform into tears of joy. Joshua creates euphoria in all.

Solitary yelps and cheers begin to be heard as the crowd intensifies.

"Tonight, we celebrate our liberation! We shout to God, and to the ears of our brothers and sisters of the Earth! We will be so loud, and so full of life, that even our pathetic leaders of old, out there, floating in the cosmos, desperate and rotting, will hear our cries! But I say! This is our world now, and this world will remain a part of us, until time ceases to be!

"And this day will be remembered through our descendants as a day of Elation! A day of triumph and victory! Let us celebrate as a new civilization! As the free peoples of Earth — as *The Abandoned*!"

Cheers drown the remaining words:

"Let the Angels of Heaven join us in celebration; and let the tormented souls of the UNA hear us in Hell! For if we greet their spirits, in this life or the next, we will mock them in our final testimony!

"WE ARE ETERNALLY FREE!"

Cheers were sounded, thunderous clapping and heavy voices shook the earth as Joshua stepped down from the judge's position, front and center, facing the wave of people rising up along Mount Sinai.

A steady chant of, "We are free! We are free!" was heard among the people, as the fire pit was instantly lit. The blue glow mingled with the setting sun, adding an orange hew to the faces of young and old as the great party began.

Dancing and cheering erupted with the drums, silencing the stringed instruments. The vibrant beat mixed with the movement of the earth as people romped to the rhythm, entranced by the beauty. The musicians continued for hours, later to fade into a soft medley.

There, in the nosebleed section, sitting on the eastern side of my ancestral hill, I watch. The men and women dance promiscuously, many leaving shortly thereafter. The young boys and girls, excited and laughing as they played and wrestled, stomping their feet through the music. The teens stood awkwardly in pods, gay and bright, as they wandered and mingled, attempting to woo the opposite sex. Parents gazed, vicariously enjoying life through the young. And the old (not that there were many) sat as I did. With no words or ways, or laughter, or expressions of any kind. We simply observed. And as the music faded I sat in solitude, awaiting my favorite artist.

As I observed in silence at the ways of our people, I more so sat in quiet anticipation. The young woman, Madison, a remarkable cellist, would soon begin.

The night was dark but still full of vigor. The beginning of winter's chill was felt, and the few young who had been dancing now in small numbers either left, perhaps to join Seven where the party inevitably would last, or huddled tight together. Many were chatting and laughing, some crying and the occasional burst from the bubbly teens. But as Madison was seen, cello in one hand, and bow in the other, all I could hear was the crackling and popping of the bon-fire.

She looked like a skeleton in rags, the pale and gaunt figure miraculously carried the large instrument with ease. Her hairless head, a great symbol of her dedication, as she fashioned her bow from the long and thin hair that recently occupied her head.

I stood in awe of her beauty. Nothing physically attractive about her features, but her soul sent goosebumps though my being. As she sat down with bow in hand, I awaited her genius, and wondered why I was so beguiled to such obvious sorrow.

A great artist can reveal any emotion, but the greatest artists brings one into internal realization.

Within such a pit, pulling out all the cares and worries, allowing one to truthfully accept who they are, I sit and listen.

Music is simply the philosopher's cry for help.

No words can describe what one feels as the long and greasy hair touched the thick strings, but her deep and melodious notes could make one feel misery and delight simultaneously. Her expression as she played struck deep within me, and as I had long awaited her rhapsody to end the night, I was not disappointed.

Madison, it would seem, I love more than any other. And as my eyes wallow up, and my breathing deepens, I feel a sense of bliss; as if nothing in the world mattered; not the past, the present, nor the future. Not even *Solei.*

I was just one entity among many, and the music took me. Far from the weight of the world I travel, and the struggle of life I fight so earnestly to maintain.

Chapter Seventeen

Torn

"And I know that the spirit of God is the eldest brother of my own.

And that all men ever born are also my brothers.... And the women my sisters and lovers,

And that a Kelson of the creation of love;

And limitless are the leaves stiff or drooping in the fields,

And brown ants in the little wells beneath them,

And mossy scabs of the wormfence, and heaped stones, and elder and mullen and pokeweed.

A Child said, 'What is the grass?' fetching it to me with full hands;

How could I answer the child? .... I do not know what it is any more than he.

I guess it must be the flagship of my disposition, out of hopeful green stuff woven.

Or I guess it is the handkerchief of the Lord,

A scented gift and remembrancer designedly dropped,

Bearing the owner's name someway in the corners, that we may see and remark, and say 'Whose?'

Or I guess the grass is itself a child... The produced babe of the vegetation.

Or I guess it is a uniform hieroglyphic,

And it means, sprouting alike in broad zones and narrow zones,

Growing among black folks as among white,

Kanuck, Tuckahoe, Congressman, Cuff, I give them the same, I receive them the same.

And now it seems to me the beautiful uncut hair of graves.

Tenderly will I use you curling grass,
It may be you transpire from the breasts of young men,
It may be if I had known them I would have loved them;
It may be you are from old people and from women, and from offspring taken soon out of their mother's laps,
And here you are the mother's laps."

- Leaves of Grass

After his speech Joshua walked away. He turned from the cheering crowd and didn't look back. He walked towards the creek to the East. Then, out of the darkness emerged his wife, Natalia. With a bright smile that brings light to even the darkest of moments (as so all men need from another), she greets her husband. Relief from the anxiety that was speaking in public, her beautiful appearance gave Joshua momentary peace. His sweaty palms grasped hers, cold and dry; his red and moist forehead greeted hers, dark and cool.

Her slender body, engrossed as of late, Joshua's seed developing within. His recent miracle. Surely, finally, a child to call his own.

Amongst the dead of old lay all that he had ever loved.

His first offspring, a young boy brought with him a pool of blood. Both he and the mother, Sadar, lay black and blue and red. Joshua's heart visibly shattered.

He miraculously recovered. Pressing on, Joshua continued in his tireless responsibilities; a mysterious internal purpose, allowing him to endure.

The next tragedy, Isabelle in labor, but pushing ceaselessly! The women and men of medicine, along with Joshua, made a decision to cut out the babe. Reluctantly, Joshua watched as the dull blade entered the screaming woman, and the cry of his daughter Madilyn, heard.

The cries were short lived. Joshua later would have wished the little girl born in horror would have died during such a gruesome entry to the world. Her death, after only half of a year alive, sent Joshua into long lasting despair. The virtuous man would never be the same. And for years he dedicated himself to the hunt, and to his brothers in blood, seeking to flee the inner torment.

Although this took place more than ten years previous, birthing was still a major concern for our people. And as of late, for Joshua and Natalia, it was a growing concern.

The horrors still preside within his memories. The cries of pain, and blood poured out as he witnessed all he had loved meet the Sea of Rorschach.

And as for Natalia, witnessing hundreds of women she'd loved over the years, crying in pain and screaming in labor, she was understandably dreading the day of such woe. She recalls too many faces, white as ghosts' as the offspring regrettably extracted from the tortured remains of family or friend. Her soul ached at the thought of so many who left their flesh in agony and terror.

As the two walked away from the party, seeking rest under the stars, and comfort in each other's arms, they find an accepting welcome from the cover of an old maple tree. The quietness rang out as the dull light of the setting sun found its way through the red and yellow leaves. Both hearts ached noticeably to each other. A beautiful understanding existed between these two new lovers, one that many under such circumstances could never know.

The two made passionate love, feeling a deep connection to each other and the earth, as their backs itch in disregard.

The grass, a flagship of their disposition.

Joshua's mind at ease as the calm eyes of his mate drift off into a different realm. As he fell to his side, and his love wrapped around him, chest to chest, he could feel her heavy heart beating. Poetry becoming his latest passion, he wished he had ink and paper with him to write down his thoughts:

"This I note as you lie here in my arms.
A feeling of bliss rushes over me,

A spirit of comfort and exception;

A warm embrace felt on a level beyond the realm of words or understanding.

Your breath moves in and out, filling the air with such peace.

Peace, the only word that could describe such a feeling,

Yet falls short of this emotion I so embrace with wonder.

No matter what causes us to part,

Be it our own folly, or the departure of our fleshly vessels;

No matter what the outcome,

I'll forever have this moment.

It stamps itself in my memories and will occupy a home in my heart,

Forever and for always.

And no matter where we end up,

I'll never stop loving you."

Neither the painful thoughts of Joshua's past, nor the frightening future of Natalia's kept the two from slumber.

They let go of all they could not control, and for the moment, just are.

Chapter Eighteen

The River Styx

I stand as a man and approach my father. He stands not as he was, but as he is — upright and full of vigor. Not the same man I buried years ago, but a manmade anew. And although I stand erect, as tall as he, I feel as though in the body of my former self. We discuss matters of old, and of new. Matters I cannot recollect as of late, but knew to be of importance.

As things pursue, and my mind wonders, suddenly I realize my position, and ask a bold question:

"Aren't you supposed to be dead?"

His eyes intensify. His manner, a reminder of who he was; the man I feared and revered.

"That's not something we talk about," he said, engaged and apprehensively.

And suddenly I travel, mind, body, and spirit, out of the otherworldly realm, and into the present misery.

***

Joshua woke with a start! Breathless with the feeling of falling, he sprung upright in forgetful terror. As the memory of a dream quickly faded, he took a few deep breaths, closed his eyes and calmed himself.

Upon re-opening, he felt the cool early morning breeze; the crickets chirped and the mosquitos buzzed as he stood up slowly, careful as to not wake the angel sleeping below.

The breath of Natalia covered the ground. Her mind still in the otherworldly realm.

Walking the way Joshua had walked so many mornings before, a comforting place to collect his thoughts and revel in the present, as the maple leaves of red and yellow dropped to the ground, the sun's early glow began to light the sky of blue variety, and he approached a large evergreen among the flames of the maple leaves.

Every man needs a tree to sit underneath.

His best thinking was done among the wisest of all earth dwellers. Here, he would allow his mind to wander and explore, amid his worries and cares.

He was a man of great responsibility, and this was his time of rest. His mind ceaselessly dealt with the burden that is life, and in this atmosphere his mind was free to just be. He was a morning person, and when the world slept, he felt that all was right, everything's the way it ought to be, and the world seemed more beautiful through this lens. In all life's difficulties, from Joshua's abandonment of self pursuit, to the divine duty of community and preservation, here he could breathe.

Some days he wished he could run away, join the animal kingdom and live within the state of mind as he did during these moments. Free of all his liability towards his kin, and living a life in such beautiful solitude.

The thought entered his mind consistently throughout his days, but never did he act upon them. This is what made him such a great leader. The ability to survive and thrive of his own accord, yet daily sacrificing his energy towards the future of his community, and surely one day, his own offspring.

But these moments were very dangerous for Joshua. Many a times he found himself boiling over the past, or re-living horrors of old. His mind ceaselessly evaluated and speculated. These mornings by himself opened him up to a new way of living, at ease with all and connected to all, in a metaphysical way he would not dare attempt to describe. But, this left him vulnerable. Many mornings he found himself engrossed on philosophical thoughts.

What was his purpose? Is there a God? If so, how could he discover such a being?

Theology, a common discussion amongst the Abandoned.

As he continued on his way, he forgot such former thoughts – in fact, he lost all thoughts together! This moment of bliss was what he longed for. The chirping of the early risen birds, and the sound of running water from the nearby river quietly appeared, and grew... then became deafening.

His mind at peace as the rushing rapids became his every thought. He breathed deeply, stood upright, and approached a site deemed too dangerous for anyone to approach alone.

Many of his fellow Abandoned had fallen here. The rushing rapids and frequent sighting of predatory animals deemed this a location for Warriors alone. Along with the rushing rapids over a hundred feet below, the River Styx demanded respect. The earth became louder as Joshua approached the cliffs.

A network of rock and root became the floor. The large slit in the roof revealed an array of blue, along with orange and grey clouds high in the sky. Joshua controlled his heartbeat as he approached the cliff face. Rolling to his belly, moving backwards feet first, he prepared to climb down the treacherous cliff-face.

He closed his eyes, and settled himself, knowing adrenaline can cause one to move too hastily. Precision and strong will was needed to make it down the embankment. His eyes still closed, he took several minutes to calm himself, feeling the breeze and listening to the rushing water.

As he opened his eyes he gasped in silent horror! Losing his grip, he frantically grabbed at whatever he instinctively could, as the visage of a wild animal stared him face to face not two feet away!

Normally such a presence would be sighted by the man of instinct; but the calming nerve and rushing rapids hid the presence of the animal. All men make mistakes, and this one could easily prove fatal to anyone of small character.

Gasping for breath and struggling to grab hold of anything, Joshua started to fall as the great beast lunged toward him.

Grabbing hold of its long black hair, Joshua caught the side of a recognizable face, the animal yelped as it began to pull its master up and safely onto his back!

For a moment Joshua could only hear the sound of his adrenalized breath among the rapids below. His heart beat heavy, and his mouth shot smoke.

There on his back, Joshua began to laugh. He rolled over, lifted himself to one knee, and still catching his breath, greeted his best friend.

"Buck! What were you thinking?" Joshua yelled trying to outdo the rapids below.

He proceeded to scratch his best friend's head, a heavy hand, powered by the nearly fatal fall.

As Joshua took a moment to calm his nerves, and Buck enjoying the playful scratch – all of a sudden the beast recoiled and stumbled backwards with a great *Yelp*!

Joshua pulled his hand back on instinct! The dog turned in a circle or two, yelping profusely, decreasing to a light hum, then sundered to the floor.

And before Joshua could comprehend what was happening, all began to haze. The light softened, and in a moment, Joshua noticed he was lying on the ground; vision blurred, and the sound of voices approaching – a faint echoing euphoria set in.

And then, darkness – the otherworldly realm greets.

Part III

"And the woman said to the serpent, 'We may eat the fruits of the trees of the garden; but the fruit of the tree which is in the midst of the garden, God has said, "You shall not eat it, nor shall you touch it, lest you die."'

Then the serpent said to the woman, 'You will not surely die. For God knows that in the day you eat it, your eyes will be opened, and you will be like God, knowing good and evil.'

So when the woman saw that the tree was good for food, that it was pleasant to the eyes, and a tree desirable to make one wise, she took of its fruit and ate.

She also gave to her husband with her, and he ate. Then the eyes of both of them were opened."

- Genesis 3:2-7

In the beginning, we came together as one, in true harmony. Using the knowledge of love and survival to expand our reaches of peace, justice and honor, influencing the weaker to the world of God's.

Many rebelled, and were cast from our presence, with whom we still fight today. The bear, the cougar, the tiger; and in the land of Eden, the ancient world of Mesopotamia, which stood the great family of Adam, it so-happened to be the snake. The most feared among enemies, it was the smartest of all and its deception lured man into a life of pride; into thinking our wants outweigh the peace and unity with all. Alone he slithers about.

We thought we were better than the laws of honesty and respect and love. We thought the day would never come, when our lust for living would falter.

The birth of civilization, trade and commerce, ownership and power.

But even at a microscopic level, given the tremendous amount of competition in all living things (including cells), how could there be such rapid and diverse growth? Has something subdued us? Some source of primary manipulation with a projected outcome?

Is this God?

Yes, it must be.

Chapter Nineteen

Mutiny on the Horizon

"The names of worldly things are utterly deceptive, for they turn the heart from what is real to what is unreal. Whoever hears the word "God" thinks not of what is real, but rather of what is unreal."

-The Gospel of Philip

"My mind, a weight.
A great weight takes hold. It crushes all it caresses.
Not freedom, but slavery, I live;
As all men who discover truth,
The nature of our slavery.

But I,
I wait for freedom."

***

Here in the clutches of my enemy I stand once again. I've lived as long as I can remember under the control of the UNA. And once more, I am dragged along The Event Horizon, towards the clutches of the supposed *best* mankind has to offer.

The great, they call him. But not me or my comrades.

The other men and women, who live in squalor at the Farm, don't seem to know of anything else. The angry group of workers, addicted, just like the rest of the *Pluggers.*

But Alexander knows not who my true comrades are.

As I limp through the dimly lit corridors, of the lower levels of The Event Horizon, I am reminded of its terror.

The sure pain I may be soon to experience — the agony that is being face to face with him, *Le bon,* Alexander.

Yet what have I done?

Nothing, I've done nothing.

These guards must be frantically pulling me because of my prediction — because of the evacuation, the prophecies, I had talked of so much before.

These so-called humans watch from above, among the toil and the tyranny enforced, the diluted peoples of earth — Alexander's army, pulling me through darkness.

Though I judge, I had been one of them long ago.

I aided in fabricating The Event Horizon, in fact! For the most part I worked on the ground. Preparing shipments to leave our atmosphere, towards another team who received it. A network of beings, the microcosm that is humanity.

But the work was good. The repetitive nature wasn't fulfilling, but wasn't terrible either. I have many fond memories of those days. I enjoyed time with my family, and drank too much with my friends. Times were good, but I lived in ignorance. I couldn't say why or how it all changed. Perhaps when I had opened my mind more towards a better way — towards the idea of good itself! I found I lived in a depressing world, one preparing to send the important people away, leaving the unimportant to its own demise.

And day after day, for years, I continued to work for the UNA, preparing shipments in the outskirts of a desert. I would regard my soul every day. That which I loved, rotting in sight. And with it, my ignorance, and my cooperation. Until the rebels came, and opened my mind to the truth lurking behind mankind.

Until the time of Adam, where consciousness was birthed, and rapid intelligence growth began, we acted on survival instincts, embedded within our souls, put there by something we understand not. Was it in fact Adam who enslaved us all to this new line of existence? In this prison of self-awareness...

Religion was our saving grace. For people to not be afraid of wrongful actions, consequence for immorality and the knowledge of sin, we would have destroyed all living things due to our need of superiority.

And I believe the ruler of such laws exists in another dimension, un-viewable by us.

He has shown many of us glimpses of his beauty and might, but we are doomed to the life of slavery and sin. Culminated, the birth of deception, greed and pride; humanity as we know it.

Yet the Idea of God, lost in the holy wars of this century. I continue my family's beliefs, a Christian man, in an agnostic world.

The new world, free of religion caused much tension. Groups like, "*The Platos*", and "*The Followers of the Way*," became the new means of people leaving the non-theistic world around them. And all people, so desperately afraid to revert back to ancient laws of combat, built itself recluse. Inwardly focused, worshiping self, creating end.

And the nations used any means needed to persuade its people into doing good, advocating their allegiance. In my country, when my grandfather was a boy, the former country of Canada still stood under the reign of the King of Britain, now belonging to history. All this before the merge. Totalitarianism. Abhorrent consumption.

A false sense of equality, as a people still abided by the rules of those in power. A false sense of importance and respect given to those who need it not. No importance in the grand scheme of things, except to eat up our resources faster, and send the world into a downward spiral quicker. The rich hoarded, and the poor shriveled.

Lost in the thought, I find myself aboard, led through the hallways of the God-Forsaken Ship I remember too well. All of a sudden, I feel a presence emerging from the darkness! With a few hard packing sounds, the heaving and huffing of a fight, and a tug and a jab; in the darkness, I am thrown to the ground!

"Come on, Maan!"

He even pronounced it right.

Wasting no time to wonder what the circumstances, I now saw the two men who once held me, bloodied and lying on the ground. Scrambling to my feet in sudden fear, the adrenaline had me behind my comrade in moments, whose movement I followed at a trot, now out of sight down the corridor.

My limp disappears. I will feel the pain later. I, in hot pursuit, nearly catch the man as we reach an old gate, reading "Servicemen only".

The gate closed behind us, and all goes dark once more.

They brought me into a room and I sit; unsure of its size; the dark cube surrounds. A solitary light emerges, burning in the middle, revealing nothing. Light reaches out to be seen, but the strength found in its endurance. I close my eyes and breath deep, taking in the feeling of being alone, just one more time.

As my eyes open, I see multiple faces in front and to my sides. Faces I know, yet different. Changed.

Like a portrait, each resembles the man of someone I once knew, yet only a glimpse as to who they are and what they may be now.

A new face emerges to the front; a face I could not forget. The war paint, a pattern totally unique unto himself. The black ink — tattoos, a ritualistic acceptance. His generation's incessant tribal needs embodied, brightening his eyes in a forceful manner. Three solitary tear drops fall on his left cheek; and his neck, wrapped in an assortment of words and pictures. I remember the phrase "Let Go"; another, "Not in rivers, but in drops", as well as a portrait of some type of angel. The sinister looking man, whom I know only as 'Sandman', stared at me, and I stared back, eager to get to work.

"There has been word, Alexander made a speech just yesterday." Sandman said, glancing now to his right.

A small man knelt near the candle, "Word is, they'll be leavin' for a new planet," he said, exactly whom, I can't quite put my recollection upon.

I decide to enter the dialogue.

"So, what are we doing?"

All the men look towards me, the eyes of the weak, the desperate. The men who I seemed to remember as vigorous, mighty, and full of passion, reduced to desperate men, waiting to die.

"We, are not on vacation any more," a lean man says to my right. A dark portrait of a dragon climbing up his arm; I don't hear what he says next, as for the moment I enjoy the thought of a comic strip playing out in real life. The dragon, and the solitary flame.

Sandman cut him off, and I jolt back to reality.

"So, now the few of us left have been trying to work out how to sabotage the ship. Nothing has changed Eurak, were still trying to save the peoples of Earth."

I almost forgot my *nom du guerre*, "Eurak."

"Who saved me?" Changing the subject, hoping to lighten the mood. I rub my head playfully. "Or should I say *hit me*? That one will probably leave a dent."

"Eurak, we don't have time!" Sandman says intently, not playing around. "Many of our men are out there, on the ship AND on the ground; Earth, our home and mother!" Sandman says in visible pain, "And now it's just us! If this ship leaves, we're at the mercy of The Event Horizon, and of course, *Him*!"

A pause, Sandman catches his breath.

"Those Gathering here, what you see in front, is the only chance left of resistance."

I look around at the dismal faction within reach.

"Alexander has wasted no time preparing, the people are already settling in for the long sleep."

How long have I been asleep?

"You've been away a long time," Sandman says as if reading my mind. Raising higher, his full body now dimly shining in the light. The grungy cloth fabric, as if thrown onto his body revealed a scarred and tattooed frame, lean yet muscular.

"Not many have been given forced labor like you. Alexander has been secretly killing anyone who associates with the so-called *Anarchists*. We've been pushed harder and harder and now is the day! But we have options. We can run to earth. If we move now, we may be able to steal a shuttle before it takes off. But I don't like this option, I'd rather fight! We can try to work the tunnels. There are ways to stop this ship!"

"The easiest way to do this..." Chimed in another, subtler voice from the shadows, not revealing himself, or herself perhaps. The voice shrouded in uncertainty, "...would be to sabotage the fuel supply; although we have yet to find it. Which is odd in and of itself. There should be mountains of it somewhere on this despicable vessel!" The articulate voice finished, bringing a new level of sophistication to the conversation it seemed. This voice was so gentle but firm; it must be that of a woman, or perhaps child. Yet I sit, more so pondering the options.

"Or..." Sandman drew my attention. "Or we do what we've never been able to do before. We make one last go of it. We cut off the head. Alexander can be defeated, we could take over this ship and bring freedom to all."

Mutiny on the Horizon.

There's nothing I'd like more than to see his face, that flawless, gauntless visage, ripped away from the body that carried it.

"This I intend to pursue, regardless of the votes outcome," Sandman finished, stepping away from the flickering light, nearly invisible now.

Ay, me too.

"Well then," said a stray voice, "Let's vote!"

Silence encompasses the darkness, yet my thoughts, loud and powerful. I weigh the options in my head for a moment, along with the interesting set of voices and faces I purposely attempt to suppress. All three options weigh heavily on my mind, yet a fourth, I ponder as well...

Is it my destiny, as is Sandman's, to see the head ceremoniously separated from the body? The king from his people, the tyrant from his peasants... Am I to risk it all for a meager shot at the impossible?

And so I sit, in the silent room, in the dark corridor, of the flying carcass, and I pray to the God of my ancestors for an answer.

We all realize the unimportance of our lives, and each find a way of coping. I now realize my destiny.
Kill or be killed.
Submission for the coward.
Glory for the brave.

Chapter Twenty

Follow the Leader

"You cannot acquire understanding unless you first know you do not have it."
        -Sextus

She told me to tell her a joke...

"Where is karma?" the boy inquired. The question, posed in such a way caused the elder to withdraw into thought.

'Where could it be? Floating above? The clouds? A flood gate inevitably to open... An order set down by the Gods, intertwined into all. Observable and experienced, perhaps?

'Or does it lie within the heart? A basic understanding of cause and effect. That the choices we make have outcomes, that we get out of life what we put into it. That the more good we propagate, outwardly and inwardly, the more good we are sure to receive and embrace.'

Lost in thought, the woman dragged by the hand; the impatient child just wanting to find the car and move along.

***

Joshua woke-up in a four-wheeled machine he had never seen before. He knew what automobiles were, and had seen the ancient vehicles in passing, but this was much different. A lower sound, a smoother ride, and an eerie feeling he was in the wrong hands. He could only see fragmented bursts of bright light down near his nose, as a white bag (or shirt) surrounded his face. It was enough for him to notice the shadows cast in the dust as they traveled down some desolate, abandoned superhighway.

The air had a faint breeze, bringing with it a punky but lustrous essence of the sea.

After another hour of driving, according to Joshua's calculations, the vehicle stopped. The air now stale and warm, big trees and lush grass gave a presence Joshua had never experience but attempted to understand. He knew the smell of these trees, and they knew him. But a stench corrupted this blissful aroma, one in which only man brings.

"What time is it?" the Warrior asked in a free manner as the two men brought him to his feet. One of them let go with a jolt – the unheard suddenly becoming human. As if the man was already dead, the two continued without a word.

"Common!" one of them said as they walked. Joshua was unsure if the man had yelled at him, or his timid partner. Joshua smirked and thought, "Must be green," As he inched forward.

The *creak* of a hinged door sent shivers up Joshua's spine. The *Clop! Clop!* of the boots on wooden floor awoke fear within the fearless man. The two men sat Joshua down in a puffy armchair. He quickly noted its comfort, cut short by the flash of light that suddenly surged into his eyes. He closed them with a wince as the blindfold comes off quick, slowly he opens them to reveal two hazy backsides – the two associates who lead him here, leaving the room.

Joshua began to calm as more and more became visible, embracing the small square with a rounded roof. What seemed roughly twenty feet up, a wondrous painting encapsulated above. His chest dropped as he noticed its beauty upon examination. His eyes felt moist and his mind attempted to unravel a deeply moving portrait of a ship, surely lost to the sea; accompanied by an unburdened host of naked, floating women. With warm cheeks and compassionate eyes, they stare into the abyss unmoved — Joshua lost within their calamity. He noted the waves, reminding him of all the solitary fiends he had heard in the past. Waves crashing in anger, frothing at the mouth! His chest sunk and heart beat heavy, Joshua closed his eyes and imagined the minds of the men on board, experiencing the dread of sure death, and the two most frightening things a man must ultimately face:

Eternal consciousness,

Or definitive end!

He breathed deeply and opened his eyes steadily. You wouldn't know whether he had just inhaled the smoke from his favorite pipe, or the definitive moment he extinguished his prey's life. He sat uneasy, yet calm.

Scanning the room, noting the pleasant color of the sky on the walls, Joshua felt quite comfortable. Suddenly feeling his bowels move, he wished he had gotten his morning squat in the bushes before being placed into his current predicament.

The door suddenly opened. A *"Thump! Thump!"* came from down the hallway. Joshua felt his heart beginning to beat but was unsure if it were of his, or infiltration.

"Thump! Thump!"

"Welcome, sir," said the timid man from before Joshua presumed, but his attention shifted as the door opened.

A creature entered the room, a dark shadow crept inside. And with it came a deep sense of respect and admiration. Silently the door was closed behind the man, and although silence itself cannot exist (It being the absence of something), it surely existed at such a moment as this.

The two stared at each other, competing alphas, neither breaking his gaze. Yet a slight fright fell upon Joshua's thoughts... The hardened eyes of the man looked at him not like any before. The eyes so bright yet aged, matured and confidant. Joshua couldn't tell whether he was a man in his sixties or mid-thirties. His salt and peppered hair hung in front of his unwrinkled forehead. His beard looked thick but was kept relatively short, neither grey nor black dominated the strong chin of the boldly postured man. Joshua felt an uneasy presence. The lack of wrinkles revealed what seemed to him like a life lived deprived of laughter.

Not necessarily a tall man, yet Joshua felt as if he were a giant! Wearing a blue garment of some foreign fabric. Barefoot, he shuffles closer to Joshua.

His eyes fell soft, transforming from a quizzical hardness to a compassionate gaze. Each seemed to realize he had been doing the exact same thing, analyzing the enemy.

"Silence is the element in which great things fashion themselves," the man broke in with, raising his muscular but smooth looking hand to the sky, as if calling upon the divine.

Joshua rebuked the comment: "Do you claim to be great?"

With a look of what can only be described of as fascination, the man replied: "Well, it is my nickname."

Joshua fell silent for a moment, he knew what this meant...

"But I would never claim something of the sort," continued the Chief. "For, making a claim of opinion is different than claiming a fact!"

Speaking as if into the air, Alexander continued, feeling his seemingly barbaric prisoner was in fact no barbarian at all.

"The truth I long for but can never find. When speaking of such things I am humbled yet perplexed! I've lived many lives, claiming to be something, but essentially am another. I have made decisions about who I am, and what I stand for; but like a tree in the fall, I shed my leaves, go to sleep and abandon all that I was."

There are deep dark places within all. Not many explore such realms of the mind. Instinct perhaps warning the host of its damnation. But, in order for one to truly know, he must explore the damnation. For who can attain knowledge if they know not the very foundations of humanity! How can one who has not experienced truly understand?

Joshua hadn't felt the presence of such speech outside of Achilles. He now looked in wonder as the speaker captivated him in the way he spoke and gestured. Alexander spoke as if he knew truth yet refused to accept his own knowledge. A true man of reason.

A man just as ourselves.

Joshua looked upon the man of history he knew to be Alexander Seyer, former soldier, turned general, turned Lord, *"Le Bon!"* Joshua recalls from Maan's *rancoeur*.

Joshua looks upon the man in anger.
I look upon him only with pity.

Does God pity us?
I surely do.

Chapter Twenty and One

Chess

"Where is my friend?" Joshua said, with power and might, not posed as a question but as a statement.

Caught off guard, Alexander caulked his head.

"I was told you came alone."

"No, they shot my friend also. His name is Buck. He is a canine."

"Your friend is safe I assure you, and will remain so, provided he and you remain civilized."

"Civilized!" Joshua's rage began to build, breathing deeply his brow widened, looking his adversary in the eyes. "I'll remain civilized with your blood under my heel!"

"Listen," said Alexander calmly, his eyes half open, looking up and directly into Joshua's. He noted the deep brown he had seen previous now drowning in white and red. The eyes of an animal glared back at his, yet he remained, steady as a rock.

"A man can go mad with the type of freedom I give! You sit across from me unchained, your friend (and you must trust me), is well. My men..." He paused momentarily, a detection of a sigh could be heard as his eyes left Joshua's for but a moment. "My men found you on our property, owned by the governance of the United Nations of Earth. And I, the caretaker.

"All that lives and breathes is under my jurisdiction, and I have every right as the head of the governing body to question my people, recorded or not, as current citizens.

"So you are aware, I have no intention of hurting you, your friend, or any more that may be from wherever you come from. But at the present time, I run this empire; and you, technically speaking, belong to me."

Joshua's anger subsided as he tried to remember his life, what seemed so long ago now, at the mercy of the UNA. Now, presumably, The UNE.

Alexander saw Joshua's anger deter, a victory in his books. But the jargon of a politician always masks deep secrets.

"Now I must ask you a question..." Alexander says, looking at Joshua. "Where are you from?"

"Why should I tell you anything?" Joshua asked in sincerity. "You shot me and my friend and brought us here unwillingly. Not only that, you and your kind abandoned me and mine twenty years ago!"

Alexander looked upset, as he began to pace the room. Joshua watched him, contemplating no doubt.

Alexander reached into his blue vest and pulled out a carved pipe, followed by a match.

He puffed on the tobacco still left in the bowl as it glowed in his palm. Putting his thumb over the top he moved towards a seat directly opposite Joshua.

"Okay then, let's not talk. How about we play a game?"

Joshua liked games, and Alexander noticed the instant perk of his brow as the word was mentioned.

"How about this," Alexander continued. "If I win the game, you give me the pleasure of showing you around the city we've built here... And you hear me out. There's a lot to be said and not enough daylight to get through all of it. I would love for you to stay as my guest."

Pause for effect.

Joshua mind raced through the scenario.

"If you win, I give you and your friend a ride back to where I found you, and we can both continue as if we had never met."

Joshua detected the subtleties of a lie under the man's breath.

"Or, of course, you may choose to stay even if you win." Alexander smiled as he felt the impossibility of refusing such an offer. He took a puff and allowed the smoke to rise out of his lungs and mouth of its own accord. Joshua pretended he didn't want a pull, but took the pipe as Alexander offered it.

"What's the game?" Joshua inquired as the smoke rose to the ceiling, masquerading as a surreal fog upon the waters-zephyr.

"House rules, so I'll pick. Would thou knowest the game of chess?"

Unsure as to what was exactly said, the foreigner felt vulnerable in his state of confusion. Without words, accepting the challenge all the same.

"Okay then, it's settled!" Alexander called for a chess board.

The game was brought in by a young man with a stern face who eagerly began to assemble the board. Joshua watched carefully as each piece was set, attempting to also listen intently to the rules Alexander professed. The young man was a bit of a distraction; he looked at Joshua just as puzzled as Joshua looked at everything — unsure of what was going on, more so pondering the intent of this summons than of the rules being verbalized.

"Honestly, I'm not that good." Joshua heard as the door slammed shut, jolting his brain back to reality. "But I find it a great way to pass the time, it's hard to keep civilized in a fallen world. So I do have practice on my side."

Joshua stared down at his army, the spurious Black.

"Good luck!" Alexander exclaimed with a sincere grin as he shot his fingertips forward with the trajectory of a spear. It met Alexander's flat palm, just before reaching the dark king on Joshua's side of the board.

I guess Alexander assumed all had known the common gesture.

***

165

"Check mate!" Alexander exclaimed as he placed his queen directly in front of Joshua's king.

In shock, Joshua scanned the board. Seeing now that he could not move his piece to the spot he planned. The diagonal moving, pointy-headed piece of his opponent blocked the escape he thought was available.

"Good win," said Joshua as he extended his muscular hand towards Alexander's. "Can we play again?"

Excited, Alexander beamed with joy as he met Joshua's hand firmly, in what he had to explain was, "*A handshake*". Alexander appreciated the grace of his opponent and was eager to set up the board once more. As he began, the carved wooden pieces placed in orderly fashion, the tiny knock each one made as it settled into its personal space – allowing Alexander to find his.

Meditating during such relaxing activities as this, emptying his mind of worries, Alexander forgetting all the horrors he had seen and lived.

This was his vacation.

"I will play again," Alexander said upon placing his final piece. "But there are some things I need to know..."

Joshua forgot about his deal in the excitement of it all. He looked at the subtle blush on his opponent's face, revealing a tender man in his mind. A man who would prefer to play, but knew the importance of business. Joshua eased off.

"What would you like to know?"

He was vague in his revelations, still unsure of what to make of the young old-man that sat directly across from him. Yet feeling an odd comfort from it all. The colors and smell of the room brought with it feeling Joshua had never known. A world of privilege he never thought possible.

As the two continued to play, Alexander now sat in silence. Digesting all that had been revealed.

The details of which, I know not.

"Do you believe in life after death?" Alexander broke the silence, asking a question Joshua had never heard before.

Joshua stared for a moment, unsure of what to say, and what he truly believed.

"I've never thought about it!" replied Joshua, squinting and looking up at the wonderful colors over-head.

He began to see not the fearful images of the deep, but the beauty of the unexplored. A silence and calm fell through the roof and penetrated the walls. The two sat across from each other, puffing and passing; life in existence, no need of speculation.

"Love is an illusion, Joshua. It is there only because the need for self-preservation has become soft, and the world simplified. I discovered no one who has truly loved in its proper form. The idea: to care for something more than the self; and thus, I have concluded that no one will ever truly love me, in the way that the word is understood, and even defined. The closest I had come to know the term, to define it if you will, would be the days spent with my brothers in arms. As we killed together, true love only discovered through death. Destruction is all I have ever known, it is what keeps the world going round – essentially! For one to survive, others must die. A sad fact of life, and essentially of fundamental importance. I find this to be a sad state of affairs, but true nonetheless! Do you understand Joshua? Do you know of what I speak?"

Indeed, he did. And within the moment his memory raced. Traveling back to a world of the past, the first of many hunts with his original companion in blood; Joshua relives his baptism into the faith...

Chapter Twenty and Two
The Primordial Hunt

"Do not fear the flesh and do not love it. If you fear the flesh, it will dominate you. If you love the flesh, it will swallow you up and strangle you."

-Gospel of Philip

On the hunt, all is distant. Far from the worries of life. Here, all is simply split in two — life or death. And here, all make the same choice. All it would seem, choose life.

Life just doesn't always choose you.

The hair on the back of Bradley stood tall; his body became stone. The rough and tattered barbarian stood concrete, the fur like the moss that grew all around. The dry forest brought a heat uncomfortably penetrating. The man sweat profusely; the beast knew better than to pant. He knew the pain of hunger, and would not risk a meal now. He hadn't eaten in six days.

Joshua stood attentively, for what seemed like an hour. He knew what impatience would encumber. In these long arduous moments of bliss, a man's mind wanders. The joy of the hunt, the uncertainty ahead, anything to distract from the pain within.

Of the companions in blood, both inwardly preparing for the sacred bond of battle. The need for violence in all species, especially the human; Joshua shares equally this solemn ground with friend and foe, and all understood the necessity of the win.

Survival depends on one to endure such hardships.

The vivid thought and exhausted helplessness is now but a memory that exists only as the mind re-lives the past. And the greatest memories known to man are memories of companionship such as these — moments of victory and accomplishment. And the euphoric high is not experienced anywhere higher than that of a successful kill; the rush of adrenaline when the deed is done, and the spoils of victory, shared by *les vainqueur*.

As the two stood still, Joshua could now see the creator of Bradley's insurrection.

A large fawn loitered in the brush. Now visible, Joshua could see what Bradley originally heard. She swayed as she walked, the doe enjoying the sheer bliss of the day, and life unalterable. The ripe leaves rustled, the taste of joy could be seen in her step.

Bradley prepared to strike. Joshua breathed deep, gripping tightly to his weapon of seemingly evil distribution. The blissful singing of birds and chirping of absent minded squirrels masked the violence and terror the small deer headed towards.

Making the first move, Bradley pounced forward, running straight at his prey! The doe stumbled out of fear, perhaps her first encounter of such veracity.

Joshua, about four steps behind, witnessed his partner leap with perfect precision – grasping the soon-to-be-loser by the scruff of her neck, quickly spinning her to her back. Joshua recalled the horror in her eyes as she spun, the fear of the unknown never quite so prevalent.

Joshua shuffled around her wild hooves, flailing and kicking about, esoterically aiming at whatever, in the instinctual fight for life.

With a deep breath and a transfer of weight, Joshua's arms plunged the rock he held down on her head. A loud *crunch* of bone and brain matter – instantaneous unconsciousness, followed by the soft and muffled thump of her head as it grooved into the earth. Joshua lifted the stone and did it once more.

He felt faintly dizzy and stood, realizing she would go nowhere. Adrenaline surging, he grabbed a knife and knelt again, holding the blade to her throat. He felt the warm red blood as it intuitively flowed to the earth. The sacred liquid given back to whence it came. He closed his eyes and internally thanked her for her sacrifice.

After his breathing began to calm, Josh felt a surge from within! Quickly, he turned to his right and dry heaved. He rose to his feet as he continued to gag and cough. Bradley appeared at his side, looking up at his master, tongue drooped in apprehensive ease. He was tired and hungry.

After a minute of settling himself, Joshua cut a strip from the thigh of his kill and began to chew, as he quickly moved to collect firewood.

As the sun dawned, he dripped with sweat. Joshua's mouth was dry and his body worn as the tough meat quenched his stomach's upheaval. This far outside of camp, they were better off staying the night.

At the fireside, eating a charred corpse and gazing into discord, the flames lit the pondering soul. The great curse of all creation, the ultimate and inevitable departure from matter. The dark world of the mind:

The flames flicker.
And the flames flicker.
And the flames flicker.

What beauty and magnificence, that so small an entity, produces such immense thought and feeling. The colors shifting, and bewildering movement; trepidation, fully enraptured.

It removes the physical and enters the spiritual. The world unseen, the world of the mind. The mysteriously dark; impossible to comprehend its perfection. An imperfect system of chaos embodied in the world of materials; yet we stare into it, so beautiful a spectacle, and fearful of the day when that flame will flicker no more.

Embedded-brethren we became as the shedding of blood spilt on both our hands and feet. The feeling one gets upon winning the greatest trophy Mother Nature has to offer: life. And in this, a brotherhood emerges, a trust that can never be broken. Not because it can't, but simply because it will not.

The moon and stars gaze upon the spectacle.

We are so small, so clueless.

The things they must observe, the death and destruction they must see.

Does the world float, drifting slowly in its sight; clueless of the things it must observe? The death and the life, like a heart, pulsating;

In and out,

In and out.

The Earth, alive and in love, attempts to home a new type of mystery...

The human mind, the immeasurable might; unfathomable tool, rivaling the power of God itself.

How the moon watches for so long I do not know. Deep wisdom, surely, the light of the lesser...

Oh, how it must understand so much. The life it has lived, the things it has seen, the ages come and gone.

And now these celestials sit in the sky, a witness to the night's events, and surely impressed with such a view as this.

Chapter Twenty and Three

Ostracized

"The duel substance of Christ — the yearning, so human, so superhuman, of man to attain to God or, more exactly, to return to God and identify himself with him — has always been a deep inscrutable mystery to me. This nostalgia for God, at once so mysterious and so real, has opened in me large wounds and also large flowing springs.

My principle anguish and the source of all my joys and sorrows from my youth onward has been the incessant, merciless battle between the spirit and the flesh."

-The Last Temptation of Christ

In solitude I seek thee. In silence I find me.

The snow caps I see. The line drawn in the trees, marking the approach and speed — the season shifts rapidly. And I with it.

So what is this?

A moment to reflect, for I, and for you as well. It is the necessity of all to seek inner knowledge. The being of our souls. The source of our code. Our deeply rooted seed, the source of humanity.

A dream of mine, I remember vividly:

I remember standing, my father sitting, as Solei slept in the room around the corner. We had a conversation, discussing what I was to do this particular night. To my right stands a mirror. This mirror, nothing particularly special, creates a movement. My eyes instinctively look upon the reflection, an image of Solei going by with an air of unease, a warped reality — a mere reflection of herself. Heart beating magnanimously, I bolt for the room in which lies the ghost. The body lie limp; the dim light reveals a deformed girl in a deep sleep.

I grab her! My tears streaming as I carry her to a bed in the open room! Her limbs elongated, and turn to a greenish hue. Her eyes black as night, as I stroke her wet and sticky hair, begging her to wake! And I still remember, screaming into her face...

"Wake up! Wake up!"

And then, all of a sudden, in a sorrowful rage, I realize my position. Without skipping a beat, I plead for mercy...

"Wake up! Wake up!"

A pause.

"God, wake *me* up."

And with that, I awoke. Drenched in sweat, alone in the dark.

***

Do you ever feel as I do?
When surrounded, utterly alone.
Surviving in a world not of your own;
A dead carcass, a floating tomb.
A mind apart, within the womb.

In between two mountains I dwell. This strangely peaceful, illuminated world.

The Golden Ears, a comfort; life promised daily and safely, in a world built on survival.

And through the clearing, Mount Red, the world unseen and mysterious; a far-off land of beauty, intrigue, and excitement. I look upon it's whitened peak and wonder of the life abiding in a world much different than mine. A world not experienced in so long. The world of wildlife, adventure – a land glowing and breezy, cool and calm.

Unsure of who I am or what I've done, I wander this life in the fetters of ignorance, and there I stand, even as of recent! So what of today? If unwise all the days of my past, how am I to believe I'm wise today? The quiet air, full of life, but only at such a foundational level.

Today is only tomorrow's yesterday.

Who is that man in the past, living in the present? Coming to terms with one's failures and faults, and idiocy and naivety, and weakness and passivity, does not make for a wise man, nor a fool; it simply makes one human, and self-aware of truth.

But alas, I sit and stare at a world just out of reach. A sheep in wolf skin, a quiet predator, hoping for disaster.

Enlightened in a darkened world.

The remnants of fear remain. But I, I fear nothing! Not man, no beast, nor spirit. Life has become death and I embrace them both.

And here I sit motionless once again upon the mount.

I have lost all ties to the material realm. I feel my doom was destined as I contemplate my believing in the human race.

How could I have been so naive?

I've lost faith in my fellow humans once again. And once again, I find myself restless. Accepting these days as my last, feeling just as spiritually confined as physically, I attempt to make my suffering true. And my spirit sits motionless, just like me. I dare not move from this spot. Here I watch the third sunrise in a row — prepared deterioration. To exit this world on my own terms, and be free of its corruptible ways once and for all; entering relation with my other brethren, molding down into the presence of the past.

The immortal must never be given to man, yet we attempt to create one ourselves.

The only thing now left in my legacy will be what they say about me. What they say about me... reduced to words and attributes. Do I know myself any other way? Can I ascribe to know who I am, apart from such frivolous banter?

And if I am condemned, I wonder, in the course of history, will my name be stamped from the records?

174

Would, like the civilizations before, I be condemned to the patriarchal past, forever known subjectively?

A power, willing to alter the human experience.

It's will over mine.

Waiting is such a hard game to play. Patience, truly a virtue as they say. And virtue I pursue, and continuously wait.

But now, with Joshua gone, and my forsaken spirit on display, I sit to my end. With my official banishment from the Abandoned, and confined to the monastic order, I fast in unjust observance, intending to make my banishment complete.

Arousing suspicion of my involvement in his disappearance, due to the opposition failing to appear at election, a question of integrity of the Abandoned's Judge (yours truly) was posed by Atenacious. I was silently appalled.

The people called for blood. And a deal with the Devil was no doubt made.

What a joke.

I know not at this time where lies the mighty warrior Joshua. But the city has been on a decline since the loss of the great man, just over a year ago. And a year of turmoil, for myself and for the people began. All have felt Joshua's disappearance. All have suffered his departure. From Natalia and her son, to the everyday-child, cold and hungry. Early frost, bitter inquisitions. The abandoned life is a demented manifesto. Its obvious air of sorrow; a people without smiles.

And I have lost patience.

Now, the people wait for a savior. Up on the hill I've witnessed many days and many nights, waiting for his return or the discovered corpse.

The only value in the world I find is in that of the other; a need to be one with all. Sadly, I am but one within all. A single cell, a separate entity. I have lived and longed; craved for such truth I know exists, yet continues to elude me. All men must make a choice, and I see no other option but detachment. I cannot care for them, destined for another disappointment.

And again my thoughts see the young child. The precious girl I once held, seeming more like a dream every day. I no longer remember the small imperfections, the color of her skin, the shade of her eyes, the glow of her hair glistening in the sun. The more my thoughts drift towards the end, towards the possibility she's gone, and my one redemptive purpose, I see that elongated corpse; that green and perspiring skin that so vividly lives in my dreams.

I feel worthless.

Now an outcast, I am controlled by the system I once controlled. So, I reminisce of my past, and once again I see little Michael's face. I have not forgotten him, the little blue boy. His cold touch and soft look, the fog in the air as I breathe upon him. The sound, I hear nothing but the heart, and the breath. These last few days, the hunger truly setting in, I see him much more. Truly, he has met God; and I, the Devil.

Chapter Twenty and Four

Call Me Ishmael

"Woe to him whom this world charms from Gospel duty! Woe to him who seeks to pour oil upon the waters when God has brewed them into a gale! Woe to him who seeks to please rather than to appal! Woe to him whose good name is more to him than goodness! Woe to him who, in this world, courts not dishonor! Woe to him who would not be true, even though to be false were salvation! Yea, woe to him who, as the great Pilot Paul has it, while preaching to others is himself a castaway!"

-     Moby Dick

The world through Ishmael's eyes was laden with wonder. A vast and eternal land, full of the unknown. Ishmael had lived a simple life thus far, as a young boy among the people known as *The Abandoned*, under the leadership of Judge Achilles, and now Atenacious. He had recently moved to Eight with his parents and three siblings.

His father, Theo, was a young builder and was eager to do his part in the new community. He loved his family and spent as much time with his boys and his girl as was possible. He was always working, a craftsman like himself endlessly busy. But even as he worked and played with the kids, he always found time for their mother. His affection was visible. His eyes were so empty of energy yet so full of love. For him, life was as it was, and could be no other way.

Carolyn was a real beauty. She always seemed to glisten to Theo. Her seemingly insurmountable joy radiated and allowed him to work as hard as he did. Often, the two would be seen sneaking off into the woods, hand in hand, leaving all behind for what any and all lovers deserve and need.

Ishmael adored his father, especially his stories. The two would stay up late under the light of the moon and the stars; sitting under the open sky, the grass would cause Ishmael to itch; and under the canvass of the millions of lights descending upon them, and the stories of adventure and mystery, Ishmael lived in ecstasy. A realm far from his, a wondrous and adventurous mind, looking at all and admiring it. The scary, and the scared. The beauty within and without.

Ishmael went exploring with the other kids of the town often. On this particular day, the pre-pubescent went with a group of his friends down by the ridge, a forested area to the south of the town (technically part of the Warriors land). It led down to the river, the dense forest and steep embankments made a dangerous, yet ideal playground.

The group of excitable boys ran their way into the dark and mysterious world of the south. The exhilaration of being in the wild, imagining themselves as the heroes of their people, the mighty and brave. Some never returned, but added to the folklore.

Ishmael walked impatiently, watching two of his brothers among the large group of boys as they walked yonder. He attempted to speed up, but an anchor kept him from such desire. His five-year-old sister, Ophelia, gripped tightly, hand tightly grasping his.

"Wait for us!" cried Ishmael. His friends couldn't hear him as they disappeared in the thicket, their voices still heard, echoing close by.

He stopped and looked down at his sister. "Let's go to the water," he said, putting his hand on her shoulder.

And so the two set-off. He encouraged her to run by tapping her arm; tongue out, he jolted ahead playfully. The young Ophelia smiled and ran slowly (as all children her age do) towards the hilariously fun joys of absolutely anything and everything, and nothing all the same. Her dimpled and red cheeks exposed almost a full set of baby teeth, a little crooked but cute on the child. Her short blonde hair waved in front of her eyes. Miraculously she didn't fall as she caught up to her brother.

"Got chu!" She said grabbing him. The two shared a laugh as Ishmael brought her to his back, traversing together the well-known route. Ishmael had been to the sacred ground, *the foot* (as he referred to it) of the River of Plenty.

As another winter had begun, the fisherman had left the waters for their allotted rest. The fish now gone to the sea. Ishmael reached the shores with his sister by means of the trail the fishermen often took with their boats.

His father built the first working boat. Theo trained many men in carpentry, and Ishmael watched his dad as he worked. Theo imagined his son would follow in his footsteps; learning everything he would need from his old man, "A chip of the old block," he would say. And Theo's excitement doubled that of Ishmael's as the two worked tirelessly on the vessels of the water. Both father and son building together. And Theo could always recall the big grin on Ishmael's face, all the days leading up to the project's conclusion.

Ishmael loved any reason to come down to the river, and today he was glad to hear nothing but the calm waters drifting by.

This boy of eleven would later recall the days as a dream. A vague understanding and acceptance of how things are, and surely must be. He felt energized and motivated at the sun's rise; tired and content at its dawn. The darkness consisted of peaceful glows and warm hearths. His father, most nights, told stories — some true, others fiction; a catalogue of intrigue for the boy. Collective joy emanated from father and son through the passion and love behind the words of the story-teller, especially during Ishmael's favorite story, the one of another Ishmael, and his exciting voyage at sea, chasing the white whale; the terrifying abyss, home to great beasts! The leviathan among them.

Carolyn would say, "Nothing scary before bed, they will not sleep!" All would accept the verdict in utter and complete silence; But some nights, Ishmael would wake in darkness to his father shaking his arm, "Shall I continue?" said Theo in a whisper.

Ishmael lived for the sea. Unlike his brothers and friends who idolized the Warriors, Ishmael would sit in silence by the water, imagining where the current led to — a world of great mysteries and fearful beasts. In Ishmael's young mind, this seemed a far more exciting life, and death, than that of the Warriors; and only recently did he become enwrapped with guilt, attempting to rationalize a way in which to tell his family, specifically his dad, that he would not be following in his footsteps. Within, Ishmael lived not as a craftsman nor warrior, but a unique will, in and unto himself;

A man among mankind.

Ishmael sat on a rock as his sister played with a stick in the dirt. Absent of care, his mind was in the sky, and on the waters, and with the breeze. He took deep breaths and relaxed in the calm, enjoying life's most precious necessities. Suddenly, his mind returned to the physical realm in front of him, and Ishmael noticed something in the water, not fifty paces upriver!

It was floating along the bank, big and black; making its presence known while scratching the brush that overhung the current. Ishmael stood instinctively! Fear pumping his blood harder and faster. He felt as if he entered a different reality, one of the animal, lacking any inner thought, based purely on instinct. Fear began taking over. The large object was now close! Ishmael, standing frozen next to the bank, and the animal, which he knew it was now, within yards from him, — held to a halt by a semicircle of rocks protruding from the agitated water.

Many, Ishmael thought, would not have the courage to approach this massive floating creature, even men of the forest, the Warriors who faced and dealt with death regularly. Fear, he realized, was in the water, and the unknown world beneath, captivated within all people,

Warrior and laity alike. "But I," he thought, "am not like them."

As he touched the cold water with his toes, working up the courage to venture into the chill of the unknown, Ishmael noticed something; it was a hand! A deathly white hand could be seen, contrasted by the dark and disturbing mass. Forgetting his sister's presence (and she in her own world), he bolted towards the human. The river was painfully cold, and the frantic sound of the splashing as he ran caught his sister's attention. Reaching the object, Ishmaels fear was replaced by a heightened sense of urgency.

The object, or man, was large, and Ishmael grunted as he used all his might to lift up. The obvious "Boy" in his grunt would call any observer to recognize a child, but in this moment, indistinguishable from any other grown man. His strength revealed what many humans fail to know of themselves. A significant strength, hidden within all; a robust vigor, only revealed when facing divinity. As he pulled the object towards the shore, the water pulled and tugged at the mass and its savior. The young girl shouted as he pulled! Her determined faith in her brother adding to his power. Miraculously, Ishmael reached the shore. Turning and unwrapping the man from his wet attire, the extrication revealed a familiar face, but, at first, no definitive name attached.

***

Ishmael's brothers, Elijah and Connor, were mid run through the forest. A distance of roughly half a kilometer lay between their start and end. The forested slope was a momentous minefield; the boys purged forward as the race was sure to reveal the greater and the lesser. A group of boys cheered from behind as they ran, another group cheered from in front as they approached the finish-line. Elijah and Connor, the family rivalry, both left no energy unexpelled as they bolted and darted through the forest. The cheers cultivated; each boy pursued the demise of his fellow kin! But, ahead of them came an unforeseen hurdle! Approaching at record speed, contact became inevitable.

Elijah attempted to stop but ran right into Ishmael! The two, fell and tumbled! Their young sister looked in silent bewilderment.

Connor, the youngest boy, crossed the finish and all cheered. He had never beaten his brother before, and as the group extolled the victor, Elijah fumed.

Out of breath, Ishmael left his angry brother on the ground, and approached the group of boys as they praised Connor. The loud cheers faded, silence fell upon them as the severity in Ishmael's demeanor revealed a story fascinating to the group.

In a mass they followed Ishmael (Ophelia on his back), traveling along the shore, excitedly reaching the naked man lying upon the banks of the river. They stood in reticence, staring at the dead hero of old — the man who had been missing for over a year, the removed savior of the *Abandoned,* the great warrior Joshua lay half frozen, back from the dead.

Chapter Twenty and Five

All's Dead on the Western Front

"Now, while the children of Israel were in the wilderness, they found a man gathering sticks on the Sabbath day.
And those who found him gathering sticks brought him to Moses and Aaron, and to all the congregation.
They put him under guard, because it had not been explained what should be done to him.
Then the Lord said to Moses, 'The man must surely be put to death; all the congregation shall stone him with stones outside the camp.'
So, as the Lord commanded Moses, all the congregation brought him outside the camp and stoned him with stones.
And he died."

-Numbers 15: 32-36

The feel of her touch brought with it a suppression of all his thoughts. The struggles, the worries that the day overflowed with; the fear and exhaustion that came with the responsibilities of a leader. A faded memory, the warm, brown eyes look deep into his. The light surrounding her causing a glow. Time seems to stand still.

And then, a shift occurs... The light dims, his heart begins to race! Fear beginning to consume all around. A realization, the inevitable separation from her, felt at the most subconscious, intrinsic level. In pang, caving to the ancient emotion, a different man contained... A man he thought lost, a lonely and broken heart, leaving the world the way he entered it, bloody, and alone.

But which man was real? He could not be sure. What remained of the man, and what of the beast, he was left to contemplate.

The lovely Natalia, bright and shimmering, now dark and sinister. She screams causing a ring so loud, forcing him to cover his ears! Through his fearful eyes, and rigid body, she turns black! Burning from the inside, charred and ash, embers for eyes; the dust, her frame. Reeling in agony, his dead eyes half open, revealing the end — only the beginning. The powerful push of man's will to survive, the only thing keeping him from allowing the temptation of final rest – freedom from the world, But which one?

And with it, the powerful sorrow he felt – a life without her. A world absent of her, and the sudden realization, the insurmountable desire for reunion. The fear felt added to the energy. A surge of sudden power felt from within. The idea that he must make it back to her caused torment as his body urged him to go. Yet, in his unwavering faith, to his people and to his love, he pushes through an invisible, and unconceivable wave. Like swimming in an ocean opaque, waters clear as crystal; surrounded by peace, he did what only those with life do... He risks all that is left, just to see her.

And with that, Joshua gasped for air. The world suddenly rushing back, and the vision of his love was met instead with faces of angels, young and bright, white as ghosts', as the dead man was reborn, wet and naked, surrounded by children he half recognized.

***

Excerpt from Rorschach's Journal:

"A world at war, but what of me?
I lack the means of understanding;
The lack, a means of getting by.

The Ignorant prosper unaware of the world and its finality.
Oh, how I long to live within their minds.

I dare describe the life of a tree.
It stands mighty and strong, connected to all around.

184

It's bark so rough to the touch,
It's smell so calming to the nerves.
It's presence, a blessing to all.

*Yet my words fall short, for how can you define
something that words cannot grasp? The mind is
sparked by the thought of it. I desperately seek its fond
memorials, stored away in the records of my life.*

*Being here, among the miraculous, the life blood of
the forest. The perfect architecture. So full of life, yet
calm and tranquil.*

*How I long to match the moral standards; how I
wish to be the representative in a cruel and desperate
world, so far apart from theirs!*

The life of the human... how depressing."

***

Awoken from a nap, the bright evening now darkened;
whoever suddenly controlling my thoughts:

"An emergency council meeting! You're in need, sir,"
said the young runner, out of breath from the sprint he
had just finished. And silently I arise and am led towards
Eight. A surge of urgency as we descend the slope
together; my arm gripped tightly onto his. He used the
time to inform me of Joshua's return. Or, as he put it,
"The Great Joshua's return."

The city had been all angst and dismay the evening he
was declared missing. All discussed the mysterious
disappearance of the monumental man. And with gossip,
comes rumors — a dark shadow of truth.

Joshua had been known to leave with Buck,
sometimes for days on end without so much as a good-
bye. He was a man who needed his space, and that I
understood. But even I felt it odd he would leave on such a
night, the night of great celebration; the disappearance,
following his speech — the Sea of Rorschach, over a year
ago. Along with a child soon to be birthed, the
responsibility of a wife, and the upcoming election, this

185

seemed so out of character! And after time, most hinted towards foul-play.

My assumption: he knew the weight of the world, and felt time's effect on the soul. He made a selfish decision; he cracked under the pressure.

True leaders, few and far between.

Some little ways down the hill I begin to see Eight, the city seemed desolate, yet, through the brush it suddenly revealed the solution. The people, all gathered at the amphitheater — the backside, the base of Mount Sinai.

The crowds sitting on the hill made it difficult for me to descend to my rightful spot among the other decision makers. It was loud and cramped. I felt anxious, being one cell within the organism.

I descended the steps of the bowl towards the center, eyes started to gravitate in my direction. Each step carefully placed as a fall here would prove fatal in my weak and aged condition. The crowds began to quiet; the quickened silence carried a momentum, and all suddenly grew still. Reaching the bottom, I enter the arena, where Joshua had given his speech that fateful night not long ago.

This large bowl-like back may have been crafted by men generations before, or perhaps a product of the earth's own accord... Whichever the case, this became the most monumental area in the Abandoned's history. Laws, debates, even sporting events took place here. The mob called it "The Theatre", and when talk of Joshua's return was circulated, the entire populace seemed to have migrated — hoards travel towards this known landmark. The people who condemned me to a life of exile, the hermit's life upon the sacred hill, sit in silent guilt.

My silence – nothing need be said.

Upon reaching the bottom, my guide directed me into the village. We pass stragglers, rushing towards their destination, where they must assume an announcement would be made. The long stares signaled an unease within each of them, as well as myself; as if we knew my passing to be an omen — a sign, good or bad.

I wonder which they tended towards...

Upon reaching the large triangular tent, my guide stopped and grabbed the deer-skinned flap.

"He asked for you specifically."

I swallowed my spit, uneasy and unsure of what lay within. The dark room was lit by a small fire in the middle, stoking at a slow rate, fumes climbing above and exiting out the small opening in the roof. Upon a raised bed lay a heap of fur, covering what I assumed to be the man who went missing not long ago.

My friend, brother, son... back from the dead. Resurrected.

I approached him uneasily. The jolt of adrenaline was foreign to my malnourished state, and was heightened as movement caught my eyes. Multiple orange faces standing above the rubble turned towards me. Two were women, nurses I had seen before, and could probably use now. Also behind them, in the corner stood a man I cared not to look upon. I could feel his presence, even before I saw it. I knew the smell of the man who corrupted my integrity, who questioned my morality, and led the revolt — my banishment. A traitor to the people I loved, and the place I call home. Atenacious stood silent, a look in his eyes revealed great fear. I recognized the face. It reminded me of the fear I had felt as a child, when I knew I had done something wrong; the anger and punishment I was sure to incur. The man stood, not a confident leader, but a naive child, surely to meet his demise at the hands of his former master, and the people who voted for his disturbing sovereignty.

They say, 'God lays up one's inequities for his children'; But let God recompense him, that he may know it! Let his eyes see his destruction, and let him drink of the wrath of the Almighty!

"He has cold," murmured one of the women towards my direction. "Must rest."

"I have only come because I was summoned." I say disconcerted. "If it's best I leave-"

"No!" came the faint, unrecognizable voice from the clutter. "I asked for you... Stay!" The hardly audible words reminded me of the value Joshua always gave. How, when he spoke to me, I knew it was important.

I approached with an opaque bewilderment, as if under the furs laid a beast, or ghost. Sweat protruding all over, the heat of the moment consumed me.

"Leave! Leave us!" He said with much effort. The women instantly headed towards the exit.

"You watch him," the one nurse said, getting right up close to my face. Her eyes were bloodshot and murky. The truth in her tone allowed me to understand the danger his life was in. I nodded impetuously.

"You too!" Joshua said turning aggressively towards Atenacious, the cowering man in the dark.

I could not look at the man I was learning to forgive, and as Atenacious began his exit, I stood staring only a few feet ahead of me, at the remnants of the man I so loved from before.

I was startled by his new appearance. Short hair revealing multiple scars, the pale flesh revealing a history I had not seen or had failed to recognize. His bloodshot eyes now in view, revealed a man in pain, but not the physical kind. For how can you properly separate the pain of the body with the pain of the mind?

Physical pain will end, but heartache... Everlasting.

I gathered Joshua was told, at least in part, as to how life here continued after his disappearance. The grimaced face also would not look at the man leaving the room. Atenacious, passing on his way out, his position, to me, grotesque! His eyes to the ground, sallow and sour. Joshua's eyes stare up, to the darkness ahead, and the smoke rising to the sky. My eyes neither to the ground, nor above in such a moment, but straight ahead, as they should be, upon the friend I so desperately needed to see. And perhaps purpose, to call mine once more.

Chapter Twenty and Six
Something Old, Something New

Journal of Joshua, Year 21, Day 75 of the *Abandoned* Calendar.

"The edge of Consciousness.

The ache of hunger.

I awaken violently, a pain in body and mind. My eyes blurred, an image I see. Parting my hair, now red and brown from the paint of blood upon the dripping strands; my body one big bruise, swollen and lifeless. A grunt which carried on for minutes, so it seemed, as I raise myself to my feet. Knees wobbling and the world starting to wake before me. The dark image ahead, lying at my feet like so many times before this... I see Buck, asleep by my side.

I look forward, the picture growing clearer and more colorful. And then to the ground, this black and red heap by my side. And I see not my best friend, but a mangled remain of what he once was. A disturbed mess of meat and marrow; a carcass upon a carcass.

I stumble to my knees in disbelief, landing in a red pool beside him. I grab his warm hair, the sun reflected so brightly off his beautiful coat. I smile and chuckle, tears start rolling to my hands. I think of how hot that coat must have been, in such a heat encountered.

I'm happy he left.

I'm happy he has found freedom.

But accordingly, this blissful solitude transforms. As my mind begins to awaken, a nasty scream in the ears, my pain begins to reveal a new self!

Jaw clenched shut, breathing begins to deepen. A beast is awakening...

The scream dulls, the heavy current of air through the teeth and gaps; the flow of saliva, a foam of rage!

I remember how I got here.

I remember who did this to me.

The man they call great, has detached himself from greatness.

The man building civilization is in fact a barbarian.

My eyes are filled with rage, not tears.

My mind has been made.

He must be punished!

He can't get away with this!

Anger boils within, masking the sorrow. It brings momentary peace to the cruel world of known.

Order to the realm of chaos."

***

As Joshua's return confirmed, I sat by his side as he recovered. Or, I should say, as we recovered. I encouraged him to eat, hoping to restore his health. He encouraged the same of me, and I thought of my fast.

The hours lengthened – turning into days, as Joshua began to walk. After just two nights, he even hiked with me up Mount Sinai. In my weakened state. He was an excellent partner, both of us taking breaks accordingly. Silent, catching our breath, I'm reminded of earlier times. And as we rekindle our friendship, our bond lost to embitterment, all seems long forgotten.

I let go.

But for him I feel only dismay. As we hike in silence, I think of the body lying there under the heap of warm furs;

Atenacious, surely headed to address the crowd at *The Theatre*. I recognized an emotional state in Joshua I had never seen before. The great Joshua, pale and thin, looking like a ragdoll, tears wallowing, heart visibly shrinking, hatred festering. In the heat of the moment, I too began to suppress tears, unsure why I felt such sadness, just one more broken man, life foremost shattered.

In the state of true hunger, emotions become enlarged.

The man made out one word, so low and faint I scarcely could confirm its existence. But I know what he said: "*Natalia.*" The faint whisper echoed in my mind. In my own personal discrepancies with the new leader of The Abandoned, I forgot of how the new Judge penetrated even further into the soul of Joshua.

Atenacious — the surrogate father.

As I sat beside my old friend that night, neither of us said much more. We both laid there, in and out of sleep, mourning the shattered life we now lived. His wife, and infant child, now belonging to his old friend, Atenacious. And something quite similar in my case.

I stayed with him in silence for what seemed like eternity, until one early morning, as I lay there unable to sleep, Joshua started to stand. I lay there watching him as he struggled. The struggle, not much different than mine own as I stood in such days as these. I could see a determination in his gaze, the pain suppressed what his mind must be stewing from within. The fearful unknown, the future we all must encounter. A life of living in the moment, unsure of what the day will bring. But it is Joshua who makes the move. I wake to the silence of night, accompanied by quiet expulsions of pain and effort. I go unnoticed by him as he breathes deep, concealing a grunt, the pain visible upon his face.

"Let's go for a walk," said he, not looking toward me.

With a moment to gather my exhausted mind:

"Yes... Let's..."

This place he had seen before, but now it all seemed so hollow. Joshua's eyes gazed at all things as if new, though he had only been gone a year.

That being said, the town had changed. Although the buildings upgraded, the craft excelling, and the population noticeably rising, these were not the changes that penetrated the view. His eyes wandered through a lens far different than the lens of any random man. This world, an epitaph, its presence a noble tribute; an imperfect representation of its perfect former self. Although, it was not without its faults before. Thinking of the past life he lived, here, with Buck, and Natalia, and the warrior band he loved as brothers, his former life seemed a perfect system he only wished could be experience in the present tense.

Joshua's vision seemed clearer. He now viewed all that surrounded him differently; and finally, I came to see him as his true self – a man after my own broken heart. No longer the blind man in Plato's cave, but the observer of shadows – dancing in front of us all, only visible to some.

As the sun hid behind the darkening sky, the cool breeze brought a sense of inundation in its early form. A light rain began, bringing me back to the present. But as I look again at the man, taking no notice of the impending storm, the eyes of a broken heart, and downcast soul... In this moment, I feel closer to Joshua than I ever had before. In the moment, I realize that he sees the world as I do. Not his true home, but a shadow of what truly is. And now I wonder, will he disengage from the corruption, give into its might, or fight against it; the inevitable loss unforeseen...

**

"Let's grab a pint," he says looking at me, our attire beginning to soak as we sit in silence upon the mount. Upon Sinai, where the two of us slowly ascended, alone to enjoy the air, we sit and recover.

The soft red glowing tobacco reflected on my forefinger. The swollen, charred sausage of an extremity housed the dried and tattered leaf, as I inhale the transformation. Man consists of all but one of the elements; and for a moment, I feel complete.

Light headed, I exhale.

"Well Josh, I think you've earned one!" I say with a sincere glow. An ale with a friend raises any man's spirit. The response: Joshua leads the way through the thicket. We slowly make our way back to town.

I navigate the foreign walkways for him. We come to the brick house, a new building and expansion of the old tent Joshua knew from before; this being the second of three to open. And this morning, as most, it remained nearly empty. Its tranquil solitude attracted the older generation. The young and energetic drank in tightly packed areas; the need to be surrounded, a lost thought to myself, and apparently not many others.

Shaking ourselves off, we enter the dimly lit room. Finding a seat, I notice two men sitting in quiet discussion directly in front; another two sitting near the chimney, in quiet contemplation. Another in shadows, the glow of his pipe and the puff of his smoke – a disturbing presence I quickly forget.

A young blonde near the back sees us as we enter, Joshua sits down seemingly unaware of her presence. I, raising my index and middle finger to signal for drinks.

The pretty young woman made a quizzical look. "Two beers," I say out loud, and quickly, she walks out of sight.

We sit down, and I decide to become upfront.

"So Joshua, will you tell me what happened? I want to respect your pain, but there is much to discuss, and much to shed light on... What happened? Where have you been?"

He looked up at me. His eyes, the way I once remembered them.

"Yes, yes! I must!" he said looking around. "And you must be the first to hear it!"

Our beers arrive but neither of us acknowledged them. The awkward moment, a distraction from thought. Joshua took a large gulp and made a satisfactory "Ahh!" as the mug descends from his lips. Joshua looked down and took another sip of the brew, as if he suddenly realized something.

"Alexander," is all he says at first.
My heart sinks at the name.

"They took me. I met him, face to face."

I sit in disturbance.

"He asked where I came from. I told him a little farm, up where it's a bit colder. He asked if I had family of friends, I said I did, but they had all died, this way or another."

He took a big gulp of the aged hops, quite cold and just what he felt for. The bitter taste rolled down his throat. Nostalgia, reminding him of the success of a hunt, and the joy he had, and missed so — having drinks with his comrades in victory.
Joshua continued:
"To be honest, I remember at first being upset I didn't pick a cool name to give him when he asked... I thought up some really cool names that first night that I would give myself to those who I met. I liked the sound of Urus!" Joshua said with a smile, "The sheer might, much fiercer than Joshua! I don't know why, but that's what I came up with... Urus."
He drank from his mug, leaving a frothy mustache." What were the odds I'd talk to the leader again, anyways? Haha!" he bellowed, the ale beginning to get to him.
"Would you like another?" I say quietly, almost hoping he didn't hear me.
I'm not much of a drinker.
"Or perhaps a tea?"

His grin left, he looked down at his mug, a quarter full. He spun it around and watched as it spun. He then stared into the drink and continued:

"But that ended quickly," he said not looking up. "I then began to think of my family. Of my Natalia, and my child within her."

I raised my fingers. Two more.

"I was put into a living quarter within the city. The nights were dark, the homes cramped and close together, neatly in rows. The angst of containment quickly arose. The first night, I examined the empty street, marveling at the quiet. And my home, even more so. I was left to an empty room with a small bed, and I sat there in silent morose.

"That night I lay awake in restrained panic. Breathing uncontrollable, my body in dismay. My heart ached knowing how far away I was to the people I loved so much." His eyes were downcast.

I drank in silence, hoping the pretty young woman would come to relieve the tension. I never know what to say in times of such pity.

Suddenly two more arrive, we both sat in silence drinking our beer. He in his world, and I in mine. His crashing down all around him. Mine: Still uncertain.

But I digress...

"Can we go see him?" he says in most seriousness; the ale suddenly powerless. "Can we see Isaac?"

The name of his boy, Isaac.

"Yes of course. Should we have another, first?" I say, wanting him to continue the story, but well aware, the man, currently in a fragile state.

"I've had enough; I am serious though, if you don't mind of course? Please, I feel like I must see him. I don't want him to see me though. We'll be quick, I'm sure the mere sight of him will render me speechless anyhow."

The man, at least knew himself.

"I want to be in control when he first meets me, you know?" Joshua says, hoping I'd approve. "We'll come right back and have another. I'll explain more then; we have all day to drink and chat. I'd rather not see my son for the first time any less sober."

We both smiled on our way out.

"Thanks, love," I say to the young lady, who seemed agitated on our quick departure. "We'll be back shortly, save our spot please."

"I don't plan on being here for much longer," she replied, "I'm only covering for my friend, but she'll be here soon and I can tell her for you."

I began to turn after Joshua, but suddenly a clasp of my arm! A youthful grip held me back.

"But... you must do something for me first," she adds...I must have looked as confused as I felt, not expecting a young woman as her, to speak to me in such a way. Demanding my respect, she made her inquiry...

"What's that man's name?" She said pointing towards the door, Joshua outside by now.

"That's Urus." I look to her and smile. She looks past me, beyond the threshold towards reality.

"Ahh, Urus. I thought maybe he was a ghost! He looks like a man I met a long time ago, the only name I caught was that of his dog, Buck. Although, I have wondered if the man truly exists or is nothing but a dream of mine. Perhaps nothing but the past haunting me."

I decided not to press further; her eyes far away, mine ever present, knowing Joshua was waiting for me. The girl, probably just another infatuated youth, one who loved the warriors as all others do. Their living definition of a true man.

"Well for what it's worth, would you tell him Isla says hi?"

A solemn nod as my reply.

**

196

We walked discreetly through the village. It was a cold clear day, and smoke was visible all over; the rich smell of cedar stole the senses. People young and old began to boil and bustle, paying no attention to the passersby. We made it to the outskirts of town, heading into the woods southeast.

As we left town and entered the thicket, I took a look around, revealing our dereliction. A small boy stood still, staring as his friends run by in playful banter. The boy looked towards me with eyes wide open; a lighthouse mid beacon. Joshua already in the bushes, much more subtle than I. Putting a finger to my lips, I signal the importance of his silence, only hoping he understands the message.

We walked through the brush, the shallow creek to our side creating a white noise. Soon it begins to fade as we veer to the right, coming to the destination Joshua seeks so calmly. A log cabin stood through the brush, smoke flowed from the chimney – an obvious signal to the isolated. We said nothing to each other, and I watched as Joshua crept forward (as best he could in his condition) to get a better look.

From my position, I could vaguely see someone walking about. I too approached to get a better view but found myself staring at Joshua instead. The somber face from before had vanished. As I looked upon nothing more than vestiges, a man motionless and silent, heart breaking from afar.

In reverent sympathy, I alter my gaze.

A true gentleman cries in private.

We watched for what seemed like hours as Natalia went about her business. She was moving about, in and out; her slender frame and olive skin, hair long and dark and thin as she. Her elegant ways made the work look like poetry. The smooth steps and ease in motion caused one to wonder at the mind behind such beauty. And I wonder at how one could go about such trivial matters with such eloquence and tranquility.

As if a signal to my curious heart, a faint cry could be heard. I look to Joshua, his eyes glazed and heart throbbing. Motion in my peripherals causing me to look back at the home — a woman bouncing up and down as the child's cries become louder. We both stood in fascination, watching the mother go about with ease as the terrifying shrieks could do nothing but create an anxious fear within, as if an apperception of torture.

She sat down and clutched the babe close. As she revealed her breast, the cries were replaced by a soft melody. A lovely, humming mother caressed a peaceful infant. Joshua's child, one with his creator. Isaac calmed.

Every great man deserves a good woman.

I close my eyes as the hum of Natalia's voice caused a peace within me I've so desperately longed for. The love of a mother was never something I had the pleasure of experiencing. The soft easeful love of mom, perfectly balanced with a firm, but fair dad, helps a boy cope with the hardness of life. Yet, who can call such an ideal upbringing reality. And Isaac, new to this world and its formalities – soon to be like us. Time is relative, and all eventually comes to light.

Suddenly my lament shifts. I feel joy knowing this boy will grow up with the love of a mother; a privilege I never had, and surely crave.

I didn't want to lose the feeling – a moment of conception; and so, stared forward, grasping Joshua's shoulder.

As your heart is, so your life will be.

"We should go now."

Chapter Twenty and Seven

Lever de Solei

"'And what is out there? Who is there — there beyond that field, that tree, that roof lit up by the sun? No one knows, and one longs to know; one dreads crossing that line, yet longs to cross it; you know that sooner or later you will have to cross it and find out what is there on the other side, just as you will inevitably have to learn what lies beyond death. But you are strong, vigorous, buoyant, and your blood is boiling, and you are surrounded by equally vigorous, nervously excited men.' So thinks, or at any rate feels, every man who comes in sight of the enemy, and that feeling gives a particular luster and joyous zest to one's impressions of all that takes place at such moments."

- War and Peace

An excerpt from a Journal marked as Jenna's Diary:

"I know God was watching me; I felt a stare, you know, like when you just know something is there... But turning to look, the gaze nowhere near; as one gets that sense of another — the feel of someone right there! Confirming the visual impossible, as he occupies now neither here nor there. The unseen forces alive and well.
But, I wonder: How does He watch?
In dismay, in entertainment?
Detachment? Or yearning?
Perhaps in fear?
I dare not speculate of the Almighty..."

***

Joshua now sharing in the comfort of privacy. Upon Mount Sinai we sat once again. Gus and the others recluse, tarry in the outskirts, waiting for our verdict on the matters at hand.

Joshua continues:

"Or does He participate – like a reader? Creating a story in His mind, a spawn from within? The mystery of intelligence itself... maybe this is the state of all things?"

He closes the pages, and places the journal delicately to his.

"Could you continue from before?" I say, delighting in the theology but not wishing to divulge. With a broken branch, I poke at the small fire to our side, trying to take my mind off the ache of my stomach. It's been five days since I've eaten, and today, to be frank, I'm feeling a little grumpy.

Joshua looked at me after a moment and his mood changed. The atmosphere dampened, and I felt he could see my thoughts.

"But Achilles, I am," he continued, "for you see, I was not safe there. I knew I was being watched. And all around me, I could feel nothing but the need to run! But I kept it up, I acted the part. I became a grey man."

He looked directly at me.

"So, when I was placed amongst the others, I wasn't special, I wasn't new! We all were! The great ship, The Event Horizon — only a few miles away! It housed row upon row of sleeping inhabitants. Each waking at their appointed time, resurrected from the dead, brought into the new world of Alexander."

The Event Horizon... I never thought I'd hear its name again.

"I was placed within a group of about a hundred or so; we went through a course they called "re-integration". It was like a school, ran by the leaders of their tribe, men and women just like the rest, who were awoken sometime before the rest. So, keeping my mouth shut, I decided just to listen. Most of them were so brain-dead after twenty years of sleep they had to re-learn all of history. And so I fit right in.

This is what they taught us, as they claim happened twenty years previous."

Now I'm listening.

"The plan was that all would sleep as The Event Horizon traversed space. Awake would be a handful of scientists, along with a few honorable men at arms, the captain of the ship, and the leader, Alexander, of course. Apparently, they all call him, *'The Great.'*"

His voice went deep pronouncing each word.

"Although, I felt many called him as such with a complete lack of conviction, as if it were custom to say he was great and to act like he were, but that many didn't agree, or at least unsure of such a bold label."

"But," Joshua continues, "the story goes: The Event Horizon was to traverse space, seeking a habitable home in the stars. None had been found, but all trusted Alexander and the crew to find one. As the ship prepared for the mission, something changed. Not all seemed to have voted in favor; a rebellious uprising, *'The Coup'*, planned to kill all on board and take over the ship. These savages (among whom I presume the presence of *Maan)* caused the ship nearly lost to the mutinous marauders."

Keyword: Nearly.

Joshua's downcast eyes revealed a pang of sorrow and regret – his savior surely dead.

"Alexander was the hero, killing the savages and saving those already asleep. And because of the chaos, he decided the ship's fate by coming back to Earth; an attempt to start humanity over once more."

"Like Noah, after the great flood." I sarcastically sneer. Realizing my gross misconduct, I decided it best to remain silent, allowing Joshua to continue, so as to properly digest his research.

"I knew something wasn't right. I didn't trust this view of their leader as some type of great hero; a man of God-like qualities — truth, surely masquerading in shadow. I wanted to run back, I wanted desperately to come home! Even that first night as I wept alone at my misfortune, but even more so the longer I stayed! I figured I was being watched, and I thought perhaps there was a reason fate delivered me to my disposition. Although I was brought in against my will, enslaved in the society he chose, I figured I could learn more about the people we had no clue still existed. So I decided to wait, to collect information. The longer I stayed the more I learned, and the more trust I felt I had earned. I joined the others with ease, and fit in quite easily. Although I didn't talk much, which many seemed to enjoy; the odd factions of ancient privilege enjoyed sharing way too much with me."

I grab my branch alight and lift it towards my face. Teeth clenched upon my carved pipe, the charred wood mixed with the smoke; my mind swarming with thoughts of all he had seen and heard. Passing the pipe to Joshua, he takes a pull; lightly coughing, the smoke encumbers. A moment of relief, smoke mingles with sky, and he continues...

"I learnt as they did. I joined classes – schooling, just like here. History differed from yours though," he looked at me with uncertain eyes, "but I guess the idea of history itself is that it can never be truly verified. Either way, I didn't trust anything or anyone. I went about my days, learning in the class-rooms, and joining in their games." He smiled. "They had some great games, I did quite well! My favorite was a game with a ball — a team game, and you had to put the ball into a hole dug on the opposite side of the pitch." He signaled for the pipe again. Smiling and looking neither at me, nor the pipe, nor the earth, but in the air as he reminisced.

"Ahh what fun I had. That was hard as well, leaving them.... I made friends Achilles! The people were alright you know!"

He took a moment, breathing deep. His mind flowing through the events of the last year, giving me a vague description of all he saw and did, but not getting into specifics. Even as he continued, my mind wandered, half listening. The idea of another group, much larger in populous and technology outweighing should strike fear in any man. Yet, I sat opposite Joshua, just waiting and wishing he mention one name.

"Until one day, I decided I had learnt all I could, and I prepared myself to go to the ship. I decided to sneak into The Event Horizon, learn all I could of it, then travel back here. I was excited but nervous."

"So..." I interrupted, showing my first obvious sign of impatience, "what did you find out?"

"Well, words simply can't describe it. Coming out of the wood and into the grasslands it became clearly visible. It shone, like a beacon. I had forgotten what artificial lighting could do, and I can only describe it as a simple white glow, growing as I approached.

"I felt uneasy as I advanced. My paranoia again kicking in, thoughts raced through my head on whether this was a good or bad idea. Had I waited long enough? Would they track me? Would they notice I had left sooner than I expected them to? So as I approached I stayed very low. I started to flank to the north, figuring I shouldn't come at a straight shot from the town — a direct path no doubt leading me into the eyes of the enemy.

I was able to channel all my fear and hate into one. Not the townsfolk, not the guards, not even Alexander... I hated that ship!"

Here he goes.

"Those people believed in that ship. It housed a divine thought, an eternal hope within each and all who emerged from it. No doubt I grew to love the people, but that ship remained our only internal grievance. For decades we lived under its tyranny; for decades we endured its sin! Its departure — the only gift! Yet here it lies; and so, as I walked, getting closer to the light, I felt unprotected. I figured the cover of darkness was my only friend, but the closer I got, the more visible all became. And sure enough, all of a sudden, as if they had been waiting for me all along, I heard a loud '*Halt!*'

"I stood motionless as two men approached with guns drawn. One stared at me, maybe five feet away with his finger on the trigger, as the other man searched me. I stood still and stared into the one man's eyes as he looked at me nervously – ready to shoot; probably never been in such a situation as this. I decided to let them take me, not knowing if he would pull the trigger or not. As they tied my hands together, and dragged me off, I took one last look towards the great ship. I don't know how far from it I was at that point, but I looked and marveled at its conception. I had never seen anything so big before, and couldn't believe our ancestors, with all their faults and failures, could have created such complicated machinery as this."

I tried to imagine the large steel vessel. The Ark, intended to survive the flood, built by the backs left to drown. No specific image came to mind.

He continues.

"There, in the middle of the night, in complete silence, they brought me to Alexander. But instead of the furnished home I had entered upon our first meeting, I was brought to a stone building. It was cold and dark. I had a sense of true dread, that here, many people had died before, and surely I was awaiting such a fate as they."

He grew a little pale, I could sense an unease as he traveled back, experiencing once again the horrors he had just withdrawn from.

"I was put in a cell, they punched and kicked me, even as I hit the floor! I shielded myself as best I could, but made sure not to retaliate. I could probably have taken the two but surely wouldn't be able to escape.

"We passed multiple guards through the structure. Large doors closed heavily behind as we passed through each room. I remember, as I was being beaten, thinking of my wife, and my child who was born... but perhaps would never get see..."

Hiding a tear, he stood and stretched. As did I, but ensuring he would delay no longer, I ask: "Would you like to walk a little as you continue?"

"No, I'm okay," he said untruthfully. "Just hard thinking of all that has happened. Why me, Achilles? Why did all this have to happen to me?"

I tried to act sympathetic, and indeed I was. But time warped me into something I had not thought possible in my younger years. As a boy I had been so happy and carefree, but now, with the lives I've seen lost, and the heartache I've endured, it's hard to show sympathy to one simply enduring just another stage of it.

Welcome to my world.

"Anyways, after I laid there, breathing hard and tasting nothing but dirt and blood as the two men left; not minutes later Alexander entered.

"'So, we meet again,' he said, the door shut behind him," Joshua looked at me, his eyes red and fierce, "and I went mad! Achilles, I charged him! I was up in an instant and rushed him — with hands tied behind my back I went teeth first, intending to latch onto his throat and rip him apart! I don't know why, I just couldn't return to what and who all seemed to love. In that moment, I hated him! I hated where I was, I hated that I had been taken against my will! And so, I acted on instinct."

"Did you kill him?" I ask in genuine intrigue. "Is he dead?"

He looked down and whispered, "Far from it... All I remember was waking up in a bed, a young man stitching the side of my head," (Joshua twisted, pointing towards a cut near his left temple) "...and a woman sitting across the room.

"'Good morning,' she said. I could see her through the corner of my eyes, the man's scoffing frown blocked most of her.

"'My name is Sarah, and I'm sorry to break this to you, but I will be the last person you get to talk to.'

"The man tugged hard on the last stitch, I could sense his displeasure as he cut the thread, and walked out. But I was more interested in the woman.

"'Unfortunately, you're tied down; and even more unfortunately, you have been sentenced to death. I am here because it's my job; and because even though you're a dead man, we believe you deserve what all dying men deserve.' She paused, and I looked towards her curiously.

"'Hope,' she said. And I believed her.

"Sarah told me I had been sentenced by Alexander himself. My attempted 'Assassination', left me with no chance at trial, but instant execution.

"I said nothing, indifferent to this destiny I awaited. She was talking to me, very calmly and thoughtfully, but I just lied there, waiting for her to leave and for me to be whisked away... led to the slaughter. But suddenly she caught my attention...

"'You know', I remember her saying, 'This may not be the end. This life, I mean. You never know what lies beyond the horizon... *A spark*! And life was created!'"

Eyes widened, I dare not interrupt.

"I turned sharply towards her," Joshua continued. "She paid no attention...

"'The spark ignites! Flames appearing, flexing, and dancing; chaotic yet beautifully unpredictable, relentlessly versatile, and eagerness beyond compare. The flames grow with excitement. The ever-devouring heat will not rest, it cannot sit still, it consumes until it can no longer.'"

In delighted dread, I listen as Joshua reveals the words of my one and only daughter. He could have stopped, I understood who he spoke of, but I listen, cherishing every word.

"'Such a fire can never be quenched. It is doomed to end. Without the fuel to maintain such a consumption, the flames lower. The fuel exhausted, the fire dampens, until all that is left is a soft glow, on way to its inevitable end...'

"'Ash and ember are all that's left, and then, smoke appears.'

"'In this new form, it rises to the heavens above. Swaying this way and that, but in silence it advances towards its completion.'

"'Towards the darkness above,'

"'And a world unknown.'"

Part IV

"Then the Lord God called to Adam, and said to him, "Where are you?"
So he said, "I heard your voice in the garden, and I was afraid, because I was naked; and I hid myself."
And He said, "Who told you that you were naked? Have you eaten from the tree of which I commanded you that you should not?"

"Cursed is the ground for your sake;
In toil you shall eat of it
All the days of your life.
Both thorns and thistles it shall bring forth for you,
And you shall eat the herb of the field.
In the sweat of your face you shall eat bread
Till you return to the ground,
For out of it you were taken;

For dust you are,
And to dust you shall return."

-Genesis 3: 9-11, 17-19

The dual substance of me:
A man, torn in two.

For in the life of relations, I experience nothing but great
love,
Followed by the terrifying depths of its loss.

In the solitude,
I grasp at the comfortable milieu,
The epoch of my destiny.

And the two I long for when within the other.
The grass, far greener on the other side,
And the refusal to see otherwise.

Chapter Twenty and Eight

In the Beginning

Journal entry of Michael, Father of Jonathan, Father of Achilles:

"The greatest fear of mankind has monopolized us. We live in self-induced ignorance and apprehensive realization. I fear the mystery of the cosmos, as men of the sea fear the great monsters of the eternal shores. Men lost to her might and fury, as I lost in thought.

Stories of bravery and horror captivated the young and haunted the old. Beasts swimming in a realm far from ours, in a world so fierce. Yet even now, we observe this world through a lens; resting in our dominion.

But the unknown is all around us. And I, I fear the head. The one who operates all of this. The will of humanity, at the heel of the unknown.

We can observe a cell, but it can't observe us. Billions of entities organized and working as one to sustain its host. But no matter, all is dying. My only envy is perhaps these entities cannot comprehend death.

The ultimate unknown.

An outcome in which all must face, together or alone. But in this, we are all united. In this we live our true bonds of affection, making us Gods among savages; standing alone and observing in complete darkness, we seldom remember we are the billions of organisms, working around the clock, leading our host to it's inevitable end."

***

The event known as "The Abandonment" is studied in Seven, along with some of Joshua's journal entries. Such as *'L'Empereur du Coeur',* his poetic account of events,

210

written on faded paper he found during one of his expeditions. It is read in attempt to bring life to the class of recent history. Joshua, seen as a modern day hero, enticing the young students to learn from authority admired, momentarily deflecting their attention from the opposite sex, a bursting spring guided and manipulated. His work was used not to deter young lovers, but to entice their passion.

The role of the parent, strength and direction.

The role of the leader, propagated allegiance

An excerpt from Joshua's *'L'Empereur du Coeur'*:

"As Achilles spoke, all was quiet. All but the imploding words, and simple thoughts of a mind in blossom. I could not help but feel overwhelmingly connected to the others, all sitting in silent awe as the teacher spoke.

An eruption of emotion, the words tugged at the heart, and the people: connected, for that time being, one in mind, and body, and spirit.

Feeling such power as this, I reflect on the emergence of the unseen. The motivation behind each syllable, the burst of truth."

Within our tribe, young birthing was encouraged, but the control of one's lust was highly regarded. The extreme need for population in such an environment of death was essential, but sexual possessiveness unchecked would tear a nation apart. A week into my leadership, I verbalized a set of basic rules to govern us as we went about.

Inside the walls of the farm, the dark and damp world of our oppressors, we ransacked and pillaged all and any tool that would be of aid. And as I sat on Maan's bed in the farm and read from a little brown Bible discovered under his sheets, I searched for the famous Ten

Commandments, a set of rules my father had mentioned before, but had never seen himself.

Where there are numbers, there is strength.

**

"I'm Joshua."

It was getting dark now. The day was coming to an end and the people of Seven returned to their homes; exhausted from the energy consumed during the exhilarating and inspiring day.

After the speech, discussions ensued. Names were shared and people bonded over the unfamiliar road they now headed down. An entire populous of slaves, now with no master. A people, freed from bondage, whether wanted or not.

The new life bursting like a spring! A rebirth, a resurrection of the heart. Needed in times as these. Freedom, so loved and begotten. But, as time reveals all things, with such excursions bring all the need of one thing... Rest.

But all seemed to agree on this: That this new man (Me) brought the words of a new world. One of encouragement and excitement! A new world of emotion and brotherhood. A freedom, a life, a true master. The mood of the mob was captivated, a people awakened! Not one lacked a freshness of mind and spirit, eagerly awaiting their destiny. A fresh start — some other beginning's end.

And at the end of the day, Joshua finds me:

"Come, let's wait a minute." I said as the youngster approached.

We stood facing each other silently as the people continued to walk. I looked at him as the time passed; he, timidly, to the ground.

After enough distance was covered, I felt I could talk liberally.

"Joshua!" I said in excitement, awaking the boy from a standing sleep.

"Yes, sir? That's me." He said back, in a deep, early pubescent voice.

"Ahh, I recognize you now; you're the shepherd boy. Tell me, what was that sign doing there? Do you know who may have written it? Who knows us specifically by name?

"*Maan*," was Joshua's response.

A name? A description? I didn't quite understand. Was his reference toward mankind too deep for me to distinguish, his poetic vernacular surpassing that of mine own?

As we walked apart from the group ahead, I encourage the lad to divulge, and came up with a few conclusions:

The message was clearly left by a manager, one who worked closely with the shepherd boy. His name was *Maan*. They had worked alongside each other at the farm, and supposedly, this *Maan* taught Joshua all he knew, and Josh obviously trusted him.

According to Joshua, this manager was not like the others. He was the good shepherd, watching over his flock with concealed care, and apparent love.

And he, it would seem, reciprocated Joshua's likeness.

And as we sat in discussion, I see how Maan saw.

"Boy of God," Joshua impersonating his voice as he described Maan's talk to the young orphan, teaching him about God, and about the connection they shared with the almighty, and each other. The two, it would seem, discussed life, and love, and pain, and grief. *Maan* didn't like the slave driving business; he felt more at home alongside Joshua. Both property of the United Nations of America – something I had failed to recognize in the ignorant days of my youth.

Property, the perfect word to describe it.

Through Joshua's stories, and explanations, I became afraid.

How did *Maan* discover me? And did anyone else know? Was I in danger? Never did I believe my paranoia of being discovered would come true! A terrible actor, hiding my true self.

And I was worried about Gus giving me up.

At this, I began to stew, a heat boiling up from within.

"What did you tell him about me?" I said with a hint of unwanted anger. He became wide-eyed, the fear bringing his eyes to hide in the dirt below. Joshua gulped, unsure if being questioned or threatened; he tried to say something but nothing came out. Mouth wide open and eyes moist with anxiety, he ceased to breath.

With a kind tone and a friendly touch, I grabbed the youth's shoulder. With a deep breath, and a forgiving smile, repeating:

"It's okay. What did you tell him?"

The youth smiled, took a deep breath, and began to rouge. Through pinning words and emotional manner, he told me of their friendship, and Maan's great knowledge of all things.

"He walked by workers all the time, but he saw something different in you. He mentored me, but was always mentioning you. I'm pretty sure he watched you much of the time. He sought to understand you... You never noticed him?"

Perhaps the only requiem a good man receives.

I had learnt never to look into their eyes. In our wretched world, I learned to just keep my head down — getting through it all, day-by-day. I had spent so long trying to know myself, I didn't take the time to look up and see the other.

And then, a feeling of shame from a thought: I had never looked into the eyes of young Joshua before.

In this I fear I have lost touch with humans and forgotten the strength of the other. His pursuit towards true humanity, the incessant, merciless battle between the spirit and the flesh. My eyes began to water as I realized how alone I had made myself, nothing different between me and the people I regarded to be of lesser than I.

Disgusting.

This, reminding me of a journal entry. Worn fragments of an article in one of the ancient family journals, deciphered as best as I could:

"If you haven't heard the news surrounding the hom[eless] ...

[Th]en you...

Here, the sense of brotherhood has been lost. We come home from work, lock our doors, watch T.V., go to sl[eep] ... [w]ake up and do it all again. The need for community has been abandoned, and we are concerned only for ourselves.

Is it not morally ethical to care for the poor, for those who are down-and-out, depressed, mentally ill, physically addicted, and to top it off, ostracized and criticized by their very neighbor? We talk and think about our homeless persons as "them", and in doing so, we make a separation. If there is a "them," there must be an "us."

And if we can be honest with ourselves, we see "them" not as people, but ... [D]olla[rs]

What is our interest in the future of our town, in the lives of our children's future, our friends and our family, our neighbor and fellow Americans, and simply for our fellow human beings?

Our purpose cannot be aimed towards personal wealth and excess. I feel pity for, and am ashamed of anyone whose pursuit of excess causes them to hate another. We outcast those who struggle every day with addiction, hunger, mental disease, and desertion . All because they hinder our pursuit of happiness, which evidently depends on our personal wealth.

Until we can change this, I [hate] to say it, but 'The po[or] will al[ways] be among you.'"

In deep thought, I realized my involvement towards the negative judgment my family attempted to prevent all those years. With a shudder of failure, I crawled into myself, realizing the corrupted thoughts. This changed the way I looked upon my fellow tribesman for years to come. A separate and inferior people; I chiefly among them.

Moved, I gripped Joshua's shirt a little tighter now. He would later recall such a euphoric energy flowing from my hand to himself — a primordial touch, one he had yet to experience outside of Maan's grasp.

We walked slowly up Sinai and talked passionately, revealing to each other many personal thoughts and experiences. Enthusiasm was awkwardly realized, and vividly seen on both of our faces. Although Joshua only felt such an intellectual presence from Maan, he connected well yet stumbled upon realizing our divergent thoughts; uncharacteristically different thinking, my voice he had never heard, but seemed to enjoy as one of reason and intrigue.

Although Maan chose to never speak of his time on the Farm, Joshua rather enjoyed life there, (I quickly understood). His relationship with Maan, caring for the animals, and learning the techniques of mastering submissive species gave him reason and purpose. Along with allotted *plug-in* time (which Maan also was not fond of, but realized the necessity of compromise), Joshua was living life the way he saw must certainly be. I speculate that he would spend many nights thereafter, weighing the words of two men, and considering his own – building a framework of his own reality.

All had gone to bed and plugged in. All but he and I, who spent that first night on Mount Sinai, attentively listening to the other's words, and eagerly waiting to share his own.

***

The sun began to rise over the mountains in the east, indicating the end of my story.

The one story I had never told anyone until then. The story of my greatest failure, and endless shame; a life haunted by the thought of my sweet little girl, given over to the enemy; and my daily grief in blindness, waiting and wondering if she still living, and of who I allowed her to become.

I began to stand and stretch. Joshua remained seated, letting in a sigh and embracing the early sun on his baby-faced cheeks.

"Well Joshua, we have a lot of work to do. We should get to it. But maybe for the next while we could meet here and I can teach you to read! My stories are nothing like those of the greats! Besides, I plan to share my books and teach all of them to read. I guess I just like the thought of getting you done first."

Joshua looked uneasy, so I added, "If you'd like to read, of course."

Joshua shrugged and began to stand. The youth was obviously tired from the long night of chatting. The embers of our small fire slowly lost its glow as the orange and red hue began filling the sky. The ash that was recently fire, symbolized the night and the dawn of our day. Joshua's face suddenly looked different. His young jaw looked seasoned; the eyes weary, not from lack of sleep, but painful endurance. The first of many to come.

But it's true what they say: Hardships beget friendships.

Chapter Twenty and Nine
The Theatre

"Greetings, I want you to know that all people born from the foundation of the world until now are of dust. They have inquired about God, who he is and what he is like, but they have not found him. The wisest people have speculated about truth on the basis of the order of the universe, but their speculation has missed truth. Philosophers voice three different opinions about the order of the universe, and they disagree with each other. Some of them say that the universe has governed itself, others say that divine forethought has governed it, and still others that fate has been in charge. All these options are wrong..."

-    Eugnostos the Blessed

The great wisdom proverb:
   "Know thyself."
   To me, such inspiration has led to many insightful thoughts and understandings. Two things about myself I here divulge:
   1.   I care what they say of me at my funeral.
   2.   I care what history says of me in a century.

   Time weighs on all things alike.

   No one knows the true nature of a man's character, for a true man of character contains it, free from admonition, and admiration. Because of this, men, like the warriors, remained a great mystery to the people in general, but also amongst the group itself. They lived like family, yet even they understood themselves to be incomprehensible. An air of tranquility hovered over the commune creating a lustrous glow without flaunting the stimuli, and all seemed to be attracted towards such people as these.

Always containing the popular vote, Joshua and his disappearance created aberration. Atenacious, the next in line, took control of all that was Joshua's — his followers, his warriors, and even his family. After months of indecisiveness in the courts, and a buzz in the town over the disappearance of Joshua, Atenacious was named councilor. His first appearance as one of decided authority, making a speech pronouncing my guilt over Joshua's disappearance; not only that, conspiracy to cheat the election, and charges of malpractice, referring to the days of famine from our early years; my integrity he condemned for all to see, and to believe.

The call for *"The Achilles trial"* was loudly heard within the populous. A disgusting need to see justice falsified in order to obtain not necessarily truth, but an answer.

How disgusting.

I agreed to exile.

And now, as I enter the amphitheater, the crowd early and with great attendance; the gossip surely made its round. All the councilors sitting as a panel, with Atenacious among them, sitting in my former spot, a sacred place of honor.

Democracy was a naive notion of our ancestors, a generally conceded mockery of a just livelihood. The people, manipulated by disinformation, believing so strongly in the political philosophy and failed practices of our forefathers; the elected officials, manipulated by money and power; and of the laity, the same could be said. Mankind believed in a principled speech, but not in its action;

A failed understanding of what it means to be human.

Joshua and I hobbled in like two war heroes. Both of us in rough shape, late, and with a slight air of death and decay. The contained anger within both of us demanded silence and respect, and a low rumble was heard. The crowd began to rise as we make our way. The silence said it all, and the heartbeat, essentially all that could be heard.

Thump-Thump.
Nothing.
Thump-Thump.
Nothing.

As we stop and face council, all sit down.

"I will be facilitating this call to council," came the voice of Shelley from the side. This young woman was one of the first to graduate and study law. A requirement was that all books (that is, all books kept on Mount Sinai) must be read by anyone wishing to be in such a position as hers. The young woman was a bookworm. She attended any class of literature, whether her age group or not, and finished faster than any before. In fact, she along with two others, Benjamin and Thomas, helped with council and judge to create the judicial laws. Her presence meant business, more so to all in attendance.

As she read the accounts of the last meetings dialogue, one in which so happened to be my decision of exile, I looked at each member of council... Three men, three women, and the man in the middle, the acting judge Atenacious.

Ludicrous.

None had the courage to look me in the eye. All looked empty, staring at their speaker. A sense of embarrassment was visibly seen protruding from each. Even the people, thousands in attendance, could be seen as moved by Shelley's words. I am not sure if the embarrassment was taken solely by the councilors, or if the people felt themselves equally at fault for my unjustified sentence. Either way, I fight not to condemn. I had never truly given up on them before, and I didn't wish to do so now.

A good father loves his children, even if they love him not.

My only hope is that they see my strength, and draw from it themselves.

"So," Shelley said in shift of tone, signaling the boring stuff to be done with, "today, as the sun's hidden light marks noon, we gather here to learn of Joshua's disappearance. Also, based on the account given by Joshua, we will assess the outstanding warrant of exile towards this people's former Judge; accused of foul play in multiple areas, all hinging on the assumption he had something to do with the disappearance of the present Joshua. A true and just ruling may now be determined. After that, we will question the council's decision to exile based on the information they knew then, as well as the information of current."

"Thank you," broke in Atenacious, perhaps cutting off more of her words. "We, the council, and the people would like to formally welcome our brother, Joshua, home once again."

A silence filled the air. Joshua looked down, unsure of how to pursue. But then, as he prepared to address the crowd, a slight clapping was heard. A small boy was seen and heard waving his arms back and forth among the crowd. His mother quickly grabbed his hands and a loud and authoritative *"SHH!"* was heard from their general direction.

Looking beside me to see Joshua with his head down, a slight grin was uncontainable as the simple gesture from a young fan made all the difference to him. And then, what ensued, what the boy started, his friends continued... The morose applause grew. And with that, perhaps a general realization that their true and needed Judge had finally returned, the people all arising in applause. A genuine excitement overcame the crowd; to see their savior, back from the dead — hope among despair!

A world at war, but what of me?

The thunderous sound was allowed by Shelley for a moment, as she too felt it justifiable. But the revelry was short lived, as the heavens begin to shift. The wind picked up, drops of rain were felt, and the applause dulled rapidly.

She bellowed, "As per the-" Suddenly, a deep rumble was heard! It wasn't overpowering, but the bass of the thunder could be felt in the heart. All looked up towards the clouds rolling in; all but I, staring at the masses, becoming wet as the heavy drops began to hit and scatter. The mob dispersed. My hair and beard beginning to soak, as frantically now even the council seeking shelter.

Atenacious remained seated.

The rain pouring down upon the few who remained.

Many scrambled to collect their children, or the crippled among them. I stood beside Joshua, both of us seemingly with no place to go, but enjoying the fresh scent of rain on the warmed earth; the taste of snot and ash hitting the tongue as I lick my lips in satisfaction.

Atenacious rose and Shelly made her final statement: "We will resume at dawn tomorrow!" She yelled over the sound of the pounding rain.

And then, she too was gone.

"Divine!" yelled Atenacious. "The way things work. Well, I guess the people will have to wait."

"True Dictatorship, eh old friend?" Bellowed Joshua towards the departing.

Without turning to acknowledge, Atenacious walked away.

"Well, what do we do now?" Urus says standing completely still to my side. The two of us stood erect, not moving or bending so as to minimize the effects of our waterlogged clothing.

"Brothers!"

The voice startles me, approaching from the rear. "Would you like a place to stay?" The young man was dark haired and thin. His pale face had no hairs — a fine shave, or late pubescent, I assume. The long, dark hair trickled down his forehead; black curls dripping heavy water droplets. He licked his lips, snot protruding from his nose just as mine.

I did not know what to say, and so said nothing but walked towards him. Joshua silently agreed, and the two of us followed the young man. Flashes of lightning caused us to quicken the pace, and the long, low grumbling of thunder persuaded us to listen.

As we walked past the village and continued on through the outskirts, we entered the wood just east of the Warriors land. Our wet clothes weighed heavy, sticking to the skin. The leaves and ferns, a soaked nuisance adding to our misfortune. And as if invisible within the brush, the boy suddenly pulled open a door, the dark quarter nestled within.

A large, lit candle glowed in the corner of the room as we enter. The boy grabbed it and used its flame to kindle the tinder, already prepared, sitting in a stone pit, protruding from the back of the home.

"There we are, strip if you like." he says in a melancholy tone. The boy removed his clothes revealing a frail, thin frame. He began arranging a structure near the dull flames, adding firewood as he went, showing a real vigor neither I nor Joshua could reciprocate. We took off our clothes and arranged them as neat as we could near the flames. I refrained from looking over Joshua's body, afraid to see scars I had yet to see, and feel I could not handle.

And so we sit. The heavy rain on the roof and the crackle and pop of the fire allowing for us to remain quiet – though inwardly loud. The warm room brought comfort, and for a while the three of us sit in silence. Cut from the same cloth.

"So, you're Joshua!" The boy looked eagerly at him and smiled. His front teeth resting on his lower lip. Then he turned to me, "And you, please correct me if I'm wrong... Sir! But are you the mighty Achilles?" He looked at me sporadically, I could sense the nervousness.

"Yes, we are who you say we are, but may we know your name?" I say slowly and definitively, trying not to entice the anxious.

"Yes of course..." the boy said with no hesitation. "I am Thomas! Although my friends call me Twin, mainly to distinguish me from my tutor, also named Thomas." He began to laugh as if we were a part of his social circle, and would appreciate the quip. "I am very fond of him to be honest, we're good friends now! Have you met Thomas? He works alongside council quite regularly now. Anyways, that is where I hope to be one day..."

The boy was noticeably rambling.

"Listen, Thomas," the boy smiled and blushed as Joshua used the sacred name, "we don't have a lot of time; for you see, we must proceed urgently. As soon as this rain settles, we will be on our way."

"Y-Yes," the boy stammered into realization, "of course you do. A big day tomorrow, hopefully a true day of enlightenment for all! What a dreadful shame the meeting ended before it even began!"

The boy stood. "Well, let me get you some food then."

"No thanks," I snapped. "We will be just fine, some peace and quiet is all we need. Accompanied by that lovely fire of course."

"Of course, sir."

The warm home created ease within us. Joshua and I were unsure how to take the meetings sudden end, but felt our plan must continue on even-so. As the embers remained, the flames now dull, and Thomas lay motionless in the shadows, we discuss inviting the eager boy into our conspiracy, allowing this chance encounter to serve us.

"Thomas!" I whispered towards the sleeping boy. A slight snore came from his area, a faint shadow, rising and falling.

"Thomas!" Joshua yells, absent of a whisper. The boy shook and rose instantaneously. "What? What-what is it?" he said in confusion.

Now, all I can think of is where that boy had been just seconds before awakening; where in the infinite world of dreams could he have possibly been?

"We are going to do something, Thomas, and we'd like your help."

He stood eagerly, revealing his naked body. I looked to Joshua, he seemed to have taken no notice.

"Do you still talk to Thomas? I mean — your tutor, Thomas? Or even Shelley?"

He made a slight yawn. "Well yes, yes of course."

I continued to look at Joshua. "Could you arrange a meeting with them?"

"Yes! Of course!"

So eager, so naive.

"Tonight?" Joshua finished.

"Tonight?" Thomas looked around for an indication of the state of affairs. Darkness surrounded all, no light peeked through the cracks in the corners, the imperfections of workmanship no longer visible

"But if it's all the same, with the meeting early in the morning, should we just wait until after?"

"No," I interrupt. "It must be now. We don't intend on being at the meeting, in fact we intend to be nowhere near it. Please, don't ask any more. If you could get Shelley and Thomas here as quickly as possible, we will explain then."

The boy hesitated – perhaps from the drop in adrenaline revealing the true state of affairs, or perhaps the sound of illegal activity a stimulant to the sleep deprived boy; or maybe he simply cared nothing for who we were and what we asked for — another dull and lazy son of Adam.

But without a word the boy covered his body, then his head, and left the log home.

Chapter Thirty

Parler

A poem on a loose paper, no Author or Title attached:

"A dark and clear night.
No sound but the emptiness.
No light but the stars.

You breathe in;
You breathe out.

Enter spirit;
Exit flesh.

Your only concern is for today.
Do not focus on tomorrow.
Remember yesterday no more.

Aspire to be content;
Not happy.
For seeking happiness is like grasping at air,
Or chasing after the wind.

Pursue to aid others,
And not to profit on their behalf.

Keep your obligations.
Remember your commitments.
You alone are responsible.
You alone, held accountable.

You breathe in;
You breathe out.

And suddenly the sky fills with light.
A snowfall replaces the dark and clear night.
The white fluff, a blanket.
Covering all things,
Even the footprint that mark your path;
The very track that brought you here.

'Be eager for the word. The first aspect of the word is
faith. The second, Love. The third, works. The fourth,
will. And from these comes life.'

Let the words flow from the outer,
And reflect that of the inner.
Let no lie exhale,
Only truth surrounds you.

Be one with your neighbor;
Be one with your enemies;
Be one with yourself."

***

Peace: The feeling of relief that all burden, all suffering, is over, never to return. Yet I know not such a peace, for much burden remains.

The look of frustration and curiosity emanated from the young and stern face of Shelley as she entered, hardly wet from the sporadic mist that replaced the downpour during the night. Thomas, the tutor seemed excited! Although the large, dark bags under his eyes revealed a man awoken from a deep slumber; yet his expressions seemed more alert than any other present. The melted fat of the dead lit the room, along with the dull flames from the chimney. The soft glow of fire creating a landscape of shadows; a vague and dark picture of all around. The warm, stale air exposed the small home for what it was – immaturely built and poorly ventilated.

A luminous silence was broken by the twin; his eagerness was visible but his energy lacked.

"See, I told you guys," the twin said assuredly, perhaps the two doubting his absurd request for their company. Shelley looked quizzically at the two men, not falling to the lure of fame that encompassed.

Thomas eagerly made his entrance:

"So, you've asked for us specifically. How can we be of service?"

I look to Joshua, but his eyes are neither on Thomas, nor Shelley. They drift with the flames of the dim fire.

"We... we asked you to come here," I start hesitantly, "because we won't be here in the morning."

Shelley's gaze does not vary. "But, it is the morning! The sun is sure to rise soon, and the meeting, given the weather," with a stammer she looked up, as if the room were open, "... it must start right away."

"We can't waste any more time," Joshua chimes in, his demeanor seeming oddly aggressive. Given his family belonged to another man, and his future dim and fleeting, I did not blame him. "We will be heading promptly, as soon as we're done here."

Thomas could sense the austere in Joshua's voice. "Well," he asked, "why are we here?"

"To relay to council where we have gone," I say deciding my description of our predicament would serve best. "No one knows this, but we are in danger."

Shelley's eyes turn from sullen and annoyed to unmistakably interested.

"We are not alone any more."

Joshua, in few words, describes his capture, his life this past year among the tribe of Alexander, and very briefly of his stoning and escape. Shelley looked dazed, and Thomas, like a boy — leaning in, daring not to miss a single word. Keeping the story to a minimum, a simple gist, Joshua leaves out much for time's sake.

He makes no mention of my daughter. And neither do I. As the story seemingly reveals enough information, I hurry things along: "I've decided to meet him! Alexander, that is, in an attempt to come to an agreement."

"What type of agreement?" Thomas asked.

"Well," Joshua says, "We're sitting-ducks here. Alexander leads a totally devoted and egotistical tribe. He has explored this area before, and given the fact he has surely discover my missing corpse by now, is destined to come this way! I don't think he trusted me when I told him I lived alone, in fact he would be stupid to! And I assure you, he is no stupid man. There is no doubt in my mind he will come this way. . I predict he is preparing soldiers as we speak! Surely preaching me a spy, traitor, and enemy."

Fear was visible. The three youngsters, no doubt have heard the stories of the abandonment; but history means nothing when it lives solely in memories of the old and the dead. For the last twenty years we've lived as if we were the only humans around, or even on the planet! Now, the thought of others not only alive, but possibly enemies, shakes the foundations of the young and weak alike.

"This needs to be voiced!" announced Shelley, her anxiety visible.

"That's what you're here for." I say. "You, and the Thomases are going to announce all of this. But we," I eye Joshua, "feel our best option is for me to meet with Alexander. If peace can be made, before everyone gets hot blooded and makes decisions they may regret, we must pursue such a course. I plan to enter the lion's den, alone and defenseless, with peace and freedom as my bargain."

"What if they don't accept?" the twin asked from the shadows, Shelley and Thomas turn slightly and acknowledge the inquiry.

"Then at least we know," I say. "But this way we can gauge the situation. Joshua and I both feel it's better to act quickly. This situation could break out in full on war, or even worse, we could become slaves to his advanced society! They outnumber us, and outgun us. If we sit here and wait, who knows what they'll do."

Shelley and Thomas both seemed to be deep in concentration. The facts were too hard to digest, and the possibilities of the future too unsure.

"So," Shelley says, "What if they just hold you guys, or kill you both?"

Joshua looks down as I explain.

"I go alone; Joshua will wait out of reach from them. If I don't return to him the first night, he has assured me he will leave me, returning home at once. I plan to make my plea and leave. I will refuse to stay with them, so if I am taken captive or killed then at least we can consider them hostile." (As if the attempted killing of Joshua, and the murder of Buck isn't enough proof of that.) "If any agreement foreseeable were to be had, I would be released as I command and require.

"But if I can reason with him, Alexander I mean, we may be able to live in peace apart from them. Or, even among them! That is, if a trustworthy partnership could be established."

"No," Thomas interrupted, "a partnership would be destined to fail. We would have to live apart from them or go to war. One day, either us or them, would attempt to exploit the other in some way. A just merging could never work!"

A pause.

"... In my opinion, of course."

Shelley visibly disagreed, she turned towards him to rebut: "That's not true! Trading and partnership could exist; it could be mutually beneficial to work alongside each other, regardless of size and technology... It could be done!"

Joshua entered, seeming exhausted. "We didn't ask you here to debate the outcome, for it's all useless. We don't know enough, and that is why we must go. Achilles is the best option we have towards peace. There are far too many possibilities to consider. You are simply here to explain everything to council; the three of you. And when we, or I, return in four days' time, we can discuss what must be done."

Joshua gazing into the fire pauses for a moment. His drifting thoughts on the future.

"... And surely, what will be done!"

Chapter Thirty and One

Epitaph

Journal of Jacob, Great-Grandfather of Achilles, Dated August Third, 2023

"God is a system. This system somehow created a system (Matter). Within this matter system, It created a whole series of systems to keep it stable; Earth, Wind, Water and Fire (and not necessarily in that order). And within those systems, It created more systems that consist of mixtures of such systems created.

Life.

And the system within... thought.

And each of these systems, within systems, within systems, have similarities yet differences. Unique, yet the same. Although, the unique stand apart.

So, is the original system, God, from which all other systems originate, just another system within a system? Like a memory, within my thoughts, within the earth, within the universe, within God itself? Just as we are not a system unique unto ourselves, but a unique system among many others similarly?

Perhaps multiple Gods? But then, what system do they belong to?

Perhaps It is the system.

He, the system.

And within the system of ignorance, the system of corruption and self, we speculate.

And anomalies seldom occur.

But occur, nonetheless."

***

Can God be in one element, but not another? Can this divine essence be in a certain place, but not another?

Is It a substance?

Is He a personage?

Is She invested?

The concept of a mind above our own; here but not here. Internal, yet external.

Some days one, some days another.

But what do I think now? As the clouds shift overhead, and the tall trees sway. Finding a soft piece of grass, I lay and imagine.

A world above ours,

A world above ours.

A world of virtues and ideas, uncorrupted by matter, floating about, like the wind upon my cheek.

"And what is out there? Who is there? There beyond that field, that tree, that roof lit up by the sun."

Forget it all! It's time to rise!

The heart races. Blood boils. Sweat perspiring.

The thrill of a journey at hand, and the unknown world outside our boundaries. We set out in the early morning, before anyone is awake; Joshua, with provisions slung over his shoulder — a few days' worth. Nothing but a warm pelt lay across mine.

Exploration changes a being. It brings life and intrigue to a stagnant world. The mundane eats at our minds, it causes a man to fester in his own thoughts, allowing evil to invade. Amongst the exploration of knowledge, truth... the idea of knowing all.

No one knows, and one longs to know.

And the truth... We can't handle the truth.

I haven't eaten; the sixth day.

We set out without a word to each other. The quiet morning brings peace to an otherwise chaotic world. I forget the fact that I'm traveling to the belly of the beast. The knowledge that I may never return causes me to look back shortly outside of the city. The bustling town of Eight, the world I helped build, but destined to see my end before Its. Surely, this marks my final farewell. And as the sun begins to rise in the east — the red mountains beginning to shine. Mount Sinai behind the city calls to me, the home of my true people — those living, and those dead. The great minds, at rest, their thoughts and feelings filling pages; an ancient practice, now abiding within the hills, but for how long? I do not know.

What is to come of my meeting with Alexander, with my plea for peace, and for freedom of existence? Surely it rests not within my grasp.

Will he listen, will he understand?

Will I?

The day begins to warm as we cross the bridge towards the land of the south. The ancient structure, not quite as I remember it. The last time I crossed, decades ago with my father, makes me think of a simpler time. The past is always so much clearer then the future. And the present, a complicated *milieu*.

Joshua seemed surprised at the distance I could travel. The only time we talked was when he suggested taking a break. I denied such a proposition. My legs felt weird, my body, lethargic; the lack of food, the fasting brought a tiredness unrecognizable, but my strengthened spirit pushed me forward.

Mind over matter.

Will over mind.

Spirit over will.

***

Joshua and I make camp at what he tells me is past midway.

A two-day journey he tells me, but because of my energetic mentality, we stop much earlier than sundown. He assured me I wouldn't need to help with camp, and so, I sat. A large evergreen my canopy. Its stature, taller than the others, brought comfort. And there, I remember, I sat, closed my eyes, and sunk deep into myself.

I wonder how the mornings meeting went... Shelley, and the two Thomas's.

After he collected enough of the dead foliage, we prep our camp under the large, maroon giant. The fire's warmth, a comforting privilege. Joshua told me past this point was the beginning of desert, a wasteland; the home of the Event Horizon, lay in decay. I remember learning as a kid of the expansive desert in the south, which once housed a much more prosperous landscape; stretching itself outwards, devouring life selfishly.

Darkness came, and with it a warm conversation beside the hot fire. (Although, the topic of discussion alludes me, I remember keeping it positive, trying not to think of the hurt both of us had been abiding in.)

Joshua fell asleep. Body still, the steady and solemn rising and falling of his large chest; I wondered at where his mind was, lost in another world, the chaos of the subconscious mind.

My head, too heavy for slumber.

Some reserve-adrenaline fueling my worn body — I stand and walk.

I walk for what must have been twenty minutes, until the trees begin to separate. The moon rightly shining in and out of thick white clouds; the sky opening in front of me. Like a bride, the trees unveil a beautiful sight. A mysteriously affectionate relationship, the awe and splendor of mystery; and that insatiable romance, creating poetry and madness alike. I look up to the stars. The same stars I've seen so many times before, and I realize how small I truly am.

I look to the sky for guidance. The stars reflect wisdom and beauty.

The cosmos hat is all; so huge it defies comprehension, yet here I stand and see it right before my eyes. Another great mystery to me: the cosmos within. The Universe; everything within me now. Where does it come from? Where does it go when I die? The hustle and bustle of the billions of cells. The ancient science now unseen and unbelieved. How could such an incomprehensible thought be? And here I stand, preparing to defy all, and leave survival behind.

So much devotion and selfless meandering, and yet this mystery lays down with me! With nothing but ancient stories to justify such wild thought. The ancient religion of science, now practiced only in the books that lay hidden behind the world, shared only with the minds who choose to understand.

Although my mind wanders, as it usually does on such sleepless nights as these, the stillness brought peace, not fear. Where many nights I remember being alone upon Mt. Sinai, and the fear of the unknown, a darkened path before me, bringing gloom to the path behind me.

I started to walk back to camp, the vibrant glow of the flames a beacon — the life seen within the brush. Walking absentmindedly, a large patch of grass and vines filled a void within the wood. The light of the moon and stars shone down, revealing a land of the dead...

Rows of small stones stand protruding from the earth, marking the grounds upon which many bodies lay in peace. I believe the pen is mightier than the sword; and as I stare down at the eroded hieroglyphs, a faded epitaph, I contemplate those who were mighty before me. My forebears, I owe my present position to. Life but one moment graspable, attainable; a single breath. The everyday, another battle on the grounds of perpetual being.

Looking upon the rows of ancient tombstones — this burial-ground containing many people like me. Men and women who fought for life; living in tough conditions, never giving up. The human nature, to succeed, to overcome, and to be preserved.

Why is it I feel more comfortable here with dead than I do with the living? Perhaps it is a reminder of what's inevitable, of what's real, of what lies at the end of all.

Why can I talk to those who can't listen, better than those who can?

Here I stand in the darkness, among the families of the dead – decaying below, creating life! The grass, a symbol of their renewal; and their memories, an emblem of hope. Our internal struggle, along with external ones, creating in all of us a bond. A connection to one another, no matter where or when. The ground upon which I stand, containing the lifeless bodies of men and women, boys and girls, and I feel nothing but peace... As if I belong here. As if, our inevitable end, our departure, is the unity within all. And the will to continue, such a beautiful cycle that is death, and ultimately, resurrection.

And with that, I travel back to the glow of mysterious energy and find a comfortable spot to drop. The warmth in front, the chill behind; the flames flicker as I lay beside a man I still cannot fully understand. The flames watch me as I travel to an even more mysterious realm — the dark world of dreams, as if waiting for me.

And all goes dark.

But only for a moment! As the heavens have opened to a flood of rain; I sit up, already in the bosom of the tree I know and hug. The sound so soothing, as the drops fall at a rapid pace in the open sky. The tall limbs swaying this way and that. I only wish I could observe the giant as it grows; from nut, to king of the forest. And as I look up through the branches, the rain begins to target me.

Fuck.

Such a rain has been lived before, and surely would again.

Well, maybe not as I intend to sacrifice myself to the will of Alexander. I know not still what I intend to do. The cruel man, I know too well. Falling into the same trap as I. A man of power, and perception; seeing now its corruptible ways, and either living with it, or against it.

Under the mighty tree I stand. The true king of the forest. Its arms reach out and comfort me so. Its soil holds me deep in its grasp. And the bark hides a great mystery. The shell of a beast. A hidden wisdom not spoken, yet communicated.

And who am I to know the man?

Seeing him, face to face is my last option. The only way I may truly know; or at least closure to a way of life that must be passed on. But to he, or the Abandoned? I do not know...

And so this is why I must go, and make my final decision as leader of my tribe. My children, my legacy, once again rests upon my actions.

Do I have a martyr complex? Only time can tell.

And so I sit the rest of the cold, damp night under tormenting thought, reassuring myself of my present misgivings.

What a life.

Chapter Thirty and Two

In the Court of the Crimson King

Hair raised and skin horripilating.

The breath moves over the torso to the mind of the seeker.

Finding uncertainty in the unthinkable;

Finding resurrection in the dead.

The albeit love of the enemy can seem inviting to the ignorant.

But ignorance comes at a pricc.

Failure, sure to follow.

Where do I stand? Whose breath? Whose touch? Whose love is this?

It is not mine own.

Memory fades, I walk in bliss.
To the moment of doubt,
To this vicious cycle.
Once saved, later doomed.
Then love, cursed after.

So what is this?
But a moment of reflection.
What is this, but time passing.
Where am I?
In battle, or at rest...

What if my mind were reincarnate? Just suppose...
Who have I been? What have I done?
Have I murdered, cheated, lied...
Have I loved...
And lost...

What fields have I tread, and mountains have I climbed.

What crystal lakes have I swam, and frozen rivers traversed?

Built? Inspired? Experienced, and shared?

How many hearts have I broken?

How many loved ones have I abandoned?

How many times have I seen the bloody, and the dying? The old, and the new...

And oh, how many must have grieved upon my departure...

Yet, here I am.

With memories of a vague beginning, and pulsating end.

As I now walk alone, exhausted and decrepit; this shell, the human being rots in my presence. So much energy is needed to fuel the mind to push on. The lack of nourishment sends me in a daze. Living in memories, not pictures but vague feelings. And Joshua waits, invested in my causatum.

The warm air rises, and the fresh air swoops in to instantly relax my wandering mind. I close my eyes, as I tend to do in such moments, and find myself in a new world.

Memories create my story. A vague sense of who I am and what I've seen.

Yet, it is the smell that creates this ancient philosophy. The relics of emotion;

Until my eyes reach the new world.

The shout of a predator.

The silence of the prey.

***

And there! There he was... The man I so craved to see. He stares as he enters, and tarries to his seat.

I grow concerned, and all begins to darken, and the man I was, and am, comes to greet me — at attention, standing directly in front of the judge.

Conviction of the conscience, and the perfected conscience, one that truly obtains grace, will regard his life in true morality. Where corruption is not prevalent. Where malice is dead. And our former self's nothing but corrupted vessels. Frames. An image of the real. The today, nothing but a shadow, and tomorrow not yet existing... A form from a form — an archetype, from a prototype.

From darkness I wake, the council chambers cold and dimly lit. Thin openings in the wall allowing the soft light of the winter's sun to come through – a witness to the historic meeting. The leader sat on high; a throne cushioned and colorful housed the body of a giant; a man who created and destroyed, a god in his own right.

Three older men await to his right, and one woman to his left. The guards who lead me in stood to the side, as I, the representing lord of the *Abandoned* people sit cross legged in front. It took a few moments to allow my body to sit comfortably; the onlookers stared at the sight, an unbelievable view before them.

All stood in awe. All but him.

I could feel his eyes upon me, as I stare to the front. Not looking at anything or anyone, but deflecting any and all vibrations his eyes sent my way.

A man with a grey beard just right of the leader stood to read the minutes from the last meeting – a seemingly human tradition. The words powerfully echoed through the halls; but my eyes now awaken, and look not to the speaker but meet the gaze of the gregarious bane, the man I found to be of such mystery. Who was he, and what is he after? My eyes couldn't leave the man on the throne, but my thoughts drift over his head.

I have grown too old.

I see into my own eyes.

A man who had seen so much pain, such loss. The eyes of a man, no longer able to see the light, the beauty, the hope in humanity. I have shared many a stares as his now, as he looks not at me but through me. I wonder at the things he's seen, at what his eyes have witnessed the man do, as he pursues what may rightfully be humanity's salvation. I hurt from within, realizing our brotherhood, and my numbness grows; the shadow, again following me. This darkened part of me, reminds me of the ancient world. And I realize my large role, as his, in the fate of humanity, and the unchangeable past I have created.

The offer of allegiance, a scary thought. To abandon any sense of self, any allegiance to the code of the Abandoned, which I produced, and ultimately, am charged with its fate. How could I bend to the will of this entity, this oppressive and manipulative power? The man who abandoned us so long ago; to become as dust, gone as the wind blows. But I, like him, lead a people based on my understanding of life. My imperfection resonates; it has created a society in which is all too human, lusting towards the pleasures of life, manipulation embodied, and fear mongered. But as I recognize the faults both civilizations must embody, I wonder as to whose is right and whose is wrong.

Or better, who is less right, and who is less wrong...

Him or me.

My only saving grace may be my poverty. The fact that from the beginning I was left nothing – a rotting wasteland, neglected and discarded; all because he took everything! My blossomed people from nothing, my only pardon for the guilt we both share. But share none the less.

But through the voice, a proposition is made. The offer he makes, a conceited notion, as if to absolve such betrayal, yet remain the betrayer. A pardon for all misgivings; can I give in to such facetious austere? The only true pardon lies within, the self-sense of honor, and subsequent death. Could I forsake everything I once believed in? The idea of true life, lived as I believe it should and can be?

Not the life I see in him.

Yet, not the life I see in me.

Where does my true allegiance lie? In my people, my daughter, the fate of humanity? Or perhaps my pride... That feeling I so long for in elevation of eyes — my peers' and subordinates' worship and allegiance.

No. It lies in my morals, my dignity, and my honor. In truth, in God, in the idea of Good over Evil.

And so, I remain silent.

***

My brain feels compressed, and my emotions suppressed. Muscle memory, a trait of my kin.

A length of time does something to a man. He lives and he dies many deaths, coming back in a new and inevitable way; sometimes, every day!

And two roads to choose between:

Abhorrence, or submissiveness.

Madness or ignorance.

I fester endlessly... Woe to the mind that rest does not find! Nothing can survive without proper rest. Even god needs a break.

The seventh day...

Maybe that's the answer. God currently resting. And the source of my woes, the burden of evil exposed...

So exhausting.

Joshua's mind circulated. It swayed and spun like a man with too much to drink, and more than his share of tobacco. Like this man, he could not close his eyes. He could not rest, and so continues in agitation. The interwoven distribution of goods; the Abandoned's safety net, total equality for the strong and weak alike. Although, not always adhered to.

He couldn't quite put his tongue on it, but he felt as though he had woken up from a strange dream. His life before meant nothing now. The love and elation that consumed his mind suddenly seemed like a faded dream, like that of a different person — a man running for his life.

All the stories of ancient warriors, the conquerors and commanders, revered in the eyes of men who had never

243

killed. Exalted by peers, honored by elites, these men have become immortal through legend. But as Joshua reflected on some of history's greatest warriors, he could only think of the person; the man, the mind, that must see life sucked away from another. A man who could stare so intimately into the eyes of the departing, his soul accepting the enemy's powerful might.

Could any of them sleep at night?

And suddenly it came to him. Joshua realized his lot in life. He was doomed from the beginning, born into suffering! A slave to death, Joshua realized the ways of the world. He would have to kill, or be killed. He could no longer love selfishly. His dreams of peace, or a life of love, with his precious Natalia, and his son Isaac. He realized that the Abandoned were now his responsibility. The morale and wellbeing of the entire community would rest on his shoulders. What was his motivation?

His heart paced faster than his feet as the skies darkened. The sound of the rain hitting the leaves and the brush was his only solace. The shiver of the night kept his feet in step. He floated home, lost in thought, wet and cold.

Alone he travels back to Eight; a clearer picture now of what must be done, and a reiteration of what he must say...

Chapter Thirty and Three

Tête-à-Tête

Excerpt from *Rorschach's Journal, 1985*

"The proliferate human, a potentially pointless position in my mind. Perhaps, even criminal. If not done with moral motivation.
In my opinion, the world is better off without us.
If things go back the way they were, we are destined for death. Not just ours, but of the spirit of the earth itself. God's greatest mistake, allowing Noah to survive the flood."

***

I look at the man to see nothing but a shell. An empty vessel. Reason would call this man a man, but I cannot. I see circuitry of madness; a man who had far outstayed his welcome. Father time gave him too much... Or was it taken?

I struggle to remember the vigor of my youth, the curiosity of all things from childhood. I see such a sight in the young of home. As an infant, barely able to stand, laughs at the butterfly as it flutters by. The little boy who fights his friend, perhaps not the victor, but smiling in the end. The girl who looks up and gazes at the stars, the bright lights that have inspired and awed so many before her. I would give anything to feel such happiness once more. To have an unspeakable awe of the mundane that surrounds. To see, once again, as if all were new, and exciting, and limitless.

"...The class system, interwoven through history and religion; the hierarchy: of upmost importance! What I saw was the need for a trustworthy leader. The embarrassing state of democracy of the 20th century, an entire population ruled by the things they owned, and the people who made them... What we needed was a cleanse, and a leader to guide them through it; one trustworthy, and loyal. A man to put the needs of his people, present and future, before his own. A man to care for the people, because history shows, they cannot care for themselves." Alexander, justifying the world he ruled.

"Immortality rests within my hands. Being a hero, you may be remembered, but become a legend, and you never die.

"They rely on our decisions. And the good men rely on our evil, or, their simple understanding of it. Without evil, how could one know, and even do good? It would seem I have simply bore the label in your eyes, allowing criticism and upheaval alike. And yet, in all my years, with all the chances I've given mankind, I live disappointed."

A chess board is suddenly delivered. I revel in the artistry, enclosed within the very description Joshua gave me just the other day. Alexander explains the rules of the game as I absentmindedly explore the creativity that encumbers.

This tyrant that sits before me represents a mysterious essence protruding. As if guilt brought with it a stench. I wonder at such a man, one who I assumed to be some type of monster. The words of Joshua painted a picture, and I had so invested my mind on his stories, as well as my father's. The colorful paintings of a world alongside ours emerged within me. Torn between life, and the burden I continuously find myself placed within. I, like all soldiers, come to know myself before battle. I have tasted the finality. And from within my bones, I prepare for my outcome.

"So, how much did you tell him?" I ask as the man dangles his right hand over the board, preparing his mind for the battle, no doubt. The game of chess itself was not new to me. My father had discussed the game at length by chance, and I remember his enthusiasm over it.

"I told him enough." Responded Alexander as his pawn jumped two spots ahead.

"Enough to what? Fight for you? Die for you? Why do you think I'm here?" I hear myself say as I must observably had turned red. My eyes went to the table, and I took my first move; a pawn advances.

"Did he ask you about Maan?"

Alexander tugged lightly on his small beard. The thick black and silver hair reflected a long and healthy life.

The man continued his advance.

"Maan means nothing to him now. I am his God." His knight hits the board with a loud knock.

I tried not to act startled as I continued my attempt to stay one step ahead.

"Have you pondered the thought of his patriotism? His love for his people..."

"We are his people now, don't you understand?" Alexander said now looking me in the eyes. "He surely understands truth."

"So, you've taught him truth, as if such a thing could be taught!" My bishop emerges. "And frankly, Sir, perhaps you don't know the truth about Joshua."

"Well, Achilles, I do know the truth about you. I know you would do anything to admonish the guilt you feel for your daughter."

Stunned by the flank... Joshua lied to me.

In a daze, my head scans the board looking for a kill.

"My morality guides me, and you yours. Do you expect to gain respect from me by polishing your stones?" He says looking at me with serious eyes. "You must understand, Achilles, I was put in charge of this world; and in charge of it I will remain. You will find I am a good god, and you will come to love me... All do."

He draws first blood, but my knight sets the flank.

"You think all this was easy?" Responded Alexander, showing a slight sense of humanity I had yet to see. "We were both given a burden to bear. When humanity itself rests on your shoulders, all considerations must be debated. A stoic by rights, I realize all I have done was destined to be, and all that is — predestined. For the future holds no reality; what we tend to forget – the future doesn't exist."

My mind flustered. The future would reveal it to be a welcomed disturbance; revealed truth, always exciting.

I switch tactics.

"What makes you happy?" I ask; Alexander staring at me all the while.

"God," he responded in a cold calculated manner, matter-of-factly, as if he had thought of this question before. "And you?"

"I- I never would have guessed at such an answer," I reply.

"I never would have guessed at such a question," said Alexander.

"I would give the same answer," I say in a moment of unexpected enthusiasm. I always enjoyed talking philosophy. Years of lonely nights, staring at the stars, contemplating existence. Summers of optimism, as well as winters of sorrow. I always enjoyed studying the ancient thoughts of a God, or Gods; but never could define Him (or It) myself.

"But tell me Alexander, can you explain God, and the happiness It gives you?"

No words could describe what his mind saw as divine, yet could aid in grasping such a concept. And in so, he felt a great worth, a potential to enlightening his fellow conqueror.

"God is justice, my friend. It is the only power Good has over Evil. The ability to turn suffering into greatness. To be reborn, after one has come so unpleasantly violent into such a world. The blood and cries of the mother, as an overture to the being, emerging from a world we remember nothing of, or perhaps have never seen. For no

248

one knows this mystery, and I care not waste my breath arguing it."

The demeanor of Alexander softened, which happened often of him in intimate conversations I have come to know. I felt a slight connection to the man. Feeling his hoarse voice was burdened just as mine; that the stern man who sat across from me, was just fulfilling the role he inherited. A man like any other, cursed to suffering.

"Although most cannot recall this initiating rite of passage, I pursue it to no end. I envision a true way of peace. God, in my mind, is where I aim to steer humanity. I remember the blood. I've experienced death! I am tainted, and so I must perceive God through a different focal point. I believe I see humanity not through the sight of a human but through the sight of God. *Le valeur du mon coeur,* the fate of our species, for the billions and billions that may walk this sacred ground, for millions of years to come. I cannot let my compassion for those I see now, selfishly tempt me towards momentary happiness, thus forgetting my future kin!

"I can see why you may see me as evil. But what you must understand is that humanity needs an enemy! All great stories tell of a good and moral warrior, who defies odds to defeat the evil man or nation who oppresses, or kills, or causes suffering. But I've learnt it's all simply a matter of perspective. The story could always be reversed, the warrior, seen as nothing more than an uncivilized terrorist... an agent of chaos!

"The point is, peace can never be."

Even in heaven peace was just a dream of the creator. And many times, I side with the adversary. Realizing we are doomed to suffering, he is tasked with the tormented existence connected to humanity; existing now within the world of suffering, the Bane eternally imprisoned.

"Without evil, good could never be.

"Like the Bane, or Adversary, or Devil (as some may prefer), we are doomed! Whether in life or in death, pain or pleasure, there's a deep inherent destitution within us all. Depending on which side of the conquerors story you reside, you may see me as good or evil. I am an agent of one or the other, and this idea tears me apart. I am burdened by responsibility, and do my best to think of the greater good above all else. Yet the meaning, and the stories embodied – this I search for, perhaps until the end of my days, if only they would come.

"I am one who regards life like the great leaders of old. Like Julius Caesar, I care for my people, and for their survival I fight. He died a death I am prepared for. Daily I pray for a knife to my side, to rid me of this eternal suffering I bear."

He sucks me into the tangent.

"But my honor is all I have. If it is the will of God to have me here, to lead my people to salvation, to the freedom of disease, death, suffering and pain... Well then, I will go to no end! And I will crush any who oppose it. Not because I want to, but because in the end, all is dust!

"Man has always needed his dark side to do good. In fact, without darkness, how could we come to understand light?"

The chess board, now a blur of black and white.

"So, is this the God that brings you happiness?" Alexander says, done talking it seems.

A moment to ponder.

"I think we define God differently, as well as happiness. What you described to me is Joy. The hope and belief that good may prosper, even though we can't see past the suffering resting upon our very nose.

"I asked you, 'What makes you happy?' As you have, I say God, and I will explain my understanding of that first."

Two like minds... who would have guessed.

"God is the force that is all. The ultimate mind behind all that we see and know, and perhaps beyond. We are a continuous life force, connected to all, emerging from dust to become agents of a higher realm.

"My understanding of our concept of time is that it exists apart from what we see and are taught. That all matter exists in a three-dimensional way, and that it only exists within the structured framework of time — the fourth dimension.

"Time's only purpose is for the existence of all that is under it.

"Just like an object can only exist if time allows it, so too rests the fate of the fourth dimension: Time must be under dominion. For without the fifth dimension (Mind, or Consciousness), time would cease to be. As I now travel further from knowable understanding, I am haunted by a feeling that the dimensions do not end there. Just as matter exists within time, and time exists within our perception of it, what does consciousness exist within? We lord the four dimensions, but what lords over the fifth? And how did it all come into existence? Such a complex system, even at the finite knowledge I possess, shows me I'm reaching beyond my limits...

"But I digress... What makes me happy..."

I tried momentarily not to think of words, or definitions, for God is not within words or definitions, but more like a feeling. I reach within myself, grasping towards happiness.

"Warm sunshine on my face as it rises out of the mountains, providing the earth with its daily bread. The cool breeze on a hot day, relief from the stale air, there to refresh and rejuvenate.

"...My memories! My father, sitting with me, explaining how we only have one life, with no expiry date. We will leave this world the same way we came in, completely oblivious.

"Personal creation! Not just physical procreation, well, that too, but so much more! The ideas and thoughts, and imaginative exploration. And equally the moments of ease — the silence and stillness of letting go, leaving the world behind us to live in the inner solitude.

"But within the oblivion, the chaos of existence. Wrapped in uncertainty! And because of it, we must be humble to the fact that we are but a moment, occupying a microscopic portion of the universe, for a microscopic portion of time, only to leave it the same way we entered: Naked and oblivious."

One day they will fall to the lure of comfort, to the will of the self. And they will fear their neighbor. Perhaps they are strong now, but what of the children? Or their children's children? Can you control how future generations live? How they think, feel and operate? All it takes is one ugly weed to penetrate the soil, and soon all are interlocked within its roots.

Can the reign of Alexander live forever?

Across the way from me, I peer into mine own eyes. The man who had seen much pain, and loss — no longer able to see the beauty, the hope in humanity.

I have shared many of those thoughts. I see it as he stares across the way at me, perhaps reading my epiphany. But as I look, I see his eyes not on mine, but through them; staring through me, as if I were just another invisible air particle, vanished to the sense of vision. Little or no importance.

"And happiness..." I continue. "Nothing more than perspective. And mine, a perspective bruised and tattered. The scars of the past, and the apeirophobic thoughts of the future haunt my happiness. I seek the happiness that is mindful ignorance... seemingly to no end."

I wonder at what he may have had to do, at the things he's seen; the debt of so many souls, crushing him into the pits of despair. Pursuing righteously perhaps, humanity's salvation. No penance of the past; no debt to the future.

So ignorantly mindful.

All's well that ends well.

A shadow from the ancient world hovers the cube.
The remnants of ancient civilization.
I only hope my guilt be pardoned.

Alexander takes charge.

"You are nothing but a harmless speck, a single tribe among millions before it. You should see the ruins that is a city of the previous age. A city! The word itself transformed, in the vernacular: death, despair, hatred and greed. A mass grave. "It became the symbol for corruption. The position of piety it hypocritically preached. And you are but one despicable people as before, and I with little care to the foresight of its demise. God, it would seem, has me as the favorite. But I myself welcome the day of departure. Unto my dying breath I see to it!"

"See to what?" I say aloud.

"That I will endure."

The board, ransacked and ravaged.
Alexander defeats me.

The dead eyes of the man saw me to the door. The darkness brought the night's terror, and I was led like a criminal to his predestined fate. Unsure of what the man is capable of, I am led in the dark, not knowing what to believe, or whom believable. But Alexander knows my story it would seem, and I momentarily question Joshua's, when a frightening thought protrudes: Does this man know who my daughter is? And if not, will he beat it out of me? Or is she gone? A memory re-awoken through harmful misdirection?

If only I could see, and speak to Joshua once more. But in my heart, I know that this will truly never be.

Do people deserve a second chance?
Do they deserve unending chance?

Chapter Thirty and Four

The Event Horizon

"Within all of us is a cruel world. As soon as we recognize it, we embody it.

And the moment we believe we are different, that we are not like any other:

One who meets life face to face,
A battle, a war, an apocalypse.
We die.
And from the grave, we rise.
Only after destruction can one see with scrutiny.
Only after death can one discover life."

I have yet to find the God I've been looking for. The perfect version of a love story. One that does not end in heartbreak. If I have learnt anything during my time mortal, it would be that all eventually separates. And as we tend to love only what we know, I can only place my hope in the days to come, and the endless possibilities of death and the unknown.

Truly, life has very few significant moments; and I mean the moments that are truly significant. A moment so powerful it affects the movement and outcome of so much around it. But believe me, those moments truly exist, whether we witness them, comprehend them, or not. But few, I say with conviction. For most of life is the moments in-between these; the quiet and mundane, the dark and elusive. Yet, this is where those significant moments culminate, where they eternally dwell, obedient or not. The natural human tendency – longing to escape.

I am who I am because of the choices I've made. But not only that, I am who I am because of the choices of others. It is not as simple as being in control of your own fate; it is a complex, elaborate ecosystem surviving off of chaotic growth, susceptible to outside influence.

As the door to my cell opens, the large wooden gateway creaks to reveal a dark and desolate room. The cold stone interior sent a chill, as if giving me a preview of how cold I was to become. They start to push me into the room, I turn to Alexander, "You have the opportunity to change history!" I say desperately to the man. "You can start over, change the way humans have become. You are the new Adam! A fresh start! You have the power to choose the apple, or to obey God!" The door slammed in my face. "Think about your choices!" I scream through the heavy door. "Think about the future of humanity!"

And suddenly, all was dark, all was quiet, and I stand alone.

Within the cold confines of a stone cell, I am left unattended. The darkness surrounds. I withdraw from the dark world around me, into the dark world within me.

A small cube placed by the door — I did not notice upon entry, perhaps brought within while my thoughts without. I sit down against the cold wall, a chill hits my brittle bones. Examining the cube now within my hand, a tenor articulation inadvertently protrudes – the voice of Alexander, like a journal read aloud:

"Stress is the great killer. It plagues the man, a virus of the mind.

Where does it stem from? And who can endure.

Knowledge? Perhaps not just knowledge, but a specific type? For all life must contain some form of knowledge.

But knowledge, as in, contemplation — the understanding of things unseen, the contemplation of past, future and the conscious self in-between.

Today, a coup d'état was attempted. A man wielding nothing more than a sharp piece of steel, perhaps part of the hull, as he lunged for me, leaving a bloody trail of bodyguards along the way.

The thing is, I miss those days, those early years. The immortal period of bloody battles. Brothers, all of us brothers – comrades and enemies alike. Where death ruled our lives, and the thought of past and future were null and void. What does that say of the man within? What does that say of the man I have become? The man I see today, of pure forethought, if not, vying for anything to remove me from truth and reconciliation.

Life has become a series of strategies, and thus, I long for moments like these.

And as my blood cools, the vigorous eyes begin to settle, I loosen the tattooed neck of a man I remember all too well, and check to make sure he is in fact dead.

Two fingers to the jugular, no pulse.

I only wish I could feel sorry, some form of pain or discomfort from his death. And as I walk through the corridor of corpses, some men of mine, some of his, I feel nothing but relief for the dead.

These men have left the burdening world of life. The contemplation; all mortals bound to flesh, cursed to endure. And now, where could each man be?

The endless possibilities of the afterlife, a symbol of hope for an otherwise bleak, and frankly disturbing existence.

Here, in my room, just as the night before, I record the monumental choices of a man given supreme authority. First among equals, I say with relent. I am just like any. And like any, who feel the pressure that is associated with the burden — although my weight heavier than any others, as I currently hold the destiny of humanity within my grasp. "

The recording goes silent for a moment. Then returns.

"We humans must understand, moving from our mother, Earth, and our father, Sun, is like a child, packing a bag, attempting to run away from home. We humans, in the grand scheme of things, are newborns; to Earth, to Time, and to Thought.

According to 20th century science, we have lived here for nothing more than a moment. And somehow, mankind thought it could conquer existence.

The greed of men destroyed the Earth, and I am but a laborer after an earthquake.

And as I contemplate the events of today, and the fact that I never intended us to leave; as all those men and women lay down to the world of dream; a world, just as real as this one, only to wait... They will awaken to the Earth, the way it was intended. Free of mass consumption, hate, and opposing forces. We will return, after the last of the bones return to the earth, and the rotten corpses turned fertile ground.

We will return to an earth with one purpose. To simply last. And in so doing, we may grow older in wisdom, and self-awareness. There is no hope for the flesh but the earth and sun. And our star, so young, breathes hope. Perhaps, over time, as we wait, another may come to save. Perhaps, one who looks upon us with pity, as I do. We simply lack the resources and might to rule the universe; and so, must endure in preparation, to submit to the will of whatever entity comes to pass.

As we spin and stare out into space, into the infinite resources; like a proton, fighting a neutron, within a microcosm so small we cannot see it; the making up of who we are... The infinitely small, mirrored by the infinitely large. And we the microcosm."

The tape ends and I lay it by my side in darkness. My head feeling sore as visions of the death and horror happened so long ago, yet right within this moment. The Event Horizon, the great mysterious tomb, home to nothing but death and destruction, although, according to past thought, an ark of all I hold dearly. Including Maan, surely one of those whose body lay amongst the dead.

The rejuvenation of a species in such need of despair.
And a man, sadly mirroring my inequities.
Honor among men, for the weak and the damned.

Chapter Thirty and Five

Final Thoughts

Journal of Jacob, Dated December 10, 2038:

"Did life come from competition?
Is our passion, our lust, I say, a subjugate for a life...
Bonded to our desires?

To be bigger, and better than the other, the selfishness vying within all men alike.
The seed of desperality, a life lived within the gnosis of it all.
A world for another realm...
A world no one should come to know.

If said-man lives in the world of forms, his bondage to the flesh pitiful.
And I pity all alike as myself.
The righteous, the sinner...
All are corrupted to the body.

A collective brotherhood -
A strange dimension all must adduce,
Endure,
Forsake,
And flee."

***

There's something unnerving about the night. As if the day's absence can be felt, and the silence of darkness heard. The illuminated buzz of life, awake and full of vigor, here becomes dormant.

Within darkness, surely chaos reigns.

The mystery and uncertainty ushers the feeling of absence, gloom, and above all... fear. My heart races at the thought of the unknown, the creatures surely lurking in the shadows.

The loneliness reverberates;

To conquer man is inevitable, but to conquer death, divine.

And to conquer death — to lose fear of it.

What good is a man who gains the world, yet forfeits his own soul?

Truly life is hell, and deaths rough hand our only deliverance.

One should and must never invest in the dying world. Indifference the key I painfully turn.

"It is only fate that divided us," I remember him saying.

Now, I finally understand my fate. The human spirit, reduced to crumbling bone, and weakened flesh. I have become numb, sitting here, knowing the fate he speaks of, and the inevitable suffering that is to come.

"The problem is, you don't understand people." I recall him saying as he walked me to my cell. "You persuaded a people to follow you, and so have I. Yet you have decided that your way of life is right and mine wrong? How can you decide yours is better than mine? I've seen death just as you, and I search to defeat it. I've lead the people where I feel they must be lead. You can't think your kind as sole survivors.

"Freedom itself has an accomplice, stress. And a proper hierarchy, relief from such burden of those who bear it. I take the stress of life from my people, and unburden them from it. They trust fully in me, and to this day, I have not let them down! And I have hope! — hope in me and my people. And do you know why? Because we are still here! Because we are strong!"

This place is haunted. A ghost, a mere shadow and trace of a soul and existence. Dull and fearful, a complicated array of attachment and detachment. Is it better for me to die without her knowing? The damage of cause has already been done. Is this beyond fixing?

Perhaps I should accept the truth.

Meaningless — it is all meaningless.

Do you ever contemplate the end? What the moment of departure will look like, consist of, entail?

I do. I become its beautiful disaster, its painful tear, its regretful demise.

As I foresee my destiny, one of pain and anguish, one jabbed directly toward the heart; as I calculate the days of my future, the life I am destined to finish; the destiny of it all! I realize something I had not before; the fear leaving – death, my rapidly closing friend, not foe. It embodies, becoming a present reality instead of a speculative future.

All the knowledge I possess, yet not a soul to relate. Neither in life, nor in death. This dark world of understanding and sorrow is a burden not meant for any mind to bear alone. The sheer magnitude of existence and all the mysteries it entails, were always shared as a family of humans, bonded into a brotherhood of survival.

The knowledge, the duty I worshipped, what was it for?

Here at the end, I stand once more. I live by my own laws. Look at what man has created! Regard the rising and falling of all the dominant nations!

The power, sure to crumble.

History as we know it...

The only wish, I would dare to ask, a wish of divine sentiment, would be to see my girl once more.

And as I wonder, the thought of such a union, could it cause her harm? What would it mean to see a man, who gave you up, left you for dead, only to appear in such a mad way? A father contrary to her culture and her upbringing; a piece of scum, left to rot on earth, never to be smelled or heard from again.

The heart begins to race. The decision has been made.

I become numb. If only I had the power to overcome.

I only wish I had the ability to recall such a time, an age where I lived without this stress of freedom. The life of luxury, where boredom takes control, and evil consumes. But all I remember is giving in, and selling my soul. *Solei,* how I wish to see her face once more.

And so it would seem, the end of the seventh day.

The sun begins to set as I remain hungry. I pull out my arm, having sat on it for so long. Raising it to my lips, teeth clenched for the last time. I feel satisfied.

The taste of flesh – a burst of life!

The holy number brings comfort in knowing the day of rest has come. I'm tired of living a life, never knowing what's right and what's wrong. Of living a life full of regrets, warn from the constant need. Rest, a thing of other worlds. And throughout my life my brain has never experience such stillness I am sure to encounter, as the bitter-sweet taste is felt on the tongue — the taste, the blood of a dying man. I find it ironic how once again I attempt to relieve my morals through contemplation and dialogue. Through sorrow of mind and spirit, wallowing to the self, the only one to truly understand who I was, and am, and may soon become. And so, I accept.

I accept the fact that no story has an end. That all are destined to look one last time upon the earth of mystery and intrigue. A world ongoing, no conclusion attained, no end in clear sight.

The need for closure; all men succumb to this sorrowful position.

Yet in my desperate need for purpose, I hope this reaches you...

Solei, perhaps alive and well, I pray you come to know who I am, and judge me not for the sins of my youth. May you feel me in places of love, and thought, and will. May the nature of all that I thought to be good, and right, and worthwhile flow towards you as I pass.

And do not weep for me, for my death occurred oh, so long ago. Rejoice! For I am finally free.

If you die, but your ideals live on, in the heart and the mind of those you know... The lives you've changed, for the better, of course! If our words and our actions effect and encourage, then can you truly say you have in fact died? What am I? Just flesh and bone? Or am I more? Am I the ideals I pass on? Surely, I am so...

I look up to the slit in the wall — ventilation. The sun, my momentary beacon, the orange glow taking its place beyond the hills, and my energy begins to deplete.

The Eighth day.

Only the sky rains down truth! Only the wind speaks clarity! Only the sea moves peacefully!

Worlds collide as I fester and die... A slave to the mind; consciousness — free will or slavery? Oh, the Irony!

My day of rest has come. The end of my flesh, but what of my mind? The eighth day begins, and my duty subsequently manifests. The fate of mankind now rests not within my midst, but the cold grasp of *The Great* — Alexander, and Urus, the rightful Judge of the abandoned, formerly known as Joshua.

And as the blood drips, within the pool of red I sit. Finally, I shed this despicable vessel! This samovar of perspirant. Light fading, the last sensory emanating. Nothing left but the smell at death's fateful meeting.

Euphoria greets – a smile from cheek to cheek

Chapter Thirty and Six

Epilogue

"The Soul replied, saying, 'what binds me has been slain, and what surrounds me has been destroyed, and my desire has been brought to an end, and ignorance has died. In a world, I was set loose from the world. And in a type, from a type that is above, and from the chains of forgetfulness, which exists in time, from this hour on, for the time of the due season of the age, I will receive rest in silence.'"

- Gospel of Mary

How do you encapsulate the human experience? In a song, or an equation? In an experience, or a thought? A time, a place, another dimension perhaps?

The sad state: All seek a means of escaping reality. This itself is the beauty of art. To simultaneously put someone in a place, absent of realism, but also directly in the midst of it.

The art of storytelling connects us in a primitive way. We all yearn for a good story; a life is not truly lived if not riddled with adventure and intrigue. One lives his day's in search of such stories that remind him of his own — of the excitement of experience. The goosebumps one gets at the touch of first love, the laughs of boyhood shenanigans, and the girls reciprocating such potent signs of affection and emotion; all can carry you from one place to another. A world so complex yet simple. The experience of another — the longing of all.

And we experience our own life in such a way, seeking a source of excitement. Anything but this moment empty — the end of time itself.

One tends to also invest in the stories of sorrow. Dwelling on the past hurts and loitering aches during such difficult times. Like the first heartbreak, when original love pursues a new interest. When that friend of yours, whose misgivings have departed along with his body; or the sight of a new bruise given to your friend, as she confesses to the abuse she lives, day-in and day-out, in sheer agony. Life is remembered in these moments of emotional firsts.

The good and the bad alike.

This unites all people. A good story creates a communal experience. A unique bond is made between author and listener, between the teller and the told. Now, sharing such an experience can create a new form of brotherhood. One, as far as we know, to be a unique to the human being – perhaps the key to either our survival, or ultimate end.

Stories have the power to change people. To influence, and encourage; and one cannot help but understand, to manipulate as well. Such power in a story has created such rich and rewarding living, along with terror and corruption. Words have a unique way of creating an immortal thought, an idea that lives longer than any life lived thus far – leaving a legacy; thinking of the future, or of oneself.

I also think of all the great and inspirational minds who've lived in squalor and died in pain, with never the opportunity to express themselves, too poor for paper or too beaten from labor. The greatest stories and the most poetic words, the wisest parables and creative thoughts come not from the intellects pen, but rests silently with the dead.

Why must men be heard? Why must our story continue? Why the constant drive to be respected and understood by all? Why do we long for this immortal calling, the need for reverence?

The inability to care about the perspective of the other;

Individually.

Collectively.

The downfall of man.

And I, as many others, think of such people. Men of history and lore. Of legend and literature. Are any of them real? And if so, how real? For history cannot reveal a man fully. Ink and paper cannot show the innermost sanctuary – the heart, mind, and soul of a man. And so, the stories reflect something even greater, whether it true or not. These stories represent ideas. True realms where the impossible is possible. True men of courage, strength and virtue. And the idea that good, even though difficult to see, is beneath it all. And our collective hope, that Good, whatever that may be, will ultimately conquer all.

The need for purpose.

The worst thing a man can do, is live his life absent of purpose. Whether the world begins spontaneous, or by a creator, whether we come into chaos or predestination, we must not lose the fact that everything we do has consequence.

Cause and effect.

And we must never forget that what we choose to do in this lifetime, affects all – not just our life, but the lives of those around us. The cause and effect continues, we are the stone thrown into the pond; the ripples – an expanding outcome, one that continues for eternity, never ceasing, throughout the cosmos; the cosmos that is us, a network of living cells and organisms; each doing its part, ignorant of the world out of sight. We observe such cells; we see the protein working hard for its supreme being. It neither sees us nor understands us, as we watch it from behind a veil.

And we must also remember that we are here because of history. And as we learn of the great peoples of old, the brave and courageous lives bring enthusiasm and drive. The unrivaled respect, immortally legend. And as I am but a product of history, so too are those of the past, and the future. The cone of space time, the product of my life, the stone hitting the shoal — the ripples I see not from my watery grave.

This gives purpose, but only to the children of God.

And you? Where do you stand? Do you live mechanically, with death at hand? Have you stopped caring of your outcome? Don't tell me you've given up on freewill!

Have you allowed other to decide your fate? How can you give up so? Well, I know...

It isn't easy to care. It is not easy to invest yourself in a world fleeting. It takes courage watching all you know grow, and thrive, and peak and die. Experiencing demise — to see it fall away; this is truly a painful duty... To give all you have into the fleeting. But you must! You must! I tell you... For what else is there? A life of disgrace! Cowardice! Taking selfishly, living vindictively, hating all, even yourself! For if you took but a moment to reflect... You would see as I, that this way of demise brings only shame. It kills, and tortures, and hurts all those around you. And there will be no one to place you in the grave, and speak as your witness, your predestined departure.

When your days become numbered, and you conceive of an end, you will cling to those around you, but the feeling, perhaps less than mutual.

And you will stare at your end, in fear or content... Yet I see nothing but my life continuously flashing by.

Now but a glimpse, here in eternity. It is like a vision I recall at will. A very detailed vision, expressed in multiple, wonderful emotional creations, from the inspiring life of the senses. This experience is a reel, leaving me with a love for all things, and excitement for the unknown.

Looking backward, the view is so much clearer. It all has purpose. Nothing is for not.

I sigh in relief thinking of what may or may not be of my daughter. All I know is the innocence. All I see is the spirit. I no longer feel guilt, but curiosity — I imagine in awe and wonder; thinking about the endlessly possible opportunity of a life she gets to call her own. I no longer regret the direct influence I wish I could have made in her life. I mean, perhaps my legacy left with *the Abandoned* will one-day tie with hers or yours. The changes I made to the thousands in the now, will surely ripple to you, in some generation or another.

Life is a choice between enlightenment and sentiment, and I somehow got caught in the middle.

But death?

What can exist outside of space and time?

A thought? A memory? Can something exist absent of a mind? Can an idea exist without the thinker?

Can a memory represent a moment, if there is no mind to travel there?

The mind, a microcosm; in and of itself.

With layers that run deep, and many worlds to explore. Through the miracles of memory, and the dream world, we get a glimpse at such eternity. The constant state of uncertainty.

We all have ways of coping through the unimportance of our lives. But at the end, how do we cope with death? Have you discovered that void? The emptiness we all find. The scary loneliness we all feel, when we let all we know and love die... When we finally let go of everything — the people we love, the memories we cherish, the idea of laughter and love, the feeling of excitement, as well as anger and sorrow. The feelings of being a human, and the conscious knowledge of it all.

But we know it must end; and in our humility, in our deep understanding that all is but breath, waiting to exhale — surely to inhale no more — we are calm as we imagine 'What else?' at the possibilities of what may be in the infinite, what is sure to come in the end. Perhaps, a new beginning?

But, as usual, I digress...

One word of advice before I go:

Laugh!

Adieux, mon couer. I will never forget you.

Avec amour,
Ton Pere,

- *Achilles.*